NEW YORK REVIEW BOOKS
CLASSICS

CASSANDRA AT THE WEDDING

DOROTHY DODDS BAKER (1907–1968) was born in Missoula, Montana in 1907 and raised in California. After graduating from UCLA, she traveled in France, where she began a novel and, in 1930, married Howard Baker, a critic, professor, and editor. The couple moved back to California, and Baker completed an MA in French at UCLA, later teaching Latin at a private school. After having a few short stories published, Baker turned to writing full-time, despite, she would later claim, being "seriously hampered by an abject admiration for Ernest Hemingway." In 1938, she published *Young Man with a Horn*, a novel about a white jazz musician, which earned critical praise and eventually became a movie starring Kirk Douglas. She won a Guggenheim Fellowship in 1942 and, the next year, published *Trio*, a novel whose frank portrayal of a lesbian relationship proved too scandalous for the times; Baker and her husband adapted the novel as a play in 1944, but it was quickly shut down because of protests. Her final novel, *Cassandra at the Wedding*, examined the relationship between two exceptionally close sisters, whom Howard Baker asserted were based on both Baker herself and the couple's two daughters. Baker died in 1968 of cancer.

DEBORAH EISENBERG is the author of three collections of short stories and the recipient of a Guggenheim Fellowship, the Rea Award, and three O. Henry Awards. She lives in New York City.

CASSANDRA AT THE WEDDING

DOROTHY BAKER

Afterword by
DEBORAH EISENBERG

NEW YORK REVIEW BOOKS

New York

This is a New York Review Book
Published by The New York Review of Books
207 32nd Street, New York, NY 10016
www.nyrb.com

Reprinted by special arrangement with Houghton Mifflin Company

The Library of Congress has cataloged the earlier printing as follows:
Baker, Dorothy, 1907–1968.
  Cassandra at the wedding / Dorothy Baker ; afterword by Deborah Eisenberg.
    p. cm. — (New York Review Books classics)
  ISBN 1-59017-112-8 (pbk. : alk. paper)
  1. Women graduate students—Fiction. 2. Sierra Nevada (Calif. and Nev.)—
Fiction. 3. Mothers—Death—Fiction. 4. Ranch life—Fiction. 5. Lesbians—
Fiction. 6. Weddings—Fiction. 7. Sisters—Fiction. 8. Twins—Fiction. I. Title.
II. Series.
  PS3503.A54156C37 2004
  813'.52—dc22
                                    2004016738

ISBN 978-1-59017-601-6
Available as an electronic book: ISBN 978-1-59017-612-2

Printed in the United States of America on acid-free paper.
20 19 18 17 16 15 14 13 12

In Memoriam
David Park

CASSANDRA SPEAKS

I

I TOLD them I could be free by the twenty-first, and that I'd come home the twenty-second. (June.) But everything went better than I expected — I had all the examinations corrected and graded and returned to the office by ten the morning of the twenty-first, and I went back to the apartment feeling so foot-loose, so restless, that I started having some second thoughts. It's only a five-hour drive from the University to the ranch, if you move along — if you don't stop for orange juice every fifty miles the way we used to, Judith and I, our first two years in college, or at bars, the way we did later, after we'd studied how to pass for over twenty-one at under twenty. As I say, if you move, if you push a little, you can get from Berkeley to our ranch in five hours, and the reason why we never cared to in the old days was that we had to work up to home life by degrees, steel ourselves somewhat for the three-part welcome we were in for from our grandmother and our mother and our father, who loved us fiercely in three different ways. We loved them too, six different ways, but we mostly took our time about getting home.

It wasn't three-part any more — the welcome. Our mother died three years ago (much too young but I'm not sure she thought so) and she would therefore not be present at Judith's wedding. Unlike me. If I went, and of course I had to, I'd be very noticeably present in official capacity — the bride's only attendant. She asked me by letter, and I didn't give her a straight answer, because I'm shy, particularly of weddings, but I did say I'd be home the twenty-second, and I had unconsciously cleared the way by the twenty-first, which in June is the longest day of the year. After I got back from taking the examinations to the office, it began to feel like it. I walked around the apartment and looked two or three times inside the refrigerator, so cold, so white, so bare, and more times than that out the big west window at the bay with the prison islands in it and the unbelievable bridge across it. Unbelievable, but I'd got to believing in it from looking at it so often, and it had been looking quite attractive to me off and on through most of the winter. All but irresistible at times, but so was my analyst, and they canceled each other more or less out.

I went out and stood on the deck and thought it over — how hot it would be at home, how searingly, curingly hot, and how nice it would be to see the dog and the current cat and my father and my grandmother. And my sister. Judith.

The bridge looked good again. The sun was on it, and it took on something of the appeal of a bright exit sign in an auditorium that is crowded and airless and where you are listening to a lecture, as I so often do, that is in no way brilliant. But lectures can't all be brilliant, of course; they can be sat through and listened to for what there is in them, and if the exit sign is dazzling it can still be ignored. Besides, my guide assures me that I am not, at heart, a jumper; it's not my sort of thing. I'm given to conjecture only, and to restlessness, and I think I knew all the time I was sizing up the bridge that the strong possibility was I'd go home, attend my sister's wedding as invited, help hook-

and-zip her into whatever she wore, take over the bouquet while she received the ring, through the nose or on the finger, wherever she chose to receive it, and hold my peace when it became a question of speaking now or forever holding it. I'd go, in all likelihood, and do everything an only attendant is expected to do. I'd probably *dance* attendance.

I didn't even know who the groom was beyond that he was a graduate medical student she met in New York, and his name was Lynch, or maybe even Finch. Yes. Finch. John Thomas Finch. Where'd she meet him — Birdland?

I left the deck and went back into the apartment and locked the door and pulled the cord that closed the curtain across the west window. I'd had enough of the view for this semester. I wandered around and ended up at my desk, looking at the page that was in my typewriter, specifically page fifty-seven of my brute thesis, my impressions of the novel in France — my big academic lunge. I turned on my lamp, my desk lamp of countless adjustments, and read what there was of page fifty-seven and laughed out loud, but not because it was amusing — because it was such busywork, this whole thing of writing a thesis so that I could become a teacher instead of a writer, particularly when the thesis is about writers, very current ones, women mostly and young, not much older than I am but whom I was exploiting ruthlessly to provide me with a thesis. I'd really have preferred it the other way around, to be myself the writer and have all those others writing their theses about me; but I have a peculiar problem in that my mother was a writer — author of two novels, and three plays, and quite a few screen plays, all quite well known, and it's not easy for the child of a writer to become a writer. I don't see why; it just isn't. It's something about not wanting to be compared. And not wanting to measure up, or not measure up; or cash in either. It's not that I have anything against my mother. I loved her, I think; but my mother's only been dead three years, just short of three years, and I'd rather wait a decent interval and then try. Or not try. But first write the idiotic thesis and get the gap-stopping degree.

I pulled the page out of the typewriter, crumpled it up and dropped it into the wastebasket beside the desk, shuffled the other fifty-six pages until the edges lay smoothly together, put them into a folder and then into the top drawer, and snapped the cover onto the typewriter. If the apartment should catch fire while I was at the wedding, the world would never know what it was I was at such pains to say about the novel as currently practiced in France by mere girls, and some boys. But it wouldn't catch fire. And when I got back I would undoubtedly pull the crumpled page out of the wastebasket, uncrumple it, copy it word for word, and be back in business. Two weeks from now, maybe only a week.

It was increasingly clear to me that I intended to go, that I didn't intend to spend another night, at least not this one, in the apartment. There were all kinds of indications: I stripped the sheets off my bed and put them into a laundry bag; and I folded the cover over the keyboard of the piano, a piano which was half mine, but which I'd scarcely touched, as they say of pianos, since Judith, who owned the other half, went to New York. I should have folded the cover over the keyboard nine months ago, and locked it. There was a key someplace.

But I didn't stop to look for it and by three that afternoon I was halfway home, and sitting in a bar, one of the ones we used to stop at in the old days. It was quite dark and air-cooled and I had in hand a lemon squash with some vodka in it in deference to my grandmother who hates the smell of alcohol on anyone's breath — particularly girls' breaths. I'm very fond of my grandmother, we both are, and I'd picked up a box of chocolate cherries for her before I left town. They were out in the trunk of the car, melting, while I sat here in the cold bar getting solidified and hoping that I had not put the chocolates on top of the box with the dress in it — dress I'd picked up before I left town and charged to one of my grandmother's accounts as she frequently implored me to do. It was a white dress, and it would probably do for the wedding. In fact I didn't even have to wonder about it — it was very simple and elegant and costly, it would do for anything anywhere, and my grandmother, high as her standards are, would know it when she saw it and thank me for doing her so much honor. She liked to see girls look nice, she said so all the time, and whether or not this had anything to do with it I developed a taste for sweatshirts a full ten years ahead of the trend. Also for sneakers, and if I knew my grandmother, she would love this dress. It would be a big relief to her, besides serving to keep the account active.

I looked across the space behind the bar and saw my face in a blue mirror between two shelves of bottles. The bottles looked familiar enough, but I didn't immediately recognize the face, mostly, I think, because I didn't want to. It's a face that's given me a lot of trouble.

But I looked again in a moment or two, unable not to, and this time I let myself know who it was. It was the face of my sister Judith, not precisely staring, just looking at me very thoughtfully the way she always used to when she was getting ready to ask me to do something — hold the stop watch while she swam four hundred meters, taste the dressing and tell her what she left out, explain the anecdote about the shepherd and the mermaid. They were the kind of thing a younger sister asks an older sister, and it was all right with me except that I wasn't all that much older. I was only eleven minutes older. It was on our birth certificates that way. The one named Cassandra was two ounces heavier and eleven minutes older than the one named Judith.

By a firm act of will I forced the face between the shelves to stop being Judith's and become mine. My very own face — the face of a nice girl preparing to be a teacher, writing a thesis, being kind to her grandmother, going home a day early instead of a day late or the day I said, and bringing something decent to wear. But it can give me a turn, that face, any time I happen to catch it in a mirror; most particularly at times like this when I'm alone and have to admit it's really mine because there's no one else to accuse.

I lifted my glass and said, "Here's to you, Narcissus," and it was by no means the first time I'd been called by the wrong name, though it had never been this one. Lots of people refuse to commit themselves to any name-calling at all in our case. "Now which one are you?" they say, and when I say I'm Cassandra they always say that's what they thought, which would be exactly what they'd say if it had been Judith saying she was Judith. Or for that matter Judith saying she was Cassandra, or Cassandra saying she was Judith. They'd say that's what they thought. We got very tired of it quite early in our lives. We never dressed alike. I was messy on principle, so that Judith could be neat; and then they'd forget which was the neat one, and have to ask. And we'd have to tell them. Very tiresome.

I finished off my lemon squash and moved down a few

stools to a place where the cash register cut off a direct view of the mirror, but a man sitting a couple of stools over interpreted the move as a desire for companionship, and offered, quite nicely, to buy me a drink. I'd been intending to have another, at least I'd been wondering whether another would make the rest of the trip cooler or hotter, and once you start wondering you have more or less decided in favor of another. But the offer changed all that. It made me realize I had some place to go and that I should be getting there, not consorting with strangers in bars, and I thanked him and paid up and went out into the heat without ever looking at him. The truth is, I'm afraid of men, strange men and ones I know, though I know there's nothing about them to be afraid of. But I am; they set my teeth on edge; and I got into my car and made what felt like a getaway without even waiting to fasten the seat belt. I figured that I could do that when I left the next bar.

I was driving my mother's car — a Riley she exchanged one of her last royalty checks for. It was four years old now, no, five — it was a year old when she bought it, she drove it a year and Judith and I'd had it three years, but people still looked sidewise, puzzled and interested, when it passed them — a classic that had begun to use quite a bit of oil. It was half mine and half Judith's, I supposed, but nobody had ever said so. Our father told us to drive it back to Berkeley when we went back after our mother's funeral, and we'd had it ever since and thought of it as our car. But it was not at all the same as the way we thought of our piano. We *chose* the piano. Nobody gave it to us. We found it in a Sunday *Chronicle*, slightly misspelled, but not every typesetter can be trusted with a name like Boesendorfer, it's long and you don't see it every day. We saw it, though, hiding among the classified advertisements, waiting to be identified and claimed, and we went to the address with our fingers crossed; and it was one. It was unmistakably a Boesendorfer, meant for us, and we became its co-owners right away. Without conferring. Without the slightest need to.

Next day we didn't go to classes. It was the day we took possession of what we'd bought and saw it hoisted with pulleys and a winch from the street up to the deck of our apartment. It was wrapped in thick pads, very dusty, and the winch creaked and curses rang and dignity was nowhere about. I watched from the street, because I wanted to be there if it fell. But Judith watched from the deck and she was there when it was put down, legless, on its side. I was there, too, all out of breath, a few seconds later, and we watched two men named Otis and Carl put it on a dolly and roll it into our living room, and screw the legs into it and push it to the wall we'd cleared for it. Then Otis picked up the pads and the dolly and took them out and hooked them onto the winch, and Carl looked the apartment over, and us too, while I wrote him a check.

"You girls twins?" he said when I handed it to him, and I said no, cousins — cousins-german, as a matter of fact, and then he left and so did Otis, and Judith and I were suddenly alone with it, all black and scrolled and three-legged and ours. We were quite shy in the face of it, feeling all the weight of commitment, and not able, either one of us, to find much to say. I wandered around the place, into the bedroom, back to the living room, out to the deck, and Judith was standoffish too. She ran some arpeggios, standing up, but she didn't do anything serious. And then sometime that afternoon we went down to the University, to the practice rooms and the music lockers, and Judith brought back a pile of her music and began to play the preludes and the fugues and all was well. I didn't do another thing all day; I only listened and knew how good she was and what a piano we had, and later that night when she quit playing and came out onto the deck where I was looking at the lights and listening, she said, "We ought to live this way, don't you think?" It was as if I'd been waiting all my life to hear her say it, and I said yes, oh yes, how could we imagine it ever being any other way? Let's never get stuck with outsiders, just be ourselves and keep it honest, now we've got this piano.

We stood leaning against the rail of the deck looking at the lights below and the stars above, the lights thicker and brighter and the stars cooler and more separate, and I remembered how bright the stars are on summer nights at the ranch with no ground lights to dim them out. We even had our own stars. Our father showed us how to find them at different seasons — Castor, there; Pollux, there, only we knew them by our own names. I looked now and couldn't find them. They were probably somewhere behind Grizzly Peak, so I stopped looking for them and looked at Judith instead, and began to feel myself getting star-crossed. And she knew it.

"We could live someplace else, couldn't we?" I heard her say. "We could live in Paris."

"We'd look just as much alike in Paris as we do here."

"But it wouldn't matter; they'd overlook it. That's why colored people go to Paris."

"To be overlooked?" I said. "I'm not sure I want to be overlooked. And I don't want you to be either."

"We wouldn't be. You could break down and start writing — and —"

"Start writing what?" I said, and I could feel my old chip in its place on my shoulder.

"The thing you threw away," she said, very simply and unemphatically, as if she thought I shouldn't have, and almost immediately there was no chip.

"What about you?" I said, "would you work too?" and I didn't get a fast answer but I got one that must have taken a great deal for her to put into words. She knew what she wanted, she said, at least she thought she did, and it wasn't anything very hard and specific like giving concerts and having people pay to hear her. It had more to do with belonging to a tradition in music and staying in it and working at it in any capacity you can fit into — playing what's being written, and what's been written, composing too if you want to and can, but mostly trying to keep it alive and separate the chaff from the grain and keep them separate. Know which is which, and care, and that's a life work.

While I listened to her I was wishing our father were listening too — it was so exactly the thing he'd been telling us since we were too young to remember, and not just about music, about everything. The pure faith of a skeptic. Maybe you don't believe in concerts but you believe in music; you care what happens to it and you're willing to contribute what you can for whatever it may be worth. Probably not much.

"What are we having here?" I said. "A revival meeting?" and she said very quietly that she hoped so; it was time for us to decide on one thing or another, either be what we should be or become something else.

"I don't know what you're trying to say," I said, but I did know. We'd been fraternizing, call it, with all kinds of strangers. I had, particularly, for all the good it did me. I had been thinking of it as my Rimbaud phase — period of expansion — but it wasn't only that. We had both been concentrating on going separate ways, having separate points of view, friends of our own, and likes and dislikes of our own. We'd been trying hard to break it up, and all we had to show for it was exhaustion and disgust. No other way of life would work, no other way felt right, and all it took to put us straight was a misspelled piano in a want ad. We know a misspelling when we see one, if it's important, and the air was clear now; we'd made the decision, we owned a piano. We were committed to it, and it wasn't as if it were just any piano; it was an incomparable piano, immaculate, peerless. The odd thing was that Judith is the pianist, I'm not, but I saw the ad and it never occurred to either of us to do anything but buy it together and have it be ours.

That's how clear the air was, that first night of possession. I felt intoxicated, but not from natural causes. From the preludes and fugues and the mention of Paris, where they take you in and accept the fact that you're being yourself and then overlook it, whatever it is. Wonderful city to establish one's piano in.

"Paris will do fine," I said, "though I remember when we were there they thought we were awfully cute."

"We were ten years old," Judith said. "We're not cute now."

I thought that over without looking at her to see for sure. I didn't feel cute. I never felt so serious in my life; I'd never had the excitement of an earth-shaking decision, and while I was having it the telephone rang, and I told Judith to let it ring because it would be Liz Janko. It had been being Liz Janko for two months.

"Janko Junko," Jude said, very perspicaciously, and I nodded in agreement, and we listened while the phone rang twenty times, and then quit.

"Did you ever really like her?" Jude asked me, as soon as it was quiet. It sounded like something she'd been wanting to ask me for two months.

"No," I said, "not much."

"Then why?"

"I'm polite. I was trying to stay out of your way."

"You can't be that polite," she said. "I don't have any way."

I had to wait a minute before I could talk. I walked over to the deck door and closed it in case the telephone might ring again, and when I came back I said, "It's not just her. I can't stand any of them," and I went on, because there was no reason not to now that we had a future and some plans for it, and told her as honestly as I could how I'm constituted. With men I feel like a bird in the clutch of a cat, terrified, caught in a nightmare of confinement, wanting nothing but to get free and take a shower.

"Birds don't take showers," Jude said, and I had to give her instances of birdbaths and lawn sprays and sprinkling systems and fountains in parks, before I could get to what I had to tell her, which was nothing so simple as the cat-and-bird relationship, even without the shower, because I'm not afraid of women; they don't terrify me slightly. Up to a point they fascinate me, and I said so.

"Up to what point?" Jude said, really wanting to know, and so I dredged for it, and said it seemed to have something to do with the old advice about not speaking to strangers and remembering that women are worse than men. Well — I could ignore the advice about women; and had. I could speak to them all right, but at the point they stopped being strangers I always wished they'd be strangers again.

"They impose themselves," I said. "I get to feeling chased."

"How?" Judith said, and I was spelling it for her when the telephone rang again, not more than ten minutes after we'd let it ring itself out.

"They take over," I said, between rings. "They get pushy."

"Do you want me to answer it?"

"No," I said, "but let's unlist it, early tomorrow. And be different. Just us. Nobody else ever."

The phone stopped after five or six rings, and Judith turned to me and said, "Thank you, thank you very much." And later, much later that night I woke up alive and went into the living room to make sure, and it was there against the white wall with a beam on it, a little halo of moonlight, or street light, that let me see J. S. Bach spelled across the book on the rack, and above the keyboard the name of the maker stretched out long in baroque lettering. Very correctly spelled. 𝕭ösendorfer.

I sat down on the bench for a while and then I went back to the bedroom and got into my bed. I was still in the revival mood, but very sleepy, and I said to myself, *This above all.* "This above all: to thine own self be true. And it must follow." But I didn't precisely know what must follow, and I didn't want to think. Just leave it the way it was, and sleep on it.

That was two years ago. Before New York, before any of this, and Judith told me sometime the next day that it had been the same for her — she got up that first night and went into the living room to see if it was really there, just to be sure she hadn't dreamed the whole thing.

I didn't stop at any more bars after the first one. Nor even at any orange juice stands. I fastened the seat belt during a red light in the next town and then kept moving because I wanted, consciously now, to get home and get it over with, the first part at least — see Judith, meet what's-

his-name, show gran the dress and give her the chocolates, and do whatever it might be with, or for, or to our
father, depending on the mood I found him in, which of
course I couldn't know until I got there, quite a moody
man. But in whatever mood I wanted quickly to see him,
get him aside and have him explain things to me, how he
felt about this wedding, mostly, and how he thought I
should feel, and what the chances were, by and large, of
Jude's going through with it. He could bring me up to
date and straighten me out quite fast if he didn't happen to
be engrossed in his work. He'd seen Judith, he'd talked
to her and to the boy, or man, he'd know how it looked.
Our father's a philosopher, retired professor, in fact, of
philosophy, but this makes him sound older than he is, he
retired at an unconventional age, unconventionally early,
and he's lived almost since we were born on our ranch,
making notes for a book on Pyrrhonic Skepticism, but
mostly thinking, and drinking. He quit teaching because
it irked him to have to meet appointments — to shave by
the clock and put on a tie and arrive at a particular place
at a particular time over and over. It wasn't that way in
Athens. A teacher in the golden age could stay in his bath
however long he happened to wish to, and when he got
out, some youth would be there with a towel and dry
him off, and by the time he was dry and robed, the word
would have got around and the young men would have
gathered to question and to be questioned and end up con-
vinced that the unexamined life is not worth living. We
were raised that way ourselves; our father was Socrates,
we were the youth and we sat at his feet. So did Jane, our
mother, when she was home, which was probably more
often than it seemed to us in those days. We liked to have
her there with us at papa's feet, because the questions

were always so much trickier. Answers too. She was an incorrigible youth, the best youth we had.

The top was down on the Riley and I knew I was getting a burn on my nose and forehead. It came out in the valley papers the next day that this was the hottest June twenty-first since 1912, and if I'd known it I suppose I'd have stopped at one of our places and had another drink and put up the top before I went on. But I didn't. It wouldn't matter too much how I looked, an only attendant doesn't have other attendants to compete with; she doesn't have to be evenly tanned; if her forehead is flaking and her nose is peeling, *tant mieux*, so much the better for the bride. It's her show anyhow. And besides, as I understood it, it wouldn't be much of a show, no wedding guests at all, just gran and papa and Judith and I, and of course the famous medical student from Medicine Hat, or wherever. Who would we invite, though, if we wanted anybody? It would have to be old friends of Jane's from Hollywood or New York, or old colleagues of papa's from Cambridge. We didn't have any friends around Putnam. Gran did, some, but we didn't. We went all through grammar school and high school in Putnam, closest town to the ranch, we swam four years on the Putnam swimming team, but we just never mingled somehow. Everybody in town spoke to us and we spoke to them, but we didn't hang around after hours. We never went to Sunday school, and not much to the movies or anybody's slumber party, and we never served any soft drinks or had anybody stay all night at the ranch. We were insular, put it that way. We always came straight home from school because we liked what we had there at papa's feet. We didn't need people.

People came in droves, nevertheless, to Jane's funeral,

but that was because she had become something of a celebrity, even in Putnam where writers don't count, and also because in our bereavement at the time of her death (though papa and gran had known for six months that she was going to die) nobody thought to tell the master of ceremonies that we naturally wanted the funeral to be private, the way we always wanted everything. We got to the chapel late, I remember, and they took us in by a side entrance and put us into a little room of our own behind a scrim and someone was playing "Sheep May Safely Graze" quite imprecisely on a Hammond organ in some other room. I felt identified with the organ, droning along unable to be very clear. But I was clear enough to know that granny was close to collapse, and I knew from the smell that our father had been seeking comfort in his accustomed way, and I was aware that we were at a conventional funeral and that it had nothing in common at all with the only other funerals we'd been to — the one for the cat, and the bird, and the various frogs, and the mouse that got drowned in the bucket. But this couldn't very well have been in that class, because Jane herself helped plan those, and this one had been thrust upon us while we weren't looking — organ, words, people and all. It was big, mainly; when we had to come out from behind the scrim and go forth into the light of day it was like Armistice Day outside, people overflowing the sidewalk and out into the street. We made an inexcusably poor appearance in the face of such a turnout, Judith and I with no hats, no gloves, no dark glasses — our father with no chlorophyl lozenge, and our grandmother unable for once to take any pleasure in a tribute to her daughter's reputation.

But that was a funeral and this was going to be a wedding. I sang a snatch of "Sheep May Safely Graze" and allowed myself to imagine how I'd handle it if it were my wedding. Not this way, I knew that much. I'd either have one or not have one. I'd either come down an aisle, all the way, stop at an altar, repeat my vows with greater unction than the unction they were given me in, and allow all the people to watch me lift the veil. And once the pronouncement had been made I'd sail, as if walking on air, back up the aisle to the Mendelssohn recessional with a smile that would exactly indicate whatever the guests might like to think of it as indicating. Let them believe in it, let them throw rice and honk horns. Or. Or make it a simple appearance before a justice of the peace, with pick-up witnesses, no exhibitionism, no intruding of this ritual on anyone except the principals. Either this or that. But. But I'd never try to have it both ways, I'd never, I swear I'd never choose to come home with a stranger and enact before our household gods the brutal double ceremony of the destruction of Athens and the founding of something that could never at its best equal it. Or come anywhere near it. Or be spoken of in the same breath. From heights you can only descend. Ask anyone. Ask me, preferably.

The sun was low now. It lay on the horizon out to my right, a little shapeless the way it gets when it hits the ground. I was close to the place where I could leave the highway and take the cross-country road to the ranch. You come to a billboard that says IN TIPTON IT's BURDICK's. The sign has been there as long as I can remember, and that's all it says. And then you come to a dairy, and very soon after the dairy you turn left across the northbound traffic, and you're on a road that goes toward the mountains. Our ranch is in the foothills.

The sun was at my back now, off my nose, off my forehead. I was fifty miles from home and I slowed down, all alone now, and let the Riley drift between fields of alfalfa, dark blue-green, like lakes, exchanging swampy breezes over my head and pulling me together. If now there would be a place to stop and have a drink, I'd stop drifting and go in. I'd find a place to comb my hair and put on some lipstick and see to my forehead and my nose and then I'd go out to the common room and take care of my thirst. I'd heed the demands, speak to a stranger and confide in him or even her that I was going to a wedding. But I knew this road like the place it was leading to and there were no common rooms on it, no taverns, no inns. The alfalfa fields would yield after a few miles and become cotton fields, and on beyond there would be vineyards with leafy vines delicately espaliered on a length of wire, looking young and adaptable to the basic training. I knew this road. The only buildings on it are pumphouses, unless you count as a building the emergency telephone booth at the crossroads near the power line. The one where we stopped and telephoned from the time Judith forgot her vaccination certificate on the way back to college our second year. We made the call and waited on the corner throwing rocks at targets until Jane came charging up with the certificate and quite a few other things we'd forgotten. Driving this car, too; wearing shorts, I remember, and a blue polo shirt of papa's with the tail out almost as long as the shorts.

Other times, other emergencies, and suddenly I was wondering about getting home a day early without telling anybody. Or asking. I hadn't thought about it as being anything peculiar, because I was going home, and one of the things about belonging somewhere is that you can go there without permission because it's where you belong.

But did I? Did I belong, at such a time, where plans were being made and questions of policy being decided, matters of great moment like for example do they have sterling silver or stainless steel? That kind of thing, white towels or solid colors or stripes; planned parenthood, or children? They'd need to talk. They'd want to get things straight. They hadn't known each other very long.

I heard myself dismiss John Thomas Finch and his bride-elect with a word I don't remember ever having said before or ever having wanted to, and I was shocked to hear it coming from me less than fifty miles from home with such bitterness and so little warning. What a way to talk about someone I don't even know, and someone I know quite well.

I don't know when I stopped drifting. Probably at the same time the word came out, but I was moving again, kicking up dust along the edges of the vineyards and slamming along between them, past the power line and past something green and shining. I was a good way beyond it when the green-and-shining got through to me for what it was — the old emergency booth, the one to use when in trouble. I stopped as soon as I knew it, left rubber on the road, and twisted around and looked back, and I was right. Our booth, there by the power line. I put an arm over the back of the seat and backed up the whole way and pulled in on plowed ground beside it and cut the motor. It was twilight now, or almost; vespers after a roaring day, and I let it come in on me — my homeland, after all. It was still hot, but the edge was off, and I sat quiet for a minute while the dust settled. I stripped off my gloves, pulled the belt apart, found coins for the phone, and kept hearing a sound I thought I knew and then knew it — the moan of a pump, not far away, quite close.

It wasn't far to seek, just across the road, a plank pump-house with a pipe sticking out of it spilling a clear head of water into a high cement weir, and I got out of the car and went straight to it and looked up at it — water, with-out which nothing for us farmers, and also for us vagrants. There was a sun-beat ladder leaning against the weir, and I went up four or five rungs, very gingerly on the one that was split around the nail, until I was high enough to touch the flow with a finger, and then with a whole hand. There was weight behind it, and enough force to push the hand away, so I took it away and grabbed the sides of the ladder and went on up and leaned far in. My mouth went to pieces with such a push against it but I made it hold while I drank. I made it hold again and again, and then without even deciding to I stuck my head in and let the water tear through to the roots of my hair and sluice one ear. I didn't stay long and on the way down I forgot all about the rung that was split. It was very dusty where I landed, and I'm not sure but I think I cried a little. At times like this someone like me needs to be picked up and brushed off and gently told not to be so headlong, not so intrepid, to wait for a tavern or hang on until she's at home where goblets are and monogrammed glasses, and va-grancy is something you only read about in newspapers. I looked up at the ladder from where I sat and saw that it was in worse shape than I was, with a rung hanging loose below the nail like a broken rib; and I picked myself up and brushed myself off gently enough and crossed the road to the booth and went in and remembered what to do — leave the receiver on the hook, turn a crank on the bat-tery box quite vigorously, then lift the receiver and listen for a voice to ask you what number you want and tell you how much it will cost. I did everything right and it worked.

"Yes?" I heard my grandmother say. It's what she says instead of hello, and I've never understood exactly what she means by it, so I always ask. Jane always asked too. I got it from her.

"Yes what?" I said. It should have identified me but it didn't, and she repeated the question, if it was one, and I dealt directly.

"Granny, this is Cassie," I said.

"Whom?" she said.

"Not whom," I said. "Who. Who this is is Cassandra Edwards. Of Berkeley California."

"Just a minute," she said and I heard her say: "Jim, it's Berkeley, I'm afraid something has happened to Cassie."

"No no," I called, "don't talk to papa, talk to me." But I said it to nobody, and a moment later I heard another aside, still from my grandmother. "Just get a towel," she said, "and come to the phone."

After this there was silence, nothing. I hallooed a little and swatted some mosquitoes against the wall of the booth, but only two or three out of fifteen or twenty, and the next voice I heard was the voice of my sister Judith, a little breathless but intensely recognizable. I felt my knees buckle with recognition. Then I took a deep breath and firmed up.

"What's the towel for?" I said.

"What towel?" she said, and then: "Oh, I just came in from the pool and granny didn't want me dripping all over everything."

"That's understandable," I said. "At least to us housewives."

"Where have you been," she said, "I've been trying to get you ever since morning."

"I've been away."

"I know. I rang the house down. Is anything wrong?"

"Not very," I said. "What did you want?"

"I wanted you to come home. Today. Quick."

I couldn't say anything to this, at least nothing easy, because I couldn't think what it might mean. Besides, I was suddenly aware that there was a second telephone in our grandmother's bedroom and I felt certain that someone had by this time set John Thomas Finch up at the other one to listen in on the conversation until the time was ripe to introduce him. Be prepared for gaiety.

"Is anyone else on this phone?" I said, to get it over with.

"I don't think so. Why?"

"I thought I heard a click. Did you hear a click?"

"Well, what if you did?" Judith said. "They've had the whole line to themselves all year. We get a turn."

"I didn't mean the party line," I said. "I meant the phone in gran's room. Is somebody on that one?"

"No. Granny's in the kitchen and papa's at the bar."

"Who with?"

"Nobody. He's just sitting there. On a stool, like."

I took the plunge.

"Where's what's-his-name?" I said, much too audibly.

"What's whose name?" I got back, just as audibly.

My turn.

"Oh you know," I said. "George. The sorcerer's apprentice."

I had not intended to say anything like this. It just happened and it created a silence on the other end.

"Jude," I said, "are you still there?"

"I'm not quite sure," she said. "Should I be?"

"Yes, please be."

"I was afraid you might be this way," she said. Her

voice was very sad. Very remote. But nothing like so sad as I felt, nor so remote.

"Let me start over," I said. "I was asking about — John Thomas Finch."

"The one you think of as George what's-his-name?"

"Not at all. The one I think of as John Thomas Finch — constantly."

"I call him Jack. So can you."

"Lucky day."

"Stop it."

"Oh I will. I want to. Tell me how."

I meant it, and she could tell I did, I think. But she didn't answer, and I was still afraid he might be listening.

"How will this sound to *him?*" I said.

"Sound to whom?" she said, and I was supposed to give the answer.

"To Jock," I said, "or whatever we call him. Jack?'"

"George."

"Listen, Judith, we can't both do this. Where is he?"

"He's not here. That's what I've been calling all day to tell you."

I couldn't say anything or even feel anything, but the mosquitoes lifted a song while I remained in suspension and tried for a way to speak. In the end, though, I didn't have to say anything because the telephone operator cut in to tell me that my three minutes were up and that if I wished to continue for another three minutes I should deposit thirty cents. It took me a while to find it in the right-sized coins. I had to go back to the car and root through my purse, but I got it together finally and dropped it into the slots and the line was still open. Judith spoke as soon as the ring of the last coin died.

"What's this thirty cents," she said, very full of life. "Where are you?"

"Me? You remember the place we called from when you forgot your vaccination certificate?"

"You're there?"

"Yes."

"Really?"

"Yes, really. It's all full of waltzing mosquitos and I just fell off of a ladder."

"*What?*" she said, quite a lot like granny. Concerned. I loved the sound of it. Loved it.

"Also," I said, "one of my ears has been sluiced."

"Sluiced?" she said. "What is it?"

"I'll tell you later. I just called to see if it was all right to come home tonight. I mean instead of tomorrow."

"Are you crazy?"

"It's possible I am. In fact, I —"

"Just a minute," Judith said. Then — "I just told gran and she wants to know if you've had dinner."

"Yes, indeed, but thank her." I couldn't remember ever having eaten.

"How soon can you be here?"

"It depends how fast I go."

"Go fast."

"One thing first —"

"What?"

"If he's not there, where is he, and don't ask me who, just tell me."

"Don't talk so fast. What did you say?"

"Where is Jack?" I said. "Did you hear that?"

"Yes indeed. You're coming in fine."

"I asked where he was, or where he is. Where is he?"

"He's gone to Los Angeles — West Los Angeles, to the University Hospital."

"What's wrong with him?"

"Nothing. He wants a job — for a year from now."

"Orderly?"

"No, resident. They live in."

"Intern, don't you mean?"

"The point is he's not here. He's in Los Angeles."

"When did he go?"

"This morning. Sudden decision."

"When will he be back?"

"Tomorrow sometime."

"When's the wedding?"

"Come on home and we'll figure it out."

"You don't mean I get a vote?"

"Cass — ?"

"Here."

There was no sound for a moment, but when I heard her again it was as if she had crawled inside the telephone to come closer and give the word directly to me, as if we were accomplices in a dangerous enterprise and precise instructions were of paramount, so to speak, importance.

"Here's what you do. Hang up now. Don't say one more word. Just hang the receiver on the hook and come straight home. I'll wait until I hear you hang up and then I will. Now — go!"

It was very full of life, the line between her mouth and my ear after she stopped instructing and waited for me to hang up. It was so charged up, so open, so electric, that I couldn't bring myself to kill it, and I knew she wouldn't quit until I did. It was very nice, listening to her waiting for me, and I felt very good about it because I was partly doing what she laid it on me to do. I was not saying one more word and nothing could have induced me to. But on the other hand I was not hanging up either, not while I could hear this beating silence, this close connection between where I was going and where I was now stuck, enchanted and under instructions, partly heeded. Let her wait. Let her stick it out, or let her break down and ask me if I was still there. But she didn't and I didn't really think she would. We both waited until time ran out and someone else spoke up asking me, and only me, if I wished to continue the conversation for another three minutes. I couldn't answer, of course, but Judith did, very quickly.

"Oh no, nothing more. Thank you, operator."

Then, right on top of it she tossed, obliquely, a last instruction.

"The other party," she said, as if the operator would be delighted to hear it, "is practically home."

I heard the line go dead then, really dead, and I leaned back against the wall of the booth with the receiver still against my ear. I was the other party, and how well I knew it — awaited, instructed, invited, and possessed of some priceless information having to do with Jack Lynch or Jerk Finch, a name I would never be able to master no matter how hard I might try. But I might try.

I hung the receiver on its hook, gave it a small pat, and unfolded the glass door and stood in the frame of it, looking out at my mother's car, so nicely parked, ready to take me, and beyond it at the lovely head of water spilling endlessly into such a tall cup. Then I banged myself on the ear with the heel of my hand the way they taught us years ago to break up a water lock, and got into the car and fastened the seat belt and went toward home. It was all but dark now. The country smelled hot and familiar. I followed the beam and went singing a song of good sentiment and high courage — the "Marseillaise" itself.

THE ROAD takes a slight curve just before it comes to our
buildings. It's an uphill curve and it doesn't allow for any
perspective of approach. You get to the top of the curve
and suddenly it's all there behind a fence on the left side of
the road, starting with the corral, then farther on, the
house, then the shop and garage, and beside the gate the
little adobe house where Conchita Padilla, a highly accomplished shirt ironer and floor waxer, lives with her husband, Tomás Padilla, an indifferent gardener. There's a
slightly feudal aspect here, this house by the gate. It gives
the sense of a gatekeeper, guardhouse, drawbridge, and
difficulty of access, though all you have to do is turn in at
the gate, which is always open, and crunch along the
stones of the driveway to our house, which stretches out
quite long and is made of railroad ties.

Before I hit the top of the curve I could see a glow, like
a fire, or lights above a town, and a minute later I knew
what it was — somebody's idea of leaving a light in the
window for me. Everything very bright — floodlights on
the lawn and over the corral, coach lights beside the
door, rural electrification all over everywhere, and it
stabbed me to think that someone had flipped all these
switches to guide me home and get me there. But someone had. Not my mother, for good and sufficient reasons.
Not my grandmother, because she is not prodigal with

lights the way she is with charge accounts. Not my father, because he never thinks of this kind of thing.

I gave up the "Marseillaise" at the gate and crunched down the drive, pulled up at the door, and hit the accelerator twice, quite hard, before I cut the motor. The dog came first, around the side of the house, very fierce, hackles up, but when I got out of the car she stopped barking, released the hackles and shook hands, quite cordially. By that time my father had come out and was moving around the car toward me. He was wearing white pants and a white shirt and dark glasses, and he held me off at arm's length and looked at me a minute before he spoke.

"Now which one are you?" he said. I don't know why he said it. It stopped being funny years ago; if it ever was.

"I'm Cassandra," I nevertheless said, "the one who wailed from the walls of Troy. And you stuck me with it yourself, so don't look at *me*."

He pulled me in, then, against his beautiful shirt.

"It's a good name," he said. "I like it."

"Then that's all that matters," I said. And I stayed there happily trapped against his collar and some of his neck, inhaling the pure distillation which has always, as long as I can remember, come consistently one-hundred proof from his pores to let me know who it is. For a moment I was back in Athens with the other two youths at the sage's feet, and the sage must have known how it was with me, because he released me one split second before I burst into tears. I don't know for certain what they would have been tears of if they had burst and flowed, but I suppose of relief — the relief of having some philosophical arms around me, for a change. Arms I could trust, I mean, and a distillation I could understand and identify as being something as universal as Five-star Hennessy, after a bleak sea-son of essences called Joie de Patou or Femme de Rochas that I could tell apart without greatly caring which was which. Or whom it was on.

I don't know when my grandmother came out, but when I looked around, after the release, she was standing on the bricks between the coach lamps, looking very fragile and elegant, and being battered by moths. My grandmother does not admire moths. She believes they eat people's clothes and spin webs in people's uncooked Cream of Wheat, but she waited there surrounded until papa released me and I came to release her.

"Let's go in out of the moths," I said, after I kissed her, and she was wonderfully willing, but she stopped to bat some away from the door before she opened it.

"Try to think of them as the emblem of summer," I told her, going in. "They're pretty."

She closed the door on them, though, and on my father opening the trunk of the car, and we were inside, and I was like the one who is it in a game of hide-the-thimble, look-ing around, at the piano, at the desk, at the chairs, at whatever offered while my grandmother was telling me how adorable it was of me to come home a day early; how clairvoyant for me to arrive like this, when Judy wanted so much to have me to herself for a little while be-fore the wedding, while the young man was away.

This caught my attention.

"Why would she want me to herself?" I asked. I think there may have been a small snarl in the question, but if there was, my grandmother either didn't notice it or elected not to. I walked across the living room, the full length, and looked out the big windows at the lawn, and out beyond it, at the pool, and on out farther at the river bottom which I couldn't see in the dark. These are in descending stages. The pool is two steps down from the lawn and behind a railroad tie fence, so that you can't stand at the window and look directly at it. Ties get in the way, but I could see that the underwater light was on and the water was churned up. I saw the flash of an arm, or it may have been a leg, and then a lower tie stopped it and I watched farther on in the direction I thought it was going, while my little grandmother was not exactly answering my question but talking around the edges of it in what struck me as quite a tiresome way — telling me how important it is for a girl who is going to be married to have a little last time alone with her family — particularly her mother, before she takes the big step.

"What mother?" I said. I saw the leg again, or the arm. Leg, I think. Then I stopped looking and turned to gran, who was looking as sad as I knew she would now be looking and telling me that that was what she meant. Without Jane, or as I believe she said it, with Jane gone, it put a great deal of responsibility on her, and on me too, to play a mother's part, to substitute for the loss. At such a time a girl needs advice and training.

I couldn't remember Jane ever giving either of us much advice, but I didn't say so. I went over to the piano and looked at the music on the rack. Mozart K 475.

"If she's so wild for advice," I said to gran, "why's she staying out there under water?"

"She told me to tell you to come out the minute you got here."

"She did?"

It must have sounded stiff, or unbelieving, because granny came right in on it telling me how Judith had been calling me every half hour all day long . . .

"I know," I said, "she told me."

. . . and how when the young man decided to go to Los Angeles, Judith could not be coaxed into going with him, because she wanted so much to get me home and have me to herself for a little while.

"That's what you said the other time," I said, but easily, and with no bite, or not much. "What kind of advice does she need? Like whether to get married, or what to wear to the wedding?"

"Oh," gran said, "it's all decided. We went to Fresno yesterday and got it at Magnin's. It's very plain, but she's happy with it."

"And that's what counts, isn't it?" I said.

"We'll have to find you something, too," gran said, and I told her I'd already found it, and charged it to her account also at Magnin's but in Oakland, and that I was happy with it, which is what counts.

She looked very happy, and then, suddenly, worried.

"Cassie," she said, "you look tired. Are you sure you've had dinner?"

I nodded. Papa was coming in with my things. I didn't want to display any clothes right then, and so I went and took the box of chocolates out of his hands and told him to put everything in my room and I'd unpack later.

"Here," I said to gran, and held out the box, "are some bitter chocolate cherries. But keep the box level until they settle down."

"I'll put them in the refrigerator," she said and thanked me quite lavishly for always remembering what she likes best and even what brand. I don't know why this always touches her so, if it does. There's nothing hard about it. But I seldom get praised for the hard things I do, and I do some of the hardest things. Things like waking up in the morning and going to sleep at night, all all alone except when I'm with someone; and it's getting harder and harder for me to be really with anyone. And more or less impossible, on the other hand, not to be frequently with someone. What's left is hardest of all — writing that dumb thesis, between times.

Papa came back into the living room empty-handed.

"How's your thesis?" he said, and I told him I'd tell him in minute detail some other time, but that right now I probably should go out and pay my respects to the bride. Elect.

"She can wait," he said. "Let's have a drink."

"Lovely," I said, and it did seem lovely, suddenly, the whole idea, getting here, being in this house where I know everything so well, the wastebaskets and the paintings and the herringbone wood on the ceiling; my sister out there breaking her lungs in the pool waiting for me, and me inside about to have a drink with our father.

Our house spreads around a lot. There's the big long living room with the entrance door at one end and the wall of windows at the other, then two steps up from it, like a little stage, there's a minor living room with a stone fireplace and bookshelves and a mosaic counter which marks off the limits of the kitchen without excluding it. That is to say, you can sit at the bar on the minor living room side and look into the kitchen; or you can sit at the bar on the kitchen side and look into the minor living room and on down into the major one where the piano is and most of the paintings and the headless wooden statue Jane brought back from Mexico. It's a good house, and you can look around in it for a long time without discovering whether it's predominantly Mexican, or Japanese, or Roman, or what. It's a lot of things.

My father was on the kitchen side of the counter, out of sight, down on his haunches, I suppose, getting bottles and glasses out of the cabinet underneath. And I supposed right, because bottles began to appear on the counter, and then glasses, and then my father himself rose up with a tray of ice cubes and started putting them into an ice bucket. I took a little last look out the window at the pool with the light shining up out of it and part of a human body flashing on the surface, and then I turned away, jumped up the two steps to the little living room and went to the bar and stood there running my hand over the tiles. They felt very familiar. This is where I almost always did my Latin when I was in high school, with the textbook and the note-book and the verb wheel and the props and the pencils spread out all the way from the copper sink to the last stripe of tile. Very fine place to study Latin. I leaned across the counter and turned a handle and watched a rib-bon of water unfurl from the goose-necked spigot to the little copper sink, all soundlessly and with no splash. But my father noticed it anyhow and told me to quit play-ing in the water and announce what I'd have.

"Brandy and soda, if you please," I said. It's not my favorite drink, but it's papa's, and it seemed polite to fol-low his lead, since it was just us.

"Very civilized choice," he said, and he put back two of the bottles — the gin, that is, and the vermouth — and splashed enough brandy into my glass to make my grand-mother, at the far end of the kitchen, take notice and offer me dinner again, quickly.

I declined again. I'd got more or less out of the habit of eating. I could come quite close to taking my skirt off without undoing it and the bridesmaid's dress was a size smaller than I'd been wearing for the last five years.

"I'm really not hungry. I'm just thirsty," I said, and I held my glass up while papa poured soda into it and then gave me some ice cubes.

It's true, I was very thirsty. I didn't wait to propose a

toast or clink my glass against my father's or even let him drink first. I took a drink quite fast and told my grandmother if she'd like to see my wedding shoes or the dress they were in the brown-and-white striped boxes, and that the bills were inside, or the sales slip, or whatever they call it when you don't pay cash.

"I O U," papa said, and granny left immediately for my room, while I drank again and realized my father was right, that brandy is a civilized choice, very complex and rewarding, much more twisty than scotch.

My father drank too, but deliberately, as if he had all night, and all day tomorrow — a lifetime, in fact, of nights and days. He'd made the civilized choice long ago and he could make it last as long as he lasted.

He looked very colonial with his mustache clipped so short it scarcely looked like one, and the black-and-white hair quite short too and showing more white than black, and a ruddy outdoors look which never came from outdoors. I imagined, looking at him, that I just might have an outdoors look myself. My hair had been through a long hard day of sun, wind, dust, and finally water, all the elements but fire. And so had the rest of me.

"Would you like it," I said, "if I went and combed my hair?"

"I'd like it better if you'd settle down," he said. "Your hair's all right. You look like a dryad."

He'd picked one of the very few images that might content me, and I thanked him, and relaxed. But only for the space of a swallow, because I immediately began to wonder what I could find to tell him about my thesis to give it some importance, where none was.

I sat there trying to remember what was on the page I'd pulled out of the typewriter and crumpled up before I left the apartment, before I folded the cover over the keyboard of a piano that is half mine, before I jumped ship a day early and lit out for home to let myself be introduced to someone who departed before I arrived, and whom I would now not have to meet until tomorrow. It gave me a certain freedom, the reprieve, and I decided, since I couldn't remember anything much about my thesis, to forget it.

"Well, what's he like?" I said.

My father didn't ask whom I had in mind, but he didn't answer the question either. He got philosophical instead and gave me a speech about how it's not easy to say what anyone's like, even among people you think you know well; and this hit me because, like most of papa's propositions, it was infuriatingly true. Judith Edwards, for example, whom I once thought I knew like myself, like the back of my hand, as they say. What made her decide to try New York, alone, for a year, before we tried Paris, together? Who knows what anybody's like?

I took an ice cube out of the bucket, closed my fist over it, and let it drip into the copper sink. This comes under the head of playing in the water, but papa didn't apparently notice, and it had the effect of rallying my forces and not letting me give up.

"Granting all that," I said in the way I seem to have to talk to my father, always having to grant him something before I can get on with whatever it is, "granting all you say about the difficulty of saying what anybody is like, still you must have formed some opinion about him in three days, or however long he's been around."

"Five days," papa said. "Gran and I met them at the Bakersfield airport last Sunday."

"Do they have a license?"

My father looked at me curiously and said he didn't think they needed one; it was a commercial plane; and this left me in the position of having to tell him I didn't mean a license to fly, I meant a marriage license. The law requires that you file an intention to wed at least three days before you do so, as I understood it.

My father nodded, but I couldn't tell whether it was in agreement with my understanding of the law or in answer to my question. There was nothing to do but ask again.

"Do they have a marriage license, do you know?"

"I suppose so," papa said. "They went to Visalia to the courthouse Monday."

I felt my hand tighten on the ice cube. To go to a county courthouse, sixty miles away, and apply for a license to marry is practically as serious an avowal as the very wedding. They got here Sunday. They applied Monday. They were not easily distracted from their purpose, or purposes, apparently.

I dropped the ice cube into the copper basin and it lay there in the drain looking so useless that I turned on the water to help it melt and get it over with. Papa didn't say anything, but I turned it off fairly soon and got back to my drink. And then back to my research.

"Do you like him?" I said, and I knew immediately that this was no way to have put it. My father never was one to deal in such simple terms as personal liking or disliking. He'd want to have the terms defined — by liking him did I mean did he find him congenial socially (which, of course, was what I did mean) or did he approve of him in various respects — did he approve, for example, of his attitude toward medicine, or toward monogamy, or money, or mountebanks? He'd want the terms defined, and then either broadened out or narrowed down.

But he didn't do any immediate cross-questioning. I finished my drink and set the glass down nearer to him than to me, and he interpreted the move correctly and made me another drink, this time with slightly more brandy and slightly less soda, and the same number of ice cubes. Two. It was an unfatherly amount of brandy, and while I was thanking him for it, he splashed some more into his own glass without adding any soda and answered my question in a way I hadn't at all expected.

"You shouldn't ask me whether I like him or not," he said. "The way you mean it, I don't suppose I like anybody."

It made me like him very much to hear him say that, so concisely and so briefly. I looked across at him and saw that he was looking on out behind me, quite pointedly, and I swung around on my stool and saw my grandmother coming up the steps between the lower living room and the upper one with a shoe in her hand, one of my wedding shoes.

"Rowena," my father said to my grandmother from behind me, "Cassie is very much concerned to find out what Jack Finch is like."

"He's all wrapped up in Judy," gran said in a fluty voice, "and that's the most important thing."

She was coming toward us with the shoe, and I swung the stool around toward the counter again, so that I didn't have to look at her saying things like that. They were her kind of thing, and I'd no doubt be hearing a great many of them, but I could separate them from the coquettish facial expression that went with them just by not looking at the face.

"Is Jude wrapped up too?" I said. I said it possibly a little too loudly or pointedly just to let her know how a phrase like wrapped-up sounds to the sensitive ear; but though I meant it only for her, it was my father who answered.

"I don't think we need to be too much concerned," he said. "They seem to understand each other."

This was the second time he'd used the word concerned, and I considered asking him why he kept using it on me. Was the implication that what Judith did was no concern of mine, because if that was what he meant I should make it very clear that I could not possibly be less concerned. If a person of her stature and of her gifts chooses to sell herself short and go the way of all suburbia, who am I to speak up for what I think of as virtue? Who am *I*? Or, possibly, who *am* I? Make it who *was* I, because once I was somebody.

I kept thinking things like this, but not letting them really get to me. And I didn't say a word, I know that. So I was quite surprised to hear my father speak to me in the sort of voice people use on children.

"What's the matter, Cassandra?" he said. My name sounded good and his voice saying it sounded so kind, and so full of his word, concern, that I think I might almost have told him how I felt — not just about this but about everything — my classes, my job, my entanglements, my nights turning into days and then back again with no firm markers, no dawns or sunsets or landmarks, except maybe the bridge, and the endless belt of plates and glasses and toothpaste and towels and couches. I think I might have, but I didn't, because my grandmother came up to the end of the counter and stood between us holding the shoe and saying she thought it was exquisite, beautifully made, but did the man make me step down on a measuring stick, because it looked miles too long for me.

In Rowena Abbott's feeling, small feet are an unfailing sign of gentle birth. Her daughter Jane's feet were size four and a half, quite narrow, and a great satisfaction to her.

"*Did* the man?" she said, and I gave up thinking what I could or couldn't tell my father and said yes, and then no, because it wasn't a man in the first place, it was a woman and she had simply brought out shoes she thought I might like and had me try them on to see if they fitted.

"If the shoe fits, charge it," my father said quite pleasantly, without concern, and I took the shoe out of my grandmother's hand and explained to her that the inch on the end was all design. I showed her a place an inch or so up from the end and told her I didn't go personally any farther than that, and then I kicked off my shoes and put the new one on and walked around the rug to let her see.

"Walk on out," she said, and I did, to the edge of the steps and took a quick look out the window, I saw the light coming up through the water, but nothing else.

"Beautiful," my grandmother said, "very striking," and my father said he thought I'd look even better if both my legs were the same length.

I had taken the shoe off, demonstration over, and was walking back barefooted to the bar when the telephone rang. Four short rings.

"That's for us," my father said, and sat where he was.

"Answer it, Cassie," my grandmother said.

I set the shoe down on the counter, and started toward the telephone, and then stopped. I had a quick frightened feeling it might be someone I'd neglected to say goodbye to in Berkeley, and I didn't care to say goodbye from here, nor to explain any neglect.

"You answer it, Granny," I said, "and if by any chance it's for me, say I'm not here."

The ring came again, four shorts, while my grandmother stood looking puzzled.

"They might want me to come back and correct some more examinations," I said, "and I don't want to, I want to stay home."

She moved toward the telephone then, and I sat down on the stool, and took a drink while she said yes, whatever it means, and then whom and who. It was clearly a long-distance call, with an interlocutor involved, and a faulty connection.

"What's this about your having to go back?" my father asked me, and I told him it was nothing, I'd corrected all the examinations in the world, but that I just didn't like answering telephones on my vacation, and I thought gran would answer it for me if I made it sound threatening.

Nothing much was happening on the telephone. Granny was waiting, apparently, for the operator to connect the other end.

"Where's it from?" I said, and she shook her head, nervously, as if she were trying to hear something being said to her on the line. I passed the time looking at my handsome long shoe. It was made of white ribbed silk and there was a very small gold tip on the heel which I placed in the exact center of one of the little square tiles, where it could not possibly have appeared to better advantage, round peg on a square base.

"Shoes belong in closets," my father said, "if not on feet," but I left it where it was and kept an ear cocked toward the conversation which had not begun, but appeared to be going to, and then did.

"Yes, she is," my grandmother said in a very gracious voice. Then, "Just a minute, I'll call her."

She set the telephone down on the desk and turned to me and said, "It's West Los Angeles for Judith Edwards."

There was a big beach towel on the back of the chair, and my grandmother picked it up and handed it to me.

"Call her, Cassie, and tell her to wrap up in this."

I got off the stool and stood holding the towel quite stupidly, but feeling more panic than stupidity. All this leisure I'd been enjoying, waiting for the moment when I'd go out and pay, as I'd said, my respects, what happened to it? Now I had to find her in a hurry with nothing prepared to say.

On the other hand, I didn't have to prepare anything, because it was prepared for me. All I had to say was come in, you're wanted on the telephone.

"Hurry up, Cassie," my grandmother said, "it's Jack."

"Jack who?" I said and I saw my grandmother's mouth go into a tight little line of exasperation, at the same time my father told me to do as I was told — go get Judith.

I went out by the dining room door and stood for a moment on the deck looking down at the pool. The water was calmer. Nobody was swimming. Then I saw her. She was sitting on the end of the diving board, rocking it and looking toward the house. I think we saw each other at the same time, but she spoke first — or called.

"It's about time."

There was no real impatience in the tone, just in the words. The tone was hers, very light and easy.

"I tried," I called back, "but I got held up talking to papa and gran."

"Well come on down and talk to me."

"Somebody else wants to talk to you," I said, "somebody from West Los Angeles."

"What did you say?"

"I said you're wanted on the telephone. Come on, come on."

"Me?"

"Yes, you. They're waiting for you — West Los Angeles, does it mean anything?"

I stood where I was and watched her jump up, come back to the end of the diving board, jump down to the terrace and come running. Up the two steps, across the lawn, up the steps to the deck, straight to me.

"Here, wrap this around you," I said, "for granny."

I tossed her the towel and had the feeling I get when I look at her, or when I look very self-consciously into a mirror, a feeling of being pulled apart and put together.

"You look wonderful," she said. "Which phone?"

"Desk," I said.

"Who answered — you?"

"No, gran."

"Are they talking?"

"No, it's person-to-person for you."

"Good, then I can dry my feet."

She bent down with the towel, and I took it out of her hand and sat down on one of the steps and told her to hold a foot up and I'd do it. She put a hand on my head for balance and I dried her feet, one after the other quite fast and told her to get going.

"I'll wait here," I said. She had the dining room door open and she turned and said, "Don't be crazy, come on in," and reached out and took hold of my arm and dragged me up and along with her.

She threw the towel down on the desk chair and sat down and picked up the telephone, and I walked past her to the counter where my shoe was, and my glass. My father wasn't at the counter; I looked around and saw him standing by the mantel filling his pipe from a tobacco can.

I couldn't see my grandmother either; and so I picked up the brandy bottle and poured quite an amount quite quickly into my glass.

"*This* is Judith Edwards," I heard my sister say, and I picked up my glass and started to go to my room. I didn't want to put her through the embarrassment of having me there listening to one side of a conversation, whether she wanted me or not. I walked past my father, down the two steps, looked for a moment out at the pool and then went into the hall that leads to the bedrooms, the one Judith and I share, and granny's. Granny's door was open and I looked in and saw the shoe box on her bed, and beyond it on a night stand, the telephone, the very one I was afraid they'd set Jack Finch up at when I called from the booth. I stood in the open door for a moment, not long, and then I took a drink, went inside, closed the door after me and walked around the bed to the night stand and considered, again not long. The main thing to consider in an operation of this kind is the little click a telephone makes when you pick it up. I set my glass down on the night stand and lifted the telephone straight up, very slowly and ever so gently. There was no click at all, a flawless operation, and I could hear Jack Finch's voice before I ever put the telephone to my ear — very masculine voice, clear, business-like, and doing all the talking. I sat down on gran's bed and let myself in on what was being said without much feeling one way or the other. Rather an attractive voice, and a nice unexpectedly impersonal manner, I thought, limiting the conversation to clear-cut information — he'd got the appointment set up for nine the next morning, which would make it quite easy for him to catch Flight 756 to Bakersfield, arriving at two forty-eight in the afternoon, and could Judith meet him?

"Of course I'll meet you," Judith said. "Any time, any

place, and how lovely for it to be two forty-eight tomorrow in Bakersfield."

"What's so great about Bakersfield?"

"It's where I meet you, isn't that enough?" Jude said, and after that the impersonal business was all finished and done with and the real John Thomas Finch was in there claiming his own, and telling her he could not, he simply could not, understand how anything so good could happen to him. He'd spent the whole day wondering about it, very abjectly.

"I know, I know," Jude said, very quietly, "it's been the same for me." I could imagine her looking around the room making sure I hadn't come back before she let herself say anything so private as those I knows.

I felt I'd had it and that I could now hang up and let them run the call up alone. But I didn't, because I was arrested by the next thing Jude said, and by the way she said it.

"Jack — Cass came home tonight."

"She did? I thought it was tomorrow."

"It was, only she came today."

I was very glad I hadn't hung up. Otherwise I wouldn't have known that Judith hadn't told him she'd been calling me all day to get me to come home.

"It was the oddest thing," Judith then said in a groping kind of tone, "after you left I called her in Berkeley to see if she couldn't come today. I thought it would be nice to have her here while I was waiting around. Sort of have a chance to catch up, you know?"

"Yes."

"Well I never got the call through, and just a minute ago here she came. Spooky?"

"I've heard spookier. How is she?"

"She looks spectacular."

"Just like you?"

"Oh no, not at all. We're not at all alike really, except very superficially. She's bright, for one thing."

"You're brilliant."

I shifted the telephone to the other hand while I took a drink and let them have this out about who's bright and who's brilliant. Neither of them sounded very brilliant to me — more like a couple of high school kids that get on the line and won't quit. Only this was long distance, and even less bright. I didn't know, of course, whether John T. Finch could afford it or not. Nobody had ever bothered to tell me whether he was a struggling medical student or a non-struggling one; but anyhow his fiancée was on the level with him — she hadn't let it go that I had just happened in uninvited, though in a way I actually had and there was no need to go into the intricacies of my being home early, particularly in the way she had done it, as if forcing herself to give him the precise facts. I couldn't think why this was unless they had talked me over quite thoroughly and decided what to do about me before they ever came home, or asked me to the wedding. But they couldn't have. This was just Judith being more than honest, as usual. I knew it a minute later when she asked John Thomas Finch if he wouldn't like to meet me and he said he'd like it very much and to put me on.

I hadn't expected this and I went into a small state of panic. The question would now be: where was I? And I wasn't quite sure. The big first thing was to get rid of the telephone without making a click. I set my glass down on the night stand, shifted the telephone to the right hand, stood up and lowered away, straight down, very very gently. But it didn't go well. I was shaking slightly, and

I lifted it again before I had it all the way down, and started over. I could hear Judith through the receiver calling me, telling me to come and meet Jack, and this time I lowered all the way down and let it click if it had to, and picked up my drink and got out of gran's room and across the hall and into her bathroom.

I closed the door behind me and leaned back against it and felt waves of heat rise from my heels to my head and then ripple back to my heels — a sensation very much like a chill except for the heat. The only light in the bathroom came from outside, through the window. I could see granny's towels and her shower curtain. I thought hard, or tried to, about where it would look nice for me to be found. Not in gran's bedroom, where the extra telephone is, I knew that much, but *then* where? In our own room, unpacking. But there wasn't time for me to get there. The only thing I could do was stay where I was, in gran's dark bathroom. I was still barefooted, and I stepped into the bathtub and pulled the shower curtain and stood there with my drink in my hand and my feet on the cool enamel of the tub. I thought I heard my name in Judith's voice, nearer and farther. I even heard the hall door open and close again, and then nothing, and I began to feel quite eccentric, standing fully clothed in my grandmother's bathtub with a drink in my hand and a shower curtain between me and my unmasking. Ludicrous, but I stayed there thinking it over until I realized how I'd got there, a fugitive in my own house, pushed into hiding by a conspiracy that operated by long distance telephone; and once I thought of it that way I felt free to protect myself in any way I could.

I was washing my face when the knock came at the door. The light was on, the shower curtain was pushed to the end of the rod, my drink was standing on the counter of the lavatory, and I had the water running into the bowl and was bent over toward it. I said come in, making it sound gurgly through the water, and Judith came in and told me a lot of things I already knew — how John Thomas Finch would be in Bakersfield at two forty-eight tomorrow, etc. etc., and how she'd tried to get me to say hello to him on the phone and couldn't find me.

"Oh?" I said, "where was I?"

"You could have washed your face some other time," she said. She sounded seriously disappointed. "You didn't have to run away."

"Yes I did," I said.

"But *why?*"

I turned off the water, pulled a towel off the rack and began to pat my face.

"I can't stand anything one-sided," I said, and I went on with the towel keeping my face pretty well covered.

"*What?*" I heard Judith say in a way that sounded somewhat less than fully bright, though I'd just heard Jack Finch speak of her as brilliant.

I held the towel over my eyes with both hands and told her what I meant — that I wouldn't have the smallest reluctance about listening to a conversation between her and the man she was going to marry, or anybody else, for that matter, if I could be situated where I could hear both sides, but that one half of a conversation always sounds so conspicuously obscene. A simple word like yes, for example, can take on fantastic implications if the one-sided hearer is forced to invent the question it's in answer to.

I took the towel away from my eyes and caught a quick look at her. She was all furrowed in thought and she came up with something quite good.

"It depends on who's doing the inventing," she said.

All I could do was thank her, and I did, quite graciously, while she looked into my face with a look that was somewhat maternal, one of granny's looks.

"You've got a bad sunburn, do you know it?"

I hung up the towel and took a look in the mirror. It was true, I was much too red. Jude's face over my shoulder looked like another person entirely, very smooth and the calm color of sandalwood. But there was more difference than just the difference in color; she looked a way I'd seen her look once or twice before — but not often. It could have been partly the way she had the towel draped around her neck and around her shoulders, and it could have been the expression on her face from the worry about my sunburn; but if I looked like a dryad, she looked like a madonna.

"Hadn't you better put something on it?" she said into the mirror, and I looked into it, but at her, not at myself, and told her she was going to make somebody a wonderful mother, but not to practice on me.

It was interesting what happened to her face when my message got through to her. The purely maternal look collapsed, or rather dissolved into a look that was still connected with the drape of the towel, very religious and full of sorrow, the look, as I interpreted it, of a mother whose grownup baby has suffered untold indignities at the hands of men.

"You must be dead," she said, and this called for a little interpretation too, but what she meant was that I must be quite tired after such a long drive on such a hot day.

I took my eyes off the place in the mirror where the sacred painting was, and all seven sorrows, and found my drink on the counter, and turned around and faced up direct. The full-length effect was much more secular, much more worldly, because of the bikini swimming suit below the towel, outrageously Mediterranean suit with the full umbilical exposure. I fell back a little, looking at it and asking myself why I hadn't noticed it outside when she came up the steps to the deck after I called her to the telephone.

"What's wrong with you?" she said, and I didn't want to tell her that she'd stunned me, nor ask her if this was what girls resort to to lure medical students into marriage, so I returned to the subject that caused the madonna look.

"Can you see any blisters?"

She got the look again, or a degree of it, and while she was inspecting me I told her how the day had gone — my sudden flight, then the unbelievably hot highway, worse than we'd ever known it together, and me exposed to the shriveling sun in the topless Riley. Such a day, such a day-and-a-half of ordeal by fire, with not one stop (I heard myself say) at one single bar, no turning aside, no respite, just this grinding march to Mecca through Bedouin territory. And now, Mecca.

"You won't be blistered until tomorrow, probably," she said, almost as if she hadn't heard my recital in the close inspection. Then she stepped back a little, and I saw her nostrils move as if she smelled something she couldn't at first identify.

"Are you sure you've had dinner?" she said, and I knew then that the identification had been made as brandy, and that this was the same thing I'd had from my grandmother, the womanly solicitude to urge on me the comforts of home, dainties from the refrigerator, stalled ox, every comfort except the one, or possibly two, I wanted.

I inhaled the brandy, drank some, and told her again I'd had dinner.

"But how could you if you didn't stop?"

"I don't know," I said, "now that you put it so clearly, I don't know how I could have."

I inhaled again, drank again, and told her that there were a lot of things I didn't know, and one was why women have to be the way they seem to have to be, always wanting to make somebody eat something or talk to somebody on the telephone or smear something on their sunburn. And in winter put on a coat.

"There's probably a school for wives," I said, "but you don't need to go."

I felt better, and I looked at her obliquely to see if she felt worse, but there was no sure way to tell. She looked very calm and thoughtful, and after a while she gave an answer. Quite good.

"Go ahead, blister. Blister and break."

"Good idea, I'll do it."

"And don't eat. Drink."

There again, I thought, say it twice and underline it. The emblem of good women is always this anxiety about drinking — other people's drinking. And I knew why. Because alcohol releases truth and truth is something good women never care to hear. It frightens them. They only want to hear clichés about how lovely it is to be home again, and what an exciting occasion this is, not only a glad reunion but with a wedding thrown in, and may I please take a peek inside the hope chest, Pandora's dear box? That's what they want — my sister no less than the most uxorious of them.

I was delving for something broad enough to say, something really sweet and dirty, when she came in ahead of me with something I didn't know just where to place.

"I don't care what you do. I'm glad you're here."

She looked straight at me, saying it, and then looked

down. She didn't look glad, no matter what she said, but she didn't look sad either. Something was happening to her face and it was very interesting to watch. The madonna look was no more, and the anxiety was gone, and as I watched I could feel what it was — she was beginning to look like me again, the way she was meant to. I felt the change as it came, and I saw her finally complete it in a gesture — very decisive — a matter of grabbing the edge of the towel in one hand, pulling it off her neck, holding it limp a moment and then flinging it across one shoulder like a storm trooper's trench coat. As movement, or call it choreography, it had great style and detachment, and I felt restored, watching it, but lost too, and slightly dizzied until I felt her taking my glass out of my hand and saw her tip it up and drink quite an amount for a single tip-up. Really quite an amount.

"By all means be my grasping guest," I said. "Drink me out of house and home."

"Sounds nice," she said, in a voice that was not at all the one she was asking me about dinner in. "Sounds very agreeable," she said, and drank again, though not spectacularly, and handed me back my glass, not quite empty. But close.

"What sounds nice? Me out of house and home?"

"You just got here," she said. "And I just told you — I'm glad."

She sighed a sort of resigned-sounding sigh that came from her heels, all sincerely, and said, "You're so —" and then stopped, and then went on, thinking it out as she went. "You're so exactly the way you are, the way you've always been. You never change. You never get any nicer — and you never get any worse. Let's go swimming, as long as you're here."

I ignored the invitation and passed the glass to her. She might as well finish it off, there was practically nothing in it.

"I left that for you," she said, and I told her to finish what she started, it's an old family rule, and I'd go get us a whole lot more, one all for her, and one all for me, but meanwhile not to go getting any ideas about me never changing one way or the other.

"Worse is one way I get quite easily," I said, "worse and worse and more of it. What gave you the idea I'd be any different?"

She stood there with the towel slung over her shoulder and my glass in her other hand and I felt the ancient one-ness, almost the way I used to feel it when I'd see her up on a starting block waiting for the gun in a swimming meet. I'd always feel my own toes grip the edge of the block with the towel spread on it, and when she hit the water something always happened to my stomach and then to my arms and legs. The difference now was that she wasn't about to hit the water, she was about to answer a question I wanted to know the answer to, and I felt my-self go through some of the answers she could make, the easy ones, waiting for her to make one, any one at all, just some words to tell me, in some way I could under-stand, what had happened to a perfectly balanced way of life that was only the only way I could live, that's all.

She opened her mouth and told me something, but it wasn't any of the ones I had been helping her toward.

"It was so crazy wonderful to hear you on that tele-phone," she said.

"What telephone?" I said, quite fast, and she looked puzzled but told me.

"The emergency booth, can't you remember that far back?"

"Of course I can," I said. "What did I say?"

"I don't know," she said, "it was the voice and the way it went. Like a play-back of something I'd have made up and recorded if I could have heard anything I wanted."

"Then I must have said something. What was it that was all that good?"

"Nothing. Just the dumb way you talk."

"Dumb means mute. Papa told us that when we were five."

"I know. Whatever way you talk. It sounded so good."

She drained the glass, for what there was in it, and looked down into it and said, finally, something that meant something.

"It sounded real."

I couldn't have said it better, myself, and I'm supposed to be the articulate one. I blessed her, tacitly, for the word, because, now she'd said it I could begin to believe that I was here, at last, and that this was real, this little white-tiled room with the towels and the faucets and the shower curtain. Five minutes before, I'd been behind that curtain, hiding, alone, so placeless, so undefined that it would not have seemed strange for me to have turned to liquid and gone without fanfare down the drain. But I hadn't, and now nothing seemed strange; I was out in the open — we both were, facing each other and knowing not only who we were but who the other one was — same old well-known other one, and if anybody had said the word *wire tapper* I would not have known what he was talking about, because that wasn't real, and this was.

"You want to go swimming?" I said. "Still?"

"I don't care much what we do," she said. "I like your idea better, I think."

"Which?"

"The one about you getting another glass of this for me

and one for you, and drinking it, and talking things over."

"Here?" I said, and she said no, someplace nicer, in there with granny and papa.

"Is that the kind of talking-over you've got in mind?" I said. "You want to hear about my thesis?"

"I don't mind."

"Well I do. I mind violently, so don't bring it up."

"I didn't bring it up. You did."

"Oh, well then I'll tell you about it. I'm on page fifty-seven. Where'd you get that bathing suit?"

"It's a swim suit. It said so on the sales slip."

"Papa doesn't like us to use infinitives where participles are called for, and you know it, fry-pan."

"I'm not arguing. I just told you what it said on the slip."

"All right, but don't tell papa."

We went dragging through this kind of old-home talk just to get the feel of it, but my eye was on that suit, that swimming costume from the islands, and I was feeling more and more over-dressed and landed, like somebody's mother's older sister at a beach party.

But not irrevocably. I was unbuttoning my blouse and remembering that I had a bikini of my own, somewhere. Probably in a bottom drawer in Berkeley, because I couldn't remember packing it.

"Is that my suit?" I said.

"*Your* suit? Does it look like it?"

"Yes, it does, a little. Remember my black-and-brown bikini with the drawstrings on the sides, like that?"

"Look," Jude said, "this is brown and blue, and these aren't drawstrings, they're solid. And besides that I bought it last week."

"Where?"

"Saks."

"Saks?"

"Saks. And Conchita was using your black-and-brown thing for a dustcloth three years ago."

"She was? Well then you'll have to pardon me. This can't be mine."

"You're right," Jude said, "it can't."

She stood there with the towel slung over her shoulder and looked at me with a nice look — narrowed eyes and white teeth — very fresh and amused.

"But if you'd like to borrow it," she said, "I'd be honored."

I took my blouse off and slung it over my shoulder and put my hand out toward the doorknob.

"What makes you think I'd want to borrow somebody's old soggy bathing suit?" I said. "I ought to be able to do better than that just poking through old dustcloths. Come on."

I opened the door and went down the hall to our room and she followed me.

Judith's things were all over, but my bed was clear of everything except my own things — my suitcase and my overnight case and the brown-and-white striped box with my dress in it. Gran hadn't opened it, for a wonder, and I didn't have any feeling for opening it now and getting chummy about bridesmaids' outfits. I had it, I knew I'd look good in it when the time came, which it would quite soon, and until then I wanted the whole business out of my mind. I picked up the box and slid it under my bed.

"What's in there?" Judith said, and I told her it was some stuff I'd bought in Oakland — couple of T shirts and some shorts to wear around the ranch, and a pair of espadrilles, and I'd had them all put into one box to save space and I didn't want to open it now, I only wanted to do the minimum. I opened my suitcase and wondered what had put a word like espadrilles into my mind, something so specific out of nothing at all on such short notice.

Judith sat on her bed and watched me unpack. I hadn't brought much, three skirts, three or four blouses, some shorts and a sweatshirt and some sneakers. I was holding the sneakers in one hand wondering where to put them.

"You ought to throw those away," Judith said, almost as if she were answering a question.

"Throw away my shoes?" I said. "What kind of wasteful talk is that?"

"They were falling apart three years ago. They haven't even got any tongues. Just look at them."

I looked.

"To my eye," I said, "they've got real style, or at least they're beginning to get it."

"What do you want to look like? Some kind of a prophet?"

I liked the word. She could have called me a lot worse things and got her point across less subtly. I sat down on my bed, across from her, and told her how it was. If I were a prophet, I wouldn't have a following, because my club would be too much of a miscegenation. I'm an Existentialist-Zen-Marxist, Freudian branch. Deviation, rather. It's a difficult line to hew to.

"I just bet it is," she said. She reached across the little space between our beds and took one of the sneakers out of my hand and felt down inside it — for the tongue, presumably, and there wasn't any. She was right. It wasn't just tucked under; there wasn't any.

"What do you Zen-Marxist-Existentialists of your deviation believe?" she said, and tossed the shoe back to me, and

I told her it wouldn't be fair for me to say what *we* believe, because I'm the only one in our branch, but speaking for myself, as prophet, it wouldn't be too hard to pin down.

"We believe in the moment," I said. "The here and now and what can happen in it."

She narrowed her eyes and looked across at me, a little cagily, and I went on quickly.

"But that's just one part. The other part — the Zen part, believes that it is only possible to achieve character, or style, the hard way, the slow way."

I held up one of the sneakers as a clarifying example.

"To arrive at this stage, I mean to say, takes time. It's here and now, now, but it wasn't always. It had to evolve. Do you follow me?"

"You know it," she said, "and my advice is still to throw them away and get evolving on the espadrilles."

I almost asked what espadrilles before I remembered the box under the bed. There was practically nothing to unpack. I took the overnight case, really a make-up case, to my dresser and set it on top and took out my comb and brush and toothbrush and lipsticks and a couple of paperbacks and my kimono, and then I went back to the bed and picked up my blouse and the sneakers and took them to my part of the closet. Our room has a full wall of closets with sliding doors. My side wasn't entirely empty but what was in it was mine — mostly things I didn't need in Berkeley — an old navy middy, and a leather windbreaker and some levis and a smocked dress I'd had in the seventh grade. It was my favorite dress of all time and I looked it over a minute — long enough to know again that I'd never throw it away as long as I live, and then dropped the sneakers on the floor beside my black cowboy boots and pushed everything to the end of the rod and looked at the back wall. There was a tennis racquet and a Snorkel mask with the glass broken and on a hook beside it a limp, faded swatch of something I was hoping would be there — my old high school tank suit. I held it out and looked at it, and then dropped the rest of my clothes and got into it and looked at myself in the full-length mirror on the door. It still had the Putnam swimming team insignia on the right leg, and it was quite a beautiful color, sort of a blue-gray-green that it had arrived at through seasons of chlorinated water and full-strength sun.

"Can you believe this was ever navy blue?" I said to Jude, and she said that wasn't so hard as to believe it had ever fitted me.

"What's wrong with how it fits?"

"It just hangs there."

"Hangs where?"

"Everywhere. Take it off, don't wear it."

I took a racing dive stance in front of the mirror and said, "Why?"

"Can't you *see* why? It's falling apart, and —"

"And what?"

She waited a moment before she answered, "And so are you."

I picked my things up off the floor and treated her to a period of silence, which she had to break.

"How'd you get so thin?"

"If you really want to know," I said, and then I gave it a long pause while I hung things up, "after you left me I quit eating."

She sighed. I heard it. And after a while she said: "Well, now I'm back, you'd better take it up again."

"You're not back," I said. I picked up one of the sneakers and took the shoelace out of it. It was very quiet in our room, and I could hear the sounds from outside — frogs and crickets, the full summer mixed chorus, but inside it seemed to get quieter and quieter. I didn't want to be the one to break it up. I took the shoelace over to my bed and sat down with it hanging out of my hand, then I passed it over to Judith and got up and sat down on her bed beside her, with my back to her. I didn't ask her to do anything but I thought she'd know what I had in mind, or at least be able to put two and two together and take the shoelace and tie the straps of the tank suit together across my shoulder blades. It was an old trick of the trade we'd discovered in high school — tie the shoulder straps together in back and they won't fall off your shoulders and get in the way of your arms.

"What do you want to do — race me?" Judith said. I could feel the straps come together in back, and I sat up straighter.

"I couldn't race a turtle," I said. "I just thought it might be a way of keeping it from falling off."

I got up and sat on my own bed and went on with it. "Because I want to go swimming, now. I don't want to wait until granny goes to bed and she doesn't like anybody to go swimming with nothing on."

Judith nodded, and at the same moment there was a little scratch at the door and granny came in, very cute and coy, wanting to know what we'd been whispering about for so long.

"Bickering," I said, "not whispering," but she didn't take the slightest notice of the word and went on in her favorite way with one of her favorite motifs — how good it was to have her two girls together again after so long — how long had it been?

"Nine months," I said, quite fast, and she said it was nine

months since Judith left Berkeley, but it was much longer than that since we'd both been home together.

"Twelve months and a half, almost," I said in the same way — factual information, reliably stated, and then stopped as if waiting for the next question. And got one.

"Where's your dress, dear?"

"It's put away," I said, "where the moths won't get it." But I knew I was in for it, the cracking out, the full display, including, more than likely, trying it on, along with the shoes, and probably having to comb my hair and consider some earrings and the kind of thing gran puts under the term of accessories. And properly enough, I suppose, but I never liked it as a term, and I also dislike anything that feels like a rehearsal. I believe in once-for-all, and anyhow I was ready to go swimming.

"How about tomorrow?" I said, but I could see that I could not do this to my dear grandmother after her great generosity with the account. Nor could I do it to anyone so openly eager, so full of curiosity and anticipation.

"Sure, why not?" I said, before she asked again, and got down on my knees between the beds and felt around under mine.

"Is that the best bathing suit you could find, Cassie?" gran said from above me.

"What's wrong with it?" I said, feeling for the box and not touching anything.

"It seems to have runners in the seat."

This alarmed me and I looked up from my search.

"Runners?" I said.

"Runs," she said, and then I knew what she meant. Break a thread in a nylon suit and it will unravel and run just like a stocking, and had. Often.

"Think of it as lacework," I said; and I got hold of the box and came up with it.

"That's just T shirts and espadrilles," Judith said.

"Is it? Oh dear."

"You just told me."

"Well, I could have been wrong," I said. "And one way to know is to find out."

I got my thumbnail under the tape and released one side of the lid and folded it back. Inside there was a sea of white tissue paper, systematically crumpled around the edges, and with a pretty pink sales slip on top. I picked up the slip, folded it and pushed it down along the edge of the box, out of sight, because I didn't want anybody's opinion of the dress to be influenced by what it cost. Then I broke a seal and unfolded the paper. The dress lay there quietly and unobtrusively white against the white paper, but with extreme elegance and style. Easily the best dress I'd had since the seventh grade.

I think I was expecting Judith to whistle and granny to chirp, but neither one of them made any sound at all; so I took hold of the shoulders and lifted it out of the box and told them it was the kind of dress that doesn't give the best account of itself lying in a box. Or hanging on a hanger, for that matter. The way it fits is the thing. And the way it's made.

"This back pleat, for instance," I said. I turned it over and showed granny the beautiful tailor's tacks that held the pleat at the top and the bottom, and granny looked and didn't say a thing.

"Pure silk," I said, "feel the weight of it. It crunches."

I was beginning to feel like a saleswoman making a hard sale to an unconvinced customer. Two unconvinced customers. And when I looked away from the dress I saw them looking at each other in a way that was hard to interpret. It was as if they were sharing a private joke. And they were, of course, but I had no idea what it was. All I could tell was that something was wrong with either me or my choice.

"It's obvious enough you don't like it," I said, and Jude sat there looking first at the dress and then at gran with this puzzled and puzzling look on her face, a sort of combination of astonishment and dismay.

"I didn't say I didn't like it," she said in a rather low, unemphatic voice. "I'm crazy about it. I was crazy about it before I ever saw yours."

She stopped and sat there looking somehow baffled, and then looked at gran and said: "Go ahead, Granny, you tell her."

Granny didn't look baffled. I hadn't seen her look so excited in years.

"Oh Cassie, this is rich," she said, "after all these years of you two refusing to dress alike."

I stopped breathing, and then started again. By rich, our grandmother usually means side-splittingly amusing. She says it where other people say this will kill you, and I got the idea clearly enough, what I'd done wrong, and where my gross error lay, without letting myself consciously believe it. I let everything get vague, the dress, the voice, the voices, and I sat there sullen in my tied-together tank suit and considered the part chance plays in a life, or two lives, and how little control can be brought to it. I also thought about brandy.

"Let's leave God out of this," I heard Jude say, and I sat up straighter and asked her what she'd been talking about.

"Where've you been?" Jude said, and I told her here, but not listening, and then she told me that granny had been saying it all went to prove that God had meant us to dress alike all the time. How else after twenty-four years of carefully avoiding any duplication in clothes could we have come up with the same dress, in two separate cities, all independently? And for the same occasion.

Granny was sitting at the foot of my bed now, across from Jude, looking truly triumphant. And vindicated.

"Goodness knows *I* always wanted to dress you alike, and I never could understand what Jane had against it. Or Jim either."

"I believe," I said, quite stiffly and slowly, so that she'd listen, "they were concerned to have us become individuals, each of us in our own right, and not be confused in ourselves, nor confusing to other people."

"That's right," Judith said, like an amen.

"Oh I've heard them explain it a hundred times," gran said, and she sighed. "I used to bring you the dearest outfits, everything alike right down to the little socks and panties, and every time I'd do it they'd make me send them right back."

She sighed again, and I felt a light twinge in an old war wound. I could still remember having to say goodbye to some very pretty presents, and crying with Jude after they'd been sent back.

We looked at each other now while granny went on with variations on her theme — ending where it began, with how rich it was for us to have chosen, separately, the very same wedding dresses.

And there she went too far. Mine was not a wedding dress. It was only a dress I'd bought to wear to somebody's wedding. It might have been all right for *me* to call it my wedding dress because I'd have let the irony show through good and thick, but it wasn't that way with gran saying it. It sounded indecent, and the room began to feel much too small and full of tissue paper.

"Let's have a look at yours," I said to Jude. "Maybe they aren't so much alike as you think."

"Don't be silly," she said.

"Let's see it."

She got up and slid her closet door open and brought out the dress on its hanger. Dead ringer. Identical signature. Size ten. White silk. Feel the weight of it, the intolerable crushing weight. I looked away from it and what did I see? The other one, fallen across the box on my bed. The one I'd been thinking of as mine — the one that was going to contrast so signally in its elegant simplicity with the kind of thing a bride is stuck to wear, including I hoped, the fluty corsage, the white prayer book and the fingertip veil.

I looked back at Judith holding the white flag on the hanger and it came to me that if ever there were a time when it would seem right and natural to start smoking again after an abstinence of two and a half years, it would be now.

But I couldn't get up.

Granny kept up a stream of talk, saying in quite a few new ways what she'd already said in quite a few too many ways before — that it was an amazing coincidence, wasn't it amazing? And yet, in another way of looking at it, not amazing at all; it only went to show that our dear well-meaning parents, for all their enlightenment and all their theories, had simply always pushed us in the wrong direction.

I gave her a sharp look which I think she must have construed as loyalty to our parents, because she stopped talking. And when she did, the quiet became more obtrusive than any amount of talking. There was Judith in her bikini hanging onto the hanger and me in my tank suit sitting in all the tissue paper, and our grandmother, between us, so fragile and so pretty, and none of us saying a word.

Then I decided not to start smoking again, to speak up instead from where I sat, and say something that came to me.

"You're the one that made the mistake," I said, "not me."

Judith looked down at me with the clear bland face she gets when she's waiting for more. So I gave her more.

"That's no dress for a bride, don't you know that? I'm sorry, but it just isn't."

I waited until I saw gran open her mouth to say something and then I went ahead.

"It's too God-damned simple."

I looked at gran and saw what I expected to see — the look of shock and hurt she always gets when she hears any profanity. It was a look I've seen her turn on Jane a hundred times, as if she could not believe her ears.

"Don't you know the bride is supposed to be gussied up?"

"Who says?" Jude said.

"I say," I said. "It's a rule. Nobody ever gets married in anything decent. You wear something you wouldn't be caught dead in anyplace else but your own wedding. And you never wear it again. You pack it away to show your dumb kids."

I waited just long enough to make the contrast have a chance.

"It's a very different matter with me. I bought this dress — or rather charged it to dear granny — with the idea that I'd wear it again. Frequently."

"Me too," Jude said with a show of spirit I didn't care much for.

"But where?" I said. "Where'll *you* ever go?"

It was lame, I knew, and overdone, but it was the best I could do at the time, and the whole place was suddenly so choked with tissue paper that I had to get out and away.

I folded the dress — the one lying beside me — in a way that could just barely not be called wadding it up, and then I crammed the paper in on top of it and got the lid approximately back in place and shoved the box under the bed and went out into the hall and closed the door after me.

The living room was quiet and the rug felt wonderfully soft under my bare feet. I went down to the big window and looked out at the tie timbers and the pool behind them, and then came back and stopped at the piano. It's a good piano, a six-foot Knabe Jane and papa gave Judith for her fourteenth birthday. My birthday too, of course, only they gave me a horse, a buckskin named Dan. And that's it, I thought, Dan's been dead four years and here's this Knabe still six feet long and growing in grace with each passing year. I had an instinct to kick it, in memory of Dan, but I was barefooted, and anyhow my father was talking to me. He was sitting up at the bar, with a glass in front of him, and a book open on the counter, asking me what we'd been doing.

"Making happy wedding plans," I said, and went up the two steps and stood across from him at the bar and asked him if he'd do me the kindness of making me another drink, since I seemed to have misplaced the last one and I wanted something to take out to the pool with me.

He got a glass and poured an amount of brandy into it, a fatherly amount this time, and while he was finding the soda I uncorked the bottle and eked it out a little. I was still eking, unfortunately, when he came back with the soda and looked at me in a way I thought was also fatherly.

"I'm not a minor," I said, in answer to the look, "and I find wedding plans quite exhausting."

"So do I," my father said, "even when I stay out of them."

I nodded, accepted the soda and the ice and thanked him and told him if anybody wanted me I'd be outside cooling off in the pool. I left by the dining room door, closed it behind me and stood for a moment on the deck where I'd dried Jude's feet for the West Los Angeles telephone call, how long ago? A half hour, three quarters of an hour at the most, but long enough for the world to cave in, what was left of it to cave. I walked down the steps, and across the lawn, and then down the other steps to the terrace. The underwater light was still on, and there was a little cone of moths above it glittering like the crown jewels. I was working hard to think of something besides people, something besides clothes and weddings, and I ended up thinking about bats and how they used to whip over the pool at twilight, weightless and on a fast slant, and scare us, but not much. We always accepted things like bats; they frightened granny, but she never managed to frighten us into being afraid of them. I stood on the coping at the edge of the pool and wished that a bat would skim across this very minute and get right into my hair, which is what granny really believes bats do. It would be very nice, I thought, to have a bat in my hair, and not just to prove that gran was right, after all, about bats, but simply to have something real, something tangible, to deal with. I knew what I'd do if I had one — I'd set this glass down so that I'd have both hands free, and while the bat was flinging itself around up there in my hair, getting more and more tangled up and frightened, I'd talk to it in a low, calm voice, tell it to relax, and trust me, give me a free hand, promise not to panic and bite me, and I'd have it out in no time. And then I'd work very delicately, get one wing free and give it a little reassuring pat, and then the other; and after I'd told the bat where we stood now, I'd take little sections of my hair, hank by hank, and get the little vestigial legs untangled from it, one after the other. It would take time, and patience, but sooner or later the last strand would be pulled away from the last leg, and the bat would lie there on my head, still a little fluttery, naturally, and exhausted, but with full trust now. Then I'd tell it it was out of my hair and free to go. Well it wouldn't go immediately. It would lie there resting, probably reflecting that peoples' hair isn't so bad as bats have always been taught to believe. And then I'd feel it stir, and take off, and be gone.

I took a sip and a half of brandy and realized that no matter how elaborately you try substitutions you end up thinking about people. I couldn't even think about a bat without personifying it. So I tried again, at random, as I believed, and I was thinking this time about black widow spiders, which gran also tried to teach us to beware of as deadly. But they never have shown any interest in biting anyone or causing trouble. All on earth they want is to spin a good thick web in a woodpile or under a chair, get rid of their husbands and live in peace. People again. They set the standard every time, and all lines of thought, however devious or confused, lead back to them and force them on your consciousness.

I began to look for a cap, and I couldn't seem to find any lying around on any tables or chairs, where you'd naturally expect to find a cap. No cap anywhere, and I wanted to get into the water now, way down under, and see if it might change the thinking any. I pulled my hairpins out and put them on the table, took another short drink and set my glass down, and walked to the end of the pool, the far end, opposite the diving board and the underwater light.

Our pool doesn't have a shallow end. It's six feet deep at one end and eight at the other and it drops to nine at the drain. We wanted it that way. Granny gave it to us when we were on the Putnam High School swimming team. She doesn't terribly much approve of municipal pools, and she thought if we had one of our own we could train at home. It paid off, too, I suppose. Judith at least, has a hatful of medals and two cups and a statue to show for all the home training. And I've got maybe a capful myself, though I was never much for training, at home or any place else.

I felt the bottoms of my feet push against the coping, and then the quick breath, and the lift, and the deep thrust, and no thoughts, now, just water — my element. Water doesn't change. It remains my element. I felt my hair flowing out behind me like a limp fin with each hair separate and the water pressing cool against my scalp and my eardrums and my eyes. I stayed down deep, ran my hands over the grid of the drain and then turned and planed toward the light, the little undersea moon, so smooth, so bright, so attractive to moths. And to me. When I came to it, I touched it with both hands, claimed it for Olympus (my country) and then came up and broke the surface and hung at the edge of the coping, gasping for breath the way we used to at the end of a race, with our lungs breaking and our hearts banging, and having to wait a second to look up and find out who won.

When I looked up Judith was standing on the edge looking down at me. She had a glass in her hand.

"I thought you weren't ever going to come up," she said,

and I told her it was a sort of last-minute decision, but she didn't understand it, because it was all gasps.

I put my head down between my arms again. I wanted to get out now, but I couldn't imagine pulling myself up over the side without asking Judith to give me a hand, so I pushed off, floated face-down to the ladder and climbed out. Very slowly. It scared me how shot I was. I used to be able to swim the length of the pool five times underwater.

"How many lengths did we used to do without coming up?" I said, and Jude said four, and she still could.

"Want to see me?"

"No," I said, "but it's kind of you to offer."

She handed me a towel, and when I'd dried my face and arms, she was holding out a comb.

"It's easier when it's wet," she said, and I told her I couldn't help it about my hair, I couldn't find a cap, I couldn't find anything. You come home where you've lived all your life and everything's changed, you can't find a cap, somebody swipes your drink, bats get in your hair, and it's a mess, a great big mess.

She turned away and left me with the comb, and I gave my hair a few swipes with it and then threw it against the bank of the terrace and put the towel over my head. When she came back she was carrying two glasses and she held one out to me.

"What's that?"

"Yours."

"Where'd you get it?"

"On the table."

"Well, give it to me. It's a very bad habit to latch onto other persons' drinks."

I expected an answer in kind. She's very good at answering in kind, at least she used to be, but she only passed me my glass and went over and picked up the comb.

"Would you like me to try to get through your hair?" she said, and I did want her to, I wanted her to very much, but I couldn't say so.

"It would be a lot easier if we had a brush," I said, and Judith set her glass on the table and said she'd be right back and started for the house. Except for one short rebellious period when we were about twelve, she's always been this way — a born errand runner. All I have to do is mention something I need and she's halfway to where it is, like a dog getting the evening paper. I went over to the table, set my glass down, picked up Judith's, and tasted it. Fairly strong, really quite a robust drink for her, though not in a class with mine. I set it down and poured some of mine into it, in fairness, and also because I had the feeling it might make communication easier if she and I could manage to achieve, or attain, approximately the same blood-sugar level, as the phrase goes. I'd have to talk to her, and be talked back to, and the wedding-dress affair was going to be a subject we could not easily, in a manner of speaking, skirt.

I tried not to think about it, but I couldn't think of anything else. It was a fact. It happened. We picked the same dress, and what could I do about it, except let myself be flooded with embarrassment of the most bitter kind — a burning, ulcerating invasion of second-degree shame that wouldn't subside, and couldn't be forgotten. How had I let myself get caught up in the nonsense of going and getting a dress in the first place? And then on top of that to pick the same one as the dazed, hoodwinked, marriage-prone bride. Elect.

I splashed another dollop into the bride-elect's glass, as

insurance, and then sat down on the bench and leaned back against the table to wait. There was no moon anywhere, but the stars were out all over, bright and close, ready for harvest. We used to know them by name — Cassiopeia, Arcturus, Venus . . . We could find the Northern Cross and name the stations. We knew about stars, papa taught us from a map of the heavens. Our own, for example, are close to the ground, I seemed to remember, across the river bed, over there someplace, probably blocked by a tree. I couldn't see them, so I stood up on the bench and looked, and then got up on the table and kept on looking where I knew they should be until I happened to remember that this was the wrong season. Our stars show up later, after school starts, Castor and Pollux inseparable. They stay together all the year round, but they go to China or someplace in the summer. Together, of course. And come back home in the fall.

"What are you doing up on the table?" my sister said.

I hadn't heard her come out of the house. I turned around and looked down, and there she was in her bikini, holding a hairbrush.

"Nothing special," I said.

"Well, I'm not going to get up *there* and brush your hair."

"You're not?" I said as if it was the one thing I'd counted on, but I got right down and sat on the bench and Jude got up and sat on the table above me, at my back, and started brushing. She was using a brush of Jane's with long stiff whalebone bristles. At first I thought she was scalping me, but it was a very effective brush and after a few tearing jerks it was getting through and pulling away quite smoothly and pleasantly. I was glad I hadn't yelled, because I was now wanting this to go on as long as might be — two hours, three weeks, forever. Just go on brushing, and keep on brushing off what's coming.

I don't know how long it went on, the whaleboning, nor exactly when it stopped and Judith got off the table and put down the brush and sat beside me on the bench. We'd have to do it now, I supposed, ask the natural questions — when's the wedding? What's he like? Do you have an apartment? And get the proper answers to the natural questions. But we didn't. For a while there we were quiet, perfectly quiet. The frogs weren't and the crickets weren't, but we were. We've sat quiet a lot in our time, and it was that way again. We could have been eleven years old, or seven, all at ease with our house behind us and the river bottom down there and everything together with itself. It was the way it should be, and I stopped worrying and let myself be grateful, at last, to Judith for fixing it. How had she done it? How had she managed to get it to be this way — just us — when I'd been expecting to come back home as an outsider and have to meet entrenched invaders?

I wanted to thank her, but it wouldn't have sounded right, so I didn't try, just relaxed and took a long swallow of my drink, and went back to being eleven years old, and seven, and thirteen — all the ages we've ever been. A lot of days gave their lives to get us all the way to twenty-four, and I sat here now and felt intimately the accumulation of two times twenty-four, which is forty-eight, taking us together — a double twenty-four years of facing responsibilities, learning to walk and talk, then read and write, button-up and unbutton, put on, take off, drive, dive, swim, judge, jeer, and worry. The world's gift of learning.

"Who was it said 'the unexamined life is not worth living'?" I said, for no particular reason, and Jude said, "Papa, who else?" in the easy offhand way I know so well and had missed so much for nine whole months of the worst year of my life.

I sighed, audibly, I guess, and found my glass.

"Don't take it so hard," I heard Jude say. "We can figure out something about the damned dress." And then said, "Dresses."

So all the fetching and carrying and brushing was only to make me feel better about the thing I had almost resolved not to feel any way at all about. I held my breath and heard my blood pound, and Judith put her arm around me and kept on talking and saying we could figure something out, and not to worry, not think twice about it, it wasn't so very odd or spooky or peculiar. We'd both had access to the same store, in different towns; we're both fairly discriminating and our tastes run to simplicity. We know a classic when we see it. Jane would undoubtedly have picked the same dress. So would the Bouvier sisters, and Althea Gibson and the Duchess of Windsor if they'd been limited to the same choice.

And on and on — earnestly. More and more earnestly telling me there was nothing here to indicate that we're too closely tied up, or that we're really the same person with two heads or any of the things we used to wonder about, and worry about, and sometimes feel secretly exultant about.

I think I might have been more receptive if she'd been calmer, if she hadn't seemed so serious and scared. But the way it was, I began to feel like the victim, the one who's been hauled out of the water a little late, but for whose sake the lifesaver must nevertheless do everything in the book, work and work and work and not give up until somebody in authority comes along and makes a pronouncement. But nobody came along, and she couldn't seem to stop it. She kept her arm around me, and went ahead with it, and back over it, telling me it was nothing, nothing at all. I could have hers and mine both and have one dyed and she and gran would go into Putnam tomorrow and find something more like what I'd said, myself, in the bedroom — something more traditional for a wedding dress. Something that looked more like a wedding dress.

I twitched and got her arm off my shoulder quite fast and quite suddenly. After all, I didn't have to sit here with some bride and listen to her say wedding dress over and over.

"Will you just do this," she said, and she was pleading now — "wear the dress you bought? Let me get something else, but you wear that one, will you please — for me?"

I turned and looked at her. The pounding was very strong now and my eyes felt as if they'd caught fire. I had my glass in my hand, about a fourth full.

"For you?" I said. "Who's that?" and I drained the glass at a shot and threw it as hard as I could down onto the terrace between us and the pool. It shattered with a real smash and I felt one of the pieces hit me in the leg.

"Oh God," Jude said, "why did you have to do a thing like that?"

She said it to God, not me; but a moment later she said it all to me: "Why did you do it?"

"Why'd I do what?" I said. "Smash a glass all over the terrace?" I couldn't think of an answer, but I heard myself giving quite a bold one: "Maybe I thought you might want to go out there and do a dance of penance, something good and tribal, like a Charleston, as long as you're barefooted and all."

I heard her take a quick breath, and I knew I'd hit her in the nerves, where I meant to. But I'd hit myself too, and

there wasn't much satisfaction in it. I only felt tired, terribly tired now, and I couldn't think why I'd smashed the
glass and got so wild or thought up anything I'd said.
Then I remembered — the white snare, the pure-silk booby
trap that caught me out.

I felt the bench move and saw Judith get up.

"Where are you going?"

"To get a broom."

"Don't. I'll do it."

"When?"

"Don't ask me things like when. Don't act like a wife
before you are one. Sit down."

"Oh God," I heard her say again. To herself this time,
very private-sounding. But she sat down, and I began
right away, because I was afraid she might get up again, to
lay the blame where it belonged — squarely on the dress.

"You know what I think I'll do — about mine?" I said.

I felt something run down my leg like a spider, but I
didn't look to see if I was bleeding. It might have *been* a
spider.

"I think I'll get gran's pinking shears and cut it all up into
little pieces. Not too little, not too big, just nice strewing-
sized pieces."

I heard it again, the oh-God with the private sound.

"And then I'll strew them all the way from here clear
over to the other side of the river bottom."

"Cassie, please don't. Just don't talk."

"Why not? It wouldn't be against the law for a dress,
would it, the way it was for Jane's ashes? Sooner or
later it would just be like leaf-mold, only dress-mold, all
over the whole river bottom. And it wouldn't even be
against the law."

"Don't think about it. Jane wouldn't have cared, strewn
or unstrewn. All she ever wanted to do was live."

"I know," I said, but I didn't say anything more, because all of a sudden I couldn't — the whole thing was on me, the present all hooked in with the past — the wedding, the dress, our proper grandmother, our renegade mother, our unfrocked father, then us, the two of us; then me, alone, not at all like Jane, finally, not at all wanting to live. Not at all.

It was on me, all of it, and I think Judith knew it. At least the arm was there again, and the quiet voice telling me not to cry, not to feel bad, not to think about Jane, or about any of it, just take it easy and feel at home, now we're back. And please forgive her if I could. Please try.

I caught enough breath to ask her what for, and as soon as I said it, she was crying too. I felt the tears on my forehead, and when I knew for sure they were tears I raised my head and kissed her, on the jawbone, I think, or the earlobe, just a random shot, but it spoke for me, and afterward we didn't try to stop crying, let the torrent rage until it was over and we were tired. But put back together. And cured.

The moon had come up, a shapeless late-riser that looked like a no-good orange, and the bits of glass on the terrace caught the light quite prettily. One of the guests must have broken a necklace — diamonds everywhere.

"I guess I will go get a broom," I said.

"Forget it. Tomorrow's soon enough. Here."

She handed me her glass with quite a lot in it.

"No, you drink it," I said, "it's yours."

"Who cares what's whose?" she said, "help me out."

And then I took it, of course, to be nice. I didn't need it, God knows. I didn't even want it much, but while I was working on it I saw her watching me, curiously, and it seemed to me, with something like pride. Like somebody's younger sister.

"You've always needed a lot more of everything than I do," she said. "Haven't you?"

I wanted to tell her that I didn't need much. Just a few essentials — faith in something and a little sense of location, but I didn't. I didn't because I was looking at her and seeing, again, the very face I'd seen behind the bottles in the bar this afternoon, the one that can always give me a turn when I really look at it and know who it is and why it looks back at me the way it does — as if it belonged to me.

I held the gaze for a long time and when I said, "Where've you been?" it was question and answer both, because I couldn't have said it if I hadn't felt sure she was back, at last, from wherever it was and however long she'd been there. Very far away. For a very long time. And she'd never have come back if she hadn't had to see me one last time. Any more than I'd have come here if I hadn't been crazy, as the girls say, to see her. Dying to, actually.

"For what it's worth," I said, finally, "and as who probably shouldn't say it — I still love you."

I tried to throw it away, not beat any drums about it, and keep it hidden with qualifications, but there it was — admitted and laid on the line, and after I'd said it I broke the gaze and looked away, at the ground, at the stars — anywhere. I wasn't waiting for an answer, but I got one, finally. It began with a sigh of perplexity, and then it became a voice with a little more ring to it than mine, and more direct.

"I love you too," the voice said, "damn it."

The moths were going wild in the cone of light. I got up and circled the broken glass and pulled the plunger that turns off the underwater globe. No pool needs two moons, and it was time for us to go inside and say goodnight to our father and grandmother.

3

MORNINGS on the ranch come earlier than Berkeley mornings, mostly, I think, because of the birds. I've counted as many as eight nests in the tree right outside our bedroom. It's quite easy to see them in winter when the leaves are off — old used-up launching pads exposed to the counting eye, but you can't see them in the summertime, you can only hear them, starting loud and early.

Besides this, our bedroom is on the east side of the house, and the sun bangs right in the minute it gets up. I love our bedroom, but it was designed for us as we once were, not as we are now. Most particularly not as I was the first morning after the first night home — not wishing to get up with birds, very likely unable to get up at all, and hindered by a damaged memory that kept me floating, face-down, unidentified and unlocated, for a good long time before the tides brought me my name along with some of the honors that attach to it. After that I floated again, and the birds screamed until I knew I was not going to be found in any of the three, or possibly four, places I can wake up in in Berkeley. Nice to know. If I need one thing more than another it's a whole new place to wake up in. The birds could have told me this one wasn't new, it was old, all the way back; but it was a circus poster that did it finally. I raised my head, ever so slightly, opened one eye and saw it there on the wall — a poster Jane had picked up somewhere and had framed for our room when we were very little, all those years ago — pure-white clown with a bald head, red eyes and a diamond-shaped mouth. I closed my eye, let my head fall back, knowing the older Edwards girl had been found, curiously enough in one of the last places you'd expect her to turn up, in the nursery, the children's corner suite, in her own bed.

Or on it, rather, and lying somewhat twisted up. Full of pain and joy and careful not to separate them, not right now with all the screaming going on in the tree, and the sun banging in through the window. She's been located, she's been identified, just leave her alone now, and she may get back to sleep.

But I didn't. I turned my head away from the sun and saw, not four feet away from me, my sister Judith in her bed. Not on it, in it, and covered to the chin by a white sheet. It frightened me, the sheet; it looked so careful, so unrumpled, so much as if it had been placed there, officially, by an official. I took a breath, so suddenly that it stabbed my head, and then I remembered that I was the official, I had pulled up the sheet, myself, so bravely-oh, and made it neat like that, before I gave her good night and the final assurances because that's the way I am, neat. I don't like things rumpled up. If there is tissue paper all over everywhere I shove it under the bed. I have ideas of order.

I moved my left arm until I got my wrist somewhere near my face and then I lifted my head again and made my eyes focus on my watch. Quarter to six, and the whole room blazing. If there weren't always so many distractions and so much to do at night — go get more ice, for instance, make the assurances, and try to find a toothbrush and a pillbox — a person of fair intelligence might be able to foresee that morning would arrive soon and brilliantly, and having foreseen it, draw a blind before going to sleep. But it takes more than just fair intelligence to draw a blind when it's dark, it takes an encompassing mind, a mind capable of large assumptions, and somehow I never can believe, in the darkness of night or the gentleness of moonlight, that there will ever again be such a thing as day. So I go to sleep without drawing a blind. Also, apparently, without getting into bed. But never without fulfilling the true obligation to the other one, if it's the true other one, of making the assurances, giving the goodnight, drawing the sheet to the chin. That's what it is to take full responsibility for what you believe in, and know, and trust, and will fight for. Morning's a side effect. I can't acknowledge it until it scalds my eyeballs.

I got up and drew the blind beside my bed. It didn't do much good. We need black blinds in the summertime, and ours are yellow, or buff, some insufficient color. It was better, though, and if I could have reduced the sound of the birds by as much, the noise would still have been touching intolerable but with a little of the edge off. "Whip poor Will, please do," I said to the clown with the diamond-shaped mouth, and then I picked my kimono up off the floor, wrapped myself in it and turned down my bed, properly, the way they do it in hospitals and good hotels — spread removed, sheet turned back on a diagonal fold, pillow plumped and in place. It took a great deal out of me, so much activity, especially the parts that required any bending over, and after I had also picked up a glass that was lying on its side on the floor between the beds, I sat down quickly on the foot of my bed, held on to the glass with both hands and had to concentrate to make the room stay level. I was not easily successful, but I was dealing here with a particularly vicious room and I knew that if I could last until the whistle I just might be high man in the whole rodeo. The thought sustained me, and in the end I won, but I knew it would nevertheless probably have to be a day for pills and I regretted this very much because a great deal would depend on me, today, and on my strength of character.

As soon as the room unwound I made myself look, clinically, at Judith's face above the sheet. It gave me the wrench I expected but bigger than I expected it to be. I can't be clinical when my nerves are exposed, but I looked at her asleep, and knew she really wasn't dead, just out somewhere. And she'd come back, soon. I could wake her and she would look up at me looking down at her and we'd know again who we are and how it has to be and what a fool's game it is to try to split it. We'd know this even on a day that required pills. We've proved it five hundred times: we're not slaves to be sold one here one there and carted off separately to live out separate stretches in scattered places. We've tried it how many times. Even this last one — nine months in New York, backed up by an engagement to some kind of a doctor, right to the edge of the real legal hem-in — it wouldn't work. It couldn't stand up against one real moment of certitude, the kind we get. Call it a moment of clarity, call it a recognition scene — we have them; we've had them, beginning, of course, with the beginning, the first one when we were five, or maybe four. We were chasing around the yard, out by the corral and we came on our favorite cat, the one we called Tacky, the one that had been missing for more than a week. He was covered with ants, good and dead. We saw him at the same time, understood it, and fell intuitively into each others' arms and knew for the first time what it is to feel complete together with our backs against the wall of bitter outrage. We learned, the day we found our favorite, where hurt lies and where comfort against it. And I knew right now, with the birds picking my brain, why I'd been asked to the wedding. I'd been asked because I could stop it in time, I could stage a last-minute rescue.

I looked again; it had been a long time since I'd seen her asleep, and it occurred to me that she looked more like me asleep than awake. There was a tension across her forehead, a look of pain blotted by sleep. I've seen my mother looking this way asleep in a hospital, and I felt a small rage start with a little yeasty feeling of growth, because I don't want this girl to have to blot anything. Judith's quality is serenity, she's all the eastern religions; I'm the tense one, and I can be tense for two if it will give her some immunity. This sounds heavy with goodness and mercy, but it's not really — it's just that Judith's calm is as close as I can get to any sense of quiet or ease. Let a line of tension pull across her forehead and I'm nowhere, standing on no legs.

It was there, however. It was present. Her eyelids weren't doing the good thing of lying easily over her eyes. They'd been forced, and I tried to think why this could be, after the recognition, after the night. But I wasn't in condition to reason. All I had was the glass to hold on to, and it finally gave me the hint that there was no real problem with Judith. It was only that she's given to moderation, to a decent degree, and for some reason last night she'd drunk quite a lot more than I've ever known her to. Not of course anything like what I managed to put away in the course of the night, but still well in excess of her norm, and enough to account for the close fit of the eyelids.

I thought this: maybe after we're together again someplace, wherever we decide to be — Teneriffe, possibly, for a while — I might go on to something new, try a balanced diet, get a tan, swim a lot, run up and down the beach, write from six until ten in the morning and let it well up in me the rest of the day, get a boat and sail a little, why not? And if we get to feeling too square for a round hole, blast our way out of it, comb beaches, but in general stay healthy and last out for the sake of the moments that have to come, and do, when it's us, and the world well lost.

The main thing, right now, was to quit looking at her, quit wondering why she didn't look relaxed, and she helped me by flipping, suddenly, onto her side, faced away from me. She freed one arm in the flipping and got the sheet off-center, but I decided not to try to straighten it, let her sleep with the full length of her spine uncovered, just let her flip and disarrange everything if she couldn't sleep serenely. She'd get it back, she'd find it and give me some.

I stood up slowly and stayed up. The best thing, the only natural thing, would be for me to find the pillbox I couldn't find last night, load up and go to sleep. Sleep until midafternoon, get up little by little, lie in a tub for a while and invalid it through the rest of the day, numb and comfortable — let granny feed me cinnamon rolls and Ovaltine, let papa tell me about man's incurably meager comprehension of things both great and small, let Judith drift in and out of my sight but be home, be around. A day like that. Yes indeed. But it couldn't be a day like that because this was going to have to be my day and I'd have to run the show, stay firm, call the shots, be responsible. There are pills for that, too, up to a point, and I had some, but the pillbox was in my purse, white leather purse, kind of a long narrow clutch-bag wherever it was. I didn't think I could have left it in the emergency booth or dropped it in the weir when I took the drink. And I knew I didn't leave it in the car, because we looked there, sometime in the night. I felt all over the floor and J. felt all over the seat and we never came on anything that felt like a long narrow clutch bag. No pills. Which is why the birds caught me so early.

I went into the bathroom, took a very quick look at myself in the mirror and then opened it out and looked in the medicine chest where there should have been some kind of pain killer or at the very least some flavored aspirin for children. I could remember taking flavored aspirin, but it must have been so delicious we took it all, because all there was in there was nothing I wanted, sunburn lotion, razor, razor blades, eye shadow, eyebrow pencil, no help. I closed it up and without looking at myself again splashed some water on my face. It felt good, but it required leaning over, so I gave it up. I left the bathroom, passed the gently curving groove of Judith's spine, and went out into the hall, into the living room, up to the bar.

I hadn't expected to find anybody around so early, but I reckoned without granny. She was in the kitchen, all clean and crisp and inexorably alert. Cheery and nosy and glad to see me, because she loves having someone to eat breakfast with, but she cannot wait until lunch time for the privilege, and it's a long wait between six and twelve with no breakfast.

I thought of things to say to that, suggestions like stay in bed until eleven-thirty and cut the wait down to a half hour, but I didn't say any of them, partly because I didn't feel like making my mouth open, and partly because she was pleased with me as an early riser and it felt nice to have it that way. I even walked around the bar and came up to her and held my breath and kissed her very quickly without breathing on her, because granny likes to be kissed goodnight *and* good morning, and I didn't remember about goodnight, whether I had or hadn't. Probably hadn't, and I probably shouldn't have tried it this morning, either, because it involved some leaning over and a little bending down. But I got it done and got back to the counter afterward and sat quickly on a stool and concentrated, and she paid me back with suggestions and questions expecting answers about breakfast. For instance, would I have grapefruit or orange juice?

I was concentrating, but I broke it off long enough to say neither.

"Neither?" Wildly rising inflection. (We raise oranges, also some grapefruit. It's our product. We should be consumers on principle.)

Not this morning, I had to say.

"Granny," I said, right on top of it, "have you seen my bag — white clutch bag, narrow and rather long for its height, or broad for its length?"

"You're going to have some orange juice, young lady," granny said. "It's one of the basic seven."

She had it in a glass all freshly squeezed, violent in color, and she brought it and set it on the counter in front of me.

"*You* drink it, Granny dear, you made it for yourself. You weren't expecting anybody else to get up until noon."

"I squeezed three glasses — one for you, one for Judy, one for your father. I always eat grapefruit, but if you'd like the grapefruit I'll drink the orange juice."

Granny talks plain on this kind of subject.

"All right then, leave the glass here, and thank you very much for the squeezing."

I don't know why the color should have distressed me so much, but it was so very very orange.

"What basic seven?" I said, to be chatty without saying much, and I saw my little grandmother's mouth go into a straight tight line of annoyance edging amusement. I've seen her turn this on Jane a thousand times.

"You know what basic seven. The seven you have to have every day."

I could have worked on this and gained time before the tilt with the orange juice, but it didn't seem worth it. But there was a way, a bold one, and I looked away from the glass and tried it.

"Granny," I said, not too loud, not too quietly, just very sincerely, "the truth is — I'm sick."

There was silence in the kitchen. I didn't look at my grandmother, but I heard her lay her spoon down on the grapefruit dish, and I could feel the compassion on her face.

"Sweetheart," she said, in a very quiet voice, "why didn't you tell me?"

"I'm telling you," I said.

"But last night. Why didn't you tell me then?"

I started to say I wasn't sick then, just today, but I decided against it. Let it go this way, because objectively looked at, my health had not been, through the second semester, the greatest thing in town. Very nervous health.

"It's nothing that will kill me," I said.

"You haven't started smoking again?" gran said.

"Oh no," I said, "this is nothing like Jane. I'm not in trouble. I'm just sick — of a lot of things."

"Have you been to a doctor?"

"Yes," I said, and that was true enough. I'd been spending an hour a week with a psychiatrist for the past seven months, a surpassingly understanding doctor who listened to anything I had to say and then wrote out reorders for unrefillable prescriptions.

"What does he say about you?" gran said, in the serious

sickroom voice the careless mention of a tonsil can cause in her.

"She says I'm working too hard, mostly," I said. "Sort of going on my nerve."

"I knew it the minute I saw you last night," gran said, "you looked drawn. She? Is it a *woman* doctor?"

I nodded. "Dr. Vera Mercer. She has quite a reputation."

I laughed, I'm not sure why, right out loud. It didn't do my head any good. But it helped granny.

"You just go into Putnam while you're here and talk to Dr. Barnes. He'll take a blood count and give you a tonic."

"You're sure you haven't seen my bag, Granny?"

She picked up her spoon and got back to the grapefruit.

"I'll look for it after breakfast," she said. "Drink your orange juice, Cassie."

"But this bag has got all kinds of tonic in it — everything I might need, and I pretty much have to find it."

"Drink your orange juice. We'll find it."

She finished her grapefruit, picked up her plate and went to the sink and rinsed it, and then opened the refrigerator and asked me whether I'd have bacon, ham, or sausage with my French toast.

"Granny," I said. I took a quick look at the orange-colored orange juice and found something to say. "My doctor, Dr. Mercer, thinks the trouble may be in my pyloric valve, it's what lets things into, or perhaps out of, the stomach. It's a very delicate mechanism and the idea is never overwhelm it. Now if I were to —"

I didn't follow it through, because I didn't want to think closely about parts of the body, not while my hammer, anvil, and stirrup were doing whatever it was, in there somewhere. But on the other hand there was no point, now, in being coy with gran. My problem was to get on my feet and face this day, and one way to do it would be to manage to eat a little something. Stabilize the pyloric valve and who knows but that hammer, anvil, and stirrup will fall in line.

"I'll tell you what let's try," I said, "just on speculation. Let's take this orange juice and whip an egg into it, and just see."

Granny looked puzzled, and I didn't explain the raw-egg principle to her; it soothes riots but you can't talk about it. I took my glass of orange juice over to the counter by the sink, dumped half of it into the blender, broke an egg into it, turned the switch and got noise, but also a frothy, rather bland-looking drink. Then I poured it into a smaller glass, took it back to the counter, said one, two, three, and took a swallow, three deep breaths and then another, and after the third swallow I was able to drink and think both. I couldn't remember where I'd ever heard about the pyloric valve, probably in grammar school physiology, but I was quite happy to have recalled it, because there was an intelligent mechanical theory here, one I'd ad-libbed out of nothing: don't overwhelm the pyloric valve; don't jam the lock. Work with it and it will work with you. And I knew now that if I could put the other half of the orange juice into the blender with another raw egg and a fair dollop of vodka I might become the woman I am, at least the one I had to be for this present occasion. But there was a small question how to set it up.

"Do you remember," I said to gran, "how Jude and I used to have to take a tablespoonful of port wine before meals?"

"No, when was that?" gran said.

"Dr. Barnes thought it up," I said, "when we had low blood counts, and I think that's a little bit the way my doctor is theorizing about this valve trouble of mine. The raw egg soothes, and the port wine stimulates. Let's just see what we've got here."

I looked into the cabinet under the bar, but I didn't lean over to do it. I went down with a deep knee bend, and squatted there upright but folded and looked the stock over. There was a brandy bottle, Five-star Hennessy, in the first row, uncorked, very disorderly, sticky around the neck, and I held it to the light to confirm what I suspected and half remembered — empty. I put it back, behind the others, and found a bottle of vodka, and took it over to the sink with the other half of my original glass of orange juice. My grandmother was laying some bacon into a frying pan, but she stopped and came and stood at my elbow and watched me.

"That's not port wine," she said. "Is it?"

"White port," I said, and I kept my hand over the label. "It's all we seem to have." I poured a seriously considered amount into the blender, took the bottle back, did the full *plié* again and put it away, in back someplace, and came back and dumped the orange juice on top and broke another egg into the blender and let it whirl.

"If you're ever at a loss for something to give us for our birthday," I said, "we could use a blender."

I poured the drink back into my glass, ran some water into the blender and went back to the counter and sat down.

"I thought," gran said, "we might give one to Judy and Jack for a wedding present. Jack makes delicious strawberry milkshakes. And they might enjoy something like that next winter."

The easy way she said Judy and Jack, as if they were characters in a third-grade reader. Jump, Jack, jump. Run, Judy, run. Run and jump, Jack and Judy. Drop dead, Jack. Run, run, run, Judy. Run and hide. New word.

"Why don't I buy one," gran said, "and you give it to them."

"Why?" I said, fairly loud. My pyloric valve was not sticking, but I couldn't tell what might happen if the conversation had to go this way.

"Oh, I just thought it would be nice," gran said. "Do you have something for them?"

"Naturally."

"That's nice. I didn't suppose you'd have had time to shop. What did you get?"

I neglected to answer, and neglect is something my grandmother does not condone.

"If it's not too much to ask," she brought herself to say, "I'm curious about what you got them."

I could tell her right now, how I felt, how we both felt, what we'd decided last night, and take a chance on her affection for us as a pair to put her on our side. But I didn't feel quite up to so much persuasion, nor to so much delicacy and charm as this explanation would require.

"You really want to know what I got them, don't you?" was all I said.

"Of course I do. It's like Christmas, even better."

"All right," I said. "I got stainless."

Granny turned a lovely smile on me. "You did, Cassie? Stainless what?"

Well, now to specify. I had the notion people who are in the know just might say stainless the way they say sterling. Apparently not.

"Just stainless," I said, "spotless, immaculate stainless,

and also a wall-to-wall electric blanket that doubles as a hot rug."

It took her a minute to say what I am, and always was — impossible to talk sensibly to, and impossible, but that was because she had to tighten her lips and roll up her eyes first. And then say it.

"Cassie Edwards — you're impossible."

"I suppose," I said, "but even so a lot of people have loved me, and some of them still do."

More eye-rolling. I drank some orange juice and thought over what I'd said. It was true, and I felt very grateful. I would measure up when the time came; I'd be equal to my task.

"Can't you ever be serious?" gran said, and if it had been a serious question I think I might have answered it, because all I want out of life is to find something worth being serious about. Ask me if I can ever be serious, and the only answer is that it's all I can be and all I ever am, have been, or will be. It's my whole trouble, but it's also my one certainty — to know how serious I can be about what I love. I'm so committed to true seriousness that I spend my time clearing out rubbish.

"Don't cook any bacon for me, Granny," I said. "I've had two eggs, and I'm beginning to feel — you know — less hungry somehow."

"Are you still unsettled?"

"How do you mean unsettled?" I said, quite fast. I've never admired my grandmother's frankness. As a matter of fact it isn't frankness, it's tactlessness, and I always try to point it out with snappish answers. Or looks. We all do. One of the things I remember as one of the greatest excitements of my life was papa's face when granny asked him one morning why he wore dark glasses in the house. She's like a child. A question occurs to her and she asks it. And gets, now and again, loud answers.

"You told me yourself you were feeling badly this morning," she said in a mild little voice, and I took a deep breath that came out again in the form of a sigh, because it's hopeless to try to explain to Mrs. Rowena Abbott that feeling badly comes from having something wrong with one's sense of touch. I've tried and she just won't accept it. It's like who and whom. Whom sounds nicelier.

"I've never felt badly in my life," I said. I ran one hand along the edge of the tiles, rather broadly, and finished it up: "No matter how sick I am I always *feel* well, at least. It's a riddle."

"You're a riddle," Mrs. Abbott said, "but I'm glad you're home, and I hope you'll stay long enough to let me build you up a little. I'd like to have Jack look you over when he gets back."

"You've got it wrong way around," I said. "I'm going to look him over."

Granny came toward me with a platter, really quite beautiful, of bacon and French toast.

"That's for you," I said.

"No, it's for both of us. And some for Judy too, if she gets up, but I've been encouraging her to sleep late, because she'll need it."

She set the platter down and put a plate in front of me and another beside me and poured some coffee. It looked quite violent, the coffee, but I could ignore it because I still had a little egg and orange juice and white port left in my glass. I accepted a piece of French toast, and decided not to comment on my sister's forthcoming need of present sleep. I preferred to think of her as sleeping right now the sleep of the unknotted and undeceived, the sleep of the just. She'd been more than just, and I could talk to gran about other things. But I didn't get the lead.

"When I suggested sending you to Dr. Barnes, I'd forgotten that we have a doctor of our own right in the family."

"Hmmm," was all I said. She had the lead, she could keep it.

"You wouldn't object, would you, Cassie? I don't believe I've ever known a young man who seems so wrapped up in his work."

This time I said, "Last night you said he was all wrapped up in Judith. He can't have it both ways."

"Wait until you meet him," granny said, with a little knowing smile. "You'll see what I mean."

She took a sip of coffee and sighed, a contented and rather private-sounding sigh, like an adolescent in love.

"They are so precious together," she said. "You just have to wonder how they ever found each other — Jack from Connecticut and Judy from clear out here."

The coffee looked very harsh, very direct, and of a mean color, but I drank some, because the tonic was gone, now, and I had to do something. I don't smoke.

"God's plan," I said, "direct from the great procuring house in the sky."

Granny smiled, I suppose because she listened to only the first part. "I think so too, Cassie," she said. "God's plan. You'll know it when you see them together."

I tasted the coffee again. Very harsh. Mornings like this tea is a much safer drink, and more curative.

"What do you suppose God's planning for me?" I said. "Besides poverty, chastity, obedience, brain damage and death?"

Gran batted her eyes at that, but chose to think of it as Cassie again, being impossible, bless her.

"You'll know, dear," she said. "Your day will come, and when you meet someone who is right for you, you'll know it as surely as Judy did."

"You believe that, don't you, Granny?"

She had her cup up to her mouth, but she nodded her head, and her eyes above the cup shone with spirituality.

"Well, you'd better believe it," I said, "because it's true, it's been true ever since the day we found Tacky."

Gran set the cup down and looked the way I expected she would.

"Tacky whom?" she said.

"Tacky Edwards," I said. "Only the best cat we ever had, that's who."

"Cassie, eat your French toast," gran said, "and let's get down to business. We have to make some plans."

I let this bounce off me because I was really thinking about Tacky Edwards, how tacky he was, but how understanding, how feline, peaceful and deep, and how we'd had to lose him, let him go, let him die, let the ants have him, in order to find what we already had — ourselves, together. This is all anyone needs to know, finally — if you can resign yourself to losing, you may win.

"Listen to this, Granny," I said, and I dug back into my memory for something someone had told me once — Jane, maybe, or papa — from one of the philosophers: " 'Nothing man naturally loves need go unhallowed, if only it can be in part sacrificed, and in part redeemed.' It's a quotation, and I'll tell you why I quoted it. Because whenever I feel right, you know, the way you said I might some day, I think of it."

"Cassie," gran said, "I think we should —"

"No, hold it a minute," I said. "I just wanted to tell you I don't have to wait to feel how right something is — I've already felt it — I mean I do, right now."

Granny had the look she gets when anyone talks to her at some length, the look of a woman who is inwardly making out a grocery list, pleasant enough, but not with you. She stayed quiet for a decent interval after I'd stopped talking and when it became clear that I had finished saying whatever it was, she came back.

"I'm so glad you got up and I can have you to myself a minute," she said, as a starter. "There are so many things I want to take up with you."

"You've got me," I said. "Take up."

"Is that all you're going to eat? You've always loved French toast."

"French anything," I said, "go ahead, what did you want to get me alone about?"

"The wedding."

"What wedding?"

"Cassie, please."

"Okay."

"Don't you think we should invite some guests?"

"Wedding guests?"

"Of course, wedding guests. Judy wants it to be just us — you and Jim and I and Jack and herself. But I think to keep it so exclusive is a snub to the community where she grew up."

"We never mingled what you'd call freely, as I remember it."

"You graduated from Putnam High School. You were head of your class."

"Maybe I was. Jude was fourth."

"Fourth's no reason not to invite teachers like Miss — what was her name — that took such an interest in her."

"What *was* her name?"

"Cassie, please."

"All right, but we should face the fact that if we can't think of her name how can we address the invitation?"

"We could think of it if you'd help just a little. Did Judy talk to you about it last night?"

"No, I don't think so. Last night we really said things."

"She didn't even mention it?"

"You mean wedding guests?"

"No, not just that, all of it, what they've decided."

I considered another swallow of coffee and found I was against it, and I got off my stool and put a teakettle on the stove, explaining as I did it that I'd come to prefer tea to coffee as a breakfast drink.

"Why didn't you tell me?" gran said.

I came back to the counter and sat down. "I can't remember just what the final plans are, except that I'm going to drive down to Bakersfield this afternoon and pick Dr. Lynch up at the airport."

"Dr. Lynch?"

"Finch, pardon it. John Thomas Finch."

"*You're* going to pick him up? You and Judy, you mean."

"No, me. Judith's got a lot to do and we both thought this way I could talk to him a little more — freely. Don't you think so yourself?"

Granny looked at me and bit her lower lip, and somewhat narrowed her eyes.

"Cassie," she said, "you're not going to try to pass yourself off as Judith or anything like that."

"*What?*" I said. I was truly shocked to find such a coarse streak in Mrs. Abbott as to imagine such a coarse streak in me, but I don't know that it should have shocked me so. She's always had a wild interest in how much we look alike and how we could exploit it instead of doing everything we can to deny it. I sat there drop-jawed and she went on: "He's too nice a boy to play any tricks on. Why don't you just dress more or less alike and go meet him together?"

I don't like to say anything against my grandmother. She loves us, she's the soul of generosity, but there was a time — we were around eight — when she even wanted to buy us a pair of accordions and have us work up a little act. I remember she had us pretty much interested. But Jane hit the ceiling and papa went through the roof.

I looked at her firmly, and spoke clearly.

"First you accuse us of planning a practical joke, then you want us to get fixed up like the Bobbseys. Granny, where do you stand? I'd really like to know," I said, as if I didn't.

Granny looked sad. "I've never been able to see anything wrong with your being —"

"Don't say it," I said, "don't say that word."

"Nobody else who is one feels this way about it," gran said in the aggrieved voice she always uses for this particular conversation, the conversation about our condition, so to call it. I'm sorry to grieve her or deny her her pleasure, but I have to make things clear, because no one of my grandmother's temperament and sensibilities can understand what it's like to be bound to a way of life like ours — a situation we inwardly glory in, but one that we have to protect at every turn from the menacing mass of clichés that are thrust on us from the outside. To be like us isn't easy, it requires constant attention to detail. I've thought it out; we've thought it out together. I've tried to explain to my doctor that it's a question of working ceaselessly at being as different as possible because there must be a gap before it can be bridged. And the bridge is the real project.

"Wasn't it funny last night?" granny said, no longer sad. "I just don't believe I've ever seen anything quite like your face when you saw Judy's wedding dress."

"Rich," I said. "Thank God I charged it. I can take it back."

I got up and turned the fire off under the teakettle and scalded out a teapot, and granny took it away from me and opened a box of tea.

"Judith wants to send hers back too," I said, "but I think it would be a good dress for her to have, good sort of chamber music dress. Something to play Fauré in. Informal summer chamber music."

I allowed myself to wonder what were the chances of any chamber music groups in Teneriffe, if we went there. Slim, at best, but there wouldn't be that kind of best; there wouldn't be any chamber music. However, there would be ways of having a piano of our own, something we could rent for as long as we decided to stay. I could work up one hand of some of the Mozart sonatas we used to play. The right hand, of course. I am a good deal more dextrous than sinister. We used to split up Mozart sonatas all the time; and with me playing one part, of course it was never very finished as performance, but it was exhilarating, like ping-pong, and it could be again. Come in after a day in the sun, play some Mozart sonatas, then hear Jude play solo while I combed my hair; and then we'd slope off someplace for dinner.

Granny brought the teapot to the counter and set it down quite firmly, a little in the manner of a waitress who is not ecstatically well pleased with the establishment she works for. She set a clean cup down rather firmly too, and while I was pouring my tea she said something that jarred me out of Teneriffe, or off it.

"I must say it's very gracious of you to let Judy keep her wedding dress."

I recognized irony at its highest, here, and tasted my tea.

"I'm sure she's very grateful for your kindness."

"I'm quite sure she is," I said, and I felt suddenly like a martyr and a prophet, or both, stoned out of town for the wrong reasons, feeding the ire of the righteous by only being true to my convictions and treading the strait way. It was discouraging to consider, and though the tea tasted pleasant, fresh, and mild, after the coffee, I was beginning to have a feeling that I should have had either more of the tonic in my second orange juice and egg, or none at all.

My grandmother sat down on a stool, the one beside me — sign that she intended to talk, maybe even get down to what she calls brass tacks.

"Now, what about guests?" she said, and then added: "Wedding guests," to tie me down.

"It seems to me," I said, and I meant it, "the best thing in this case would be leave them out." I left it at that, though I almost got my nerve up to question openly the advisability of inviting people to a wedding that was not going to take place — exciting for the guests, no doubt, but embarrassing for the principals, and most particularly for the bride *manquée's* grandmother.

"People are not what people used to be," Mrs. Abbott said. "It used to be taken for granted that a girl wanted to be married in a church, with a line of close friends as bridesmaids, and bridal showers for weeks before, and a rehearsal and supper for the wedding party the night before — all the things I'd like Judy to have."

"Poor Jude," I said, "she makes it easy on you and you feel cheated."

"And that's why I've been wanting so much for you to get home — so that you could help me persuade her to do it right. I'm certainly willing."

"I believe it," I said, "but you'll have to be a little —" I stopped because no good word came to me; I felt dizzy and it was now beginning to seem that the few sips of tea on top of the few sips of coffee were making rather an unfortunate marriage of their own, unlikely to succeed.

"I'll have to be a little what?" my grandmother asked, as if she were coaching me.

"A little pragmatic," I said. "You'll have to be willing to deal within the context. And a context can change character radically between one night and the next morning."

"I'm sure I don't know what you're talking about, baby," granny said, and hearing her call me baby suddenly hurt my eyes. Granny was around when I learned to talk; she herself had a big hand in teaching me my first words, pretty and naughty and peek-a-boo and good understandable words like that, and here I was confusing her with jargon. Knowingly. At breakfast. I felt all at once like cutting my throat.

"I love you, Granny," I said. "I really do, and the only thing I meant was that we have to be willing to let things go the way they have to go, the way it's right for them to go, even though it may look a little odd from the outside."

I looked into my teacup for some small sign, any slight foretelling of the future, but there wasn't a leaf in it.

"You didn't make this out of tea bags, did you?" I said.

"Of course not. Your father would die."

"I didn't know he drank tea," I said, and granny looked puzzled and said I was right, he doesn't. She was thinking about instant coffee.

I nodded my head. We're not for short cuts, we're not

for innovations, we're for tradition, and the fact that our own traditions tend to be unconventional doesn't make them any the less strictly held and seriously held to. No innovations.

"What were we saying, dear?" granny said, and when I looked lost, she did some prompting. "— something about things looking bad."

"I didn't say bad," I said, "I said we can't really worry about how we look to outsiders from the outside, as long as we know we're all right inside. Do you see?"

"Well, not exactly. Do you mean not inviting people from the town, people we've known all our life, a few personal friends of mine like Sarah Clemmons and Hannah Hagan? I couldn't feel right inside about not having them. And Kate. The four of us have played cards together every other Wednesday for almost twenty years."

"There's no reason not to keep it up that I can see. Matter of fact this is Wednesday, isn't it?"

"We played last Wednesday. It's just the second and fourth Wednesdays."

"Then what are we worrying about? Wait until a week from now and play."

"Cassie, will you settle down now and tell me what you and Judy talked about last night?"

I felt very warm. It was going to be a very hot day, and the tea was driving it home. I shifted the neckband of my kimono off my neck to let a little air get to me.

"Don't you have anything on under your wrapper, dear?" gran said. She's terribly observant.

"Not yet," I said. "I didn't really mean to get up yet; I only came out to look for my bag, kind of a long narrow white clutch bag. Have you seen it anywhere? I really need it."

"You asked me that before, and I told you I haven't."

"Sorry," I said. "My memory's shot."

"Wait until you get to my age, before you talk to me about memory," granny said, and I let her come back into my heart for that, for the candor and the understanding; and also back into my confidence. Why not, she's our grandmother, she's Jane's mother, she has a right to know how it is. It's all in the family.

"You wanted to know what we were talking about last night —"

"You sounded as if you were having such a wonderful time," gran said, and I had to wait until she finished, which was quite a wait. "I'd hear your voice, saying something, I couldn't hear what, and then I'd hear Judy laughing and laughing, the way she always does when you say any-thing —"

"How do you know she wasn't talking and I wasn't doing the laughing?" I said.

"You don't laugh that way," granny said. "I'd know Judy's laugh anywhere on earth. I lay there in bed and had to laugh just from hearing it. And then I heard you go out the front door, and stay out for quite a long time and then come in."

"We went out to the car to look for my bag," I said.

"I thought I heard you go out to the kitchen several times, too," gran said.

"We did," I said, "for ice. It was a very hot night. It's been quite cool in Berkeley. I'd almost forgotten how it can be at home. Not just heat — everything. We sat here and talked to papa until after midnight."

"About the wedding?" granny said, and I said I didn't believe we covered the wedding very thoroughly, we were talking about my thesis, for some reason, and papa was drawing a parallel between existentialism and classic skepticism.

"I want to use it. It might actually save the day for me."

I was glad I'd remembered the session with papa. It's perfectly possible I might get interested in my thesis and say something in it that would be worth saying — clear things up a little, tie up some loose philosophical ends.

I didn't exactly feel good, not all the way, but thinking about work, and ideas, and backing, made me feel a great deal better. I reached a hand out toward my grandmother and patted her on the arm.

"Granny," I said, "we — after we left papa — we did do a lot of talking, and it was mostly about ourselves and how bad it was last year with me in Berkeley and Jude in New York."

I looked up and saw Mrs. Abbott's mouth opening to say something, something which would probably be very much to the point from her side and very irrelevant from mine, and I came in ahead of her in a forestalling move.

"You're right about us, you know, the way you've always felt, that we shouldn't try so hard to go separate ways; we realize it now — it's impossible. We can't do it."

I didn't look up for a while. Let her absorb it, hear it, take it in, and then ask the close questions of me, hear the answers, make a pronouncement, get a rebuttal.

She looked at me and then came in quite close to me and kept on looking, almost as if she were trying to see into my head.

"I wanted to tell you first," I said, "before papa or before anybody else, because you've always been so understanding, and if you'd had the say things would have been different."

She blinked, and gave me a funny look, a look of sympathy and rapport, I thought, but I couldn't be sure.

"Remember the accordions we never got," I said. "They made Judith take piano lessons, instead, and got me that dumb flute."

"Whatever became of your flute, dear?" gran said.

Whatever became of *me*, I thought, but I'd started something here and I knew I'd better stay with it.

"All I'm trying to say is that I know now what you wanted and how you felt about us — that we should be ourselves, stay together, accept the problem with pride and seriousness instead of being ashamed of it, or dodging it."

I took a long deep breath, looking into the teacup, and summed up: "Well, we've accepted it. We decided, last night. We're staying together."

It was strong. I'd given it everything, considering my condition, but somehow it didn't get through. Granny stopped looking so closely at me when I was no more than halfway through my speech, and by the time I came to pride and seriousness I could tell I'd lost my audience. She was looking on out beyond me, with a little smile on her face, a little fluttery smile of welcome, very delicate and gracious. I'd lost her, and after such an uphill fight. All that hard work.

"We were just saying we hoped you'd stay in until noon, Judy, and get a real beauty sleep before your prince comes charging back, weren't we, Cassie?"

I turned on my stool and saw Jude coming up the two steps from the lower living room. Her hair was combed and she was wearing white linen shorts and a blue searsucker shirt, all very crisp and clean. She took the steps with quite a lot of bounce.

"Yes," I said, "we were saying all that prince stuff,

and all that beauty business. That's just what we were sitting here saying. You bet."

"Cassie's in a very wild mood this morning," gran said.

"Oh, ho-so, prenty wired," I said in an oriental accent that took a lot more out of me than I had to put into it.

Granny got up to get Jude's orange juice, and Jude came and stood beside me at the counter and put a hand on my shoulder and left it there. I turned and looked at her. She looked healthier than she looked happy, but she smelled wonderful.

"What have you got on?" I said, and she said, "Lime cologne, how do you feel?"

"Top-notch," I said. "Top-hole. Not too great."

"You should have let me put something on your sunburn."

"Wrong diagnosis."

"Why didn't you sleep a while? It's only seven-thirty."

"Why didn't *you?*"

"I did, a little. I got to thinking."

"Well, don't. I just told granny the plans, the new ones, and she's darling."

Granny set the glass of orange juice down in front of Judith.

"When's papa get up?" I asked, and gran rolled her eyes up very subtly and said anywhere from ten to twelve, depending.

Judith picked up her glass, all undismayed by the orangeness, and drank, thoughtfully.

"I guess we grow the best oranges in the whole world," she said, and Mrs. Abbott, across the kitchen, told her she was glad to hear her say it, because some people feel they have to put an egg in it.

"Two," I said.

"And some white port wine," Mrs. A. added.

Judith looked at me. "Really?" she said, and I said I couldn't see why people have such prejudices against raw eggs — pure blind prejudice — probably none of the ones that yell the loudest have ever tried one, even.

"What about white port wine?" Jude said, in that little-sister way she has.

"She's absolutely wrong there, at least," I said, and I let granny look the way I knew she would. "But two eggs, yes."

"Tell her what your doctor said about your what-ever-it-was — your valve."

I waited for Judith to ask, so that I could tell her it was nothing — no doctor, no valve, just Mrs. Abbott being an alarmist and a betrayer of confidence besides — but the question didn't come, and it began to seem certain that it wouldn't — that granny had, in her turn, lost her audience. Judith had taken her hand off my shoulder, had sat down on a stool and was staring across the room, out the window to the back porch. There was a cat out there, the current one, looking in. The cat and Judith looked at each other for a long time, both a little out of focus, and Judith finished her orange juice, set the glass down, and said, "We can't, that's all."

"I know," I said, "don't worry about it."

"No," she said, "I mean we can't send you to pick him up. It has to be me."

"No," I said. "I'll go. I'm all right, I mean I will be by the time I have to go."

"No," Jude said, "I don't think so. Everything's crazy. I got to thinking. I'll have to go."

"That's not the way you felt about it last night," I said. I didn't quite understand the way she was acting — that funny gazing at the cat, and a sort of vacillating manner in everything she did.

"Last night was —" She stopped and looked across the room at granny who was making more French toast, and then went on, very quietly: "Well everything was so unexpected — your coming home and the talking, and the what-was-it, brandy?"

"You didn't have much," I said.

"It was a lot for me," she said. "And then you and papa and all the philosophy, and just being home again with both of you."

She sighed, looked out at the cat, then over at granny and then closer, at me, and said: "And then you, being the way you were."

"How was I being?"

She sighed again, and said it — "The way you are. You know how you are."

"No, I don't, really," I said. "But I do know how I want to be, and how I believe I can be. That's what I was trying to tell you, how we can be."

Granny came with a fresh plate of French toast and bacon, an individual serving, and I jumped up a little too quickly and offered to help. The offer was rejected, but I brought a cup and saucer and set it in front of Judith and asked her if she'd have coffee or tea.

"Tea?" she said, "in the morning? Who drinks tea?"

"I do," I said, "not always, just sometimes."

"I don't remember that," she said, and I poured coffee into the cup, and took away both my teacup and my coffee cup, and my glass and my plate with the French toast on it, and scraped the plate and rinsed the cups and the glass and put them into the dishwasher. It wasn't easy, but nothing is.

When I went back to the counter gran was sitting across from Judith and asking her right out loud if she didn't think we owed the community something.

"Think of all the kind people who came to — to Jane's services," she said.

"That was a fluke," Judith said. "They just came because we didn't say it was private."

"That's why we should *ask* them this time," granny said.

"I don't know," Judith said in a very small perplexed voice. I could scarcely believe granny could plow right ahead with her plans after what I'd let her in on. She must have understood a little something of what I'd told her. I looked hard at Judith, and tried to get her to look at me, because if she'd look at me I could manage somehow to indicate something about granny's failure to take in the situation. I could roll my eyes up a little, and tighten my mouth into a thin line, for instance. I'd seen a lot of that done this morning. But she wouldn't look at me. She wouldn't look at granny either. She kept her eyes lowered and looked at nothing but French toast.

"I must say she has a much better appetite when Jack's here," granny said to me, and that did it for me.

"Where are you going, Cassie," granny called after me, and I called back that I was going to try to find my bag, my clutch bag, because I seriously needed it.

"Did we ever look out by the pool?" Judith said, and I didn't answer. But we hadn't.

"Go on out," she said, "and I'll come out and help as soon as I'm through breakfast."

"I don't need any help," I said.

"But I want to talk to you," she said.

I didn't answer this either, but when I went out I

closed the door firmly enough to let her know which door
I left by.

The sun hit me hard when I went out onto the deck, but
the grass was cool under my feet when I crossed the lawn,
and the birds had quieted down somewhat, and when I got
to the terrace I wheeled a chaise longue out of the sun
and under a bamboo-shaded section and lay down, exhausted, and tried to locate my bag from where I lay. It
wasn't on the table. All there was on the table was a dustpan full of pieces of glass and beside it, a whisk broom. I
couldn't remember sweeping up the glass, though it was
perfectly possible, the way I felt last night, or the way I
felt at times last night, that I might have done it. I might
have come out and done it as penance, or out of pure ex-
uberance, or gratitude. I might have, but I couldn't remember. All I knew now was that I was glad it was
done, because I didn't feel all that exuberant, or penitent, or
anything else at this point. Why shouldn't I go get the
bachelor at the airport; how did I get relieved of the
assignment I'd taken on with such solemnity and with such
a feeling of responsibility to do justice to all of us with
frankness, honesty, wisdom, largesse of spirit? I wanted
it; I volunteered for the mission because it's the kind of
thing I can do; I can feel my way with words; I'd be able
to tell this boy, where Judith couldn't. For good or ill
she's simply not so articulate as I am. When a spokesman
is required I'm the one that speaks up. It's a tradition. For
an extreme example, when Jude applied at Juilliard I
wrote the letter. I couldn't stand having her go but I
wrote the letter. I could have written something that
would have absolutely assured me of her not being admitted, but I didn't. It was a very persuasive letter, and
she got in. And left me alone with both halves of a Boesendorfer to take care of.

It was nice lying down, but I couldn't sustain it. Within two minutes I got up and took the dustpan around the corner and emptied it into the trash can — dustpan, whisk broom, glass, and all, because it was worth the price of a new pan and broom to me not to try to remember where we kept the old ones. When I came back to the terrace I went and stood by the edge of the pool. The air was very hot, hotter every minute, and I'd have dropped my kimono and gone in but granny dislikes suitless swimming even at night, if she knows about it, and so I sat cross-legged at the edge and leaned over and sank both hands to the wrists. The water was very still and I could see a couple of clouds reflected in it and the branches of the oak trees by Jane's study. Also, when I moved closer, my own face in the space between my hands. It wasn't like looking in a mirror, nothing like so sharp and precise, and I was able to look straight at it without shock. In fact, I looked good down there in the rough outline and I wish all mirrors could have this softening effect when I need them to. Papa's word dryad came back to me, and I saw what he meant — a certain wayward quality in the hair, a rather attractive kind of disarray that did more for me than a comb would have. I stayed where I was and looked and considered. The sun was hitting me on the head, directly, and though it might have done me in, still I felt better than I had all morning, and able to think a little and remember things that are soothing to think about, such as, for instance, that a hamadryad is a dryad more or less limited to trees, and a water dryad is called a naiad. They were all good things to know at a time like this, and I was looking at the naiad down there between my hands when I saw Jude's reflection beside it.

"You meditating?" she said.

"No, why?"

"You're in the position — the cross-legged bit."

"I just didn't want to get my robe wet."

"Remember when we got on the meditation kick? What was that girl's name?"

"What girl?"

"Oh you know, your Buddhist friend, Sophie somebody, Sophie — uh, Myers."

"I don't recall any Sophie Myers."

"Then don't try. It's just as well."

"You sound exactly like granny," I said. "The way you said 'your Buddhist friend' could have been granny herself."

I got my legs under me and stood up. No more naiad. I walked under the bamboo roof and lay down on the chaise, and Judith came along and sat down on the edge of it.

"I wonder who took care of the glass?" she said.

"Me. Who else?" I said. "I swept it all up and got rid of it."

"When?"

"Last night."

"No. Don't you remember? I swept it up last night and left it there on the table because I didn't want to clang around with the lid of the trash can."

"All right, maybe you did. But I put everything away where it belongs — just now."

"Thank you."

"You're welcome. Where's Conchita?"

"Granny told her to stay home mornings this week because she didn't want her roaring around with the vacuum, and anyhow granny enjoys getting breakfast."

"She certainly does."

I turned over on my stomach and lay face-down with my arms around my head to keep out the light.

"Did you find your bag?"

"No."

"I looked too. It's not out here. Funny."

"Howling." I shifted a little to find out if she was still sitting beside me.

"You want me to move?"

"No, stay here, please stay here. Don't go away ever."

I turned over on my side and got an elbow under me and propped my head up to look at her. She looked the way I wished I felt.

"Don't ever. You won't, will you, ever?"

She sat very still, looking away from me, and finally she said, "That's what I wanted to talk about."

I felt a small chill through all the heat, and I shivered in a way I couldn't have believed. Maybe I just had the shakes but it felt like a chill.

"I'm not going to let you go get him," Judith said, and I stopped shaking because a jolt like that is a thing to change the metabolism. It was the word *let* that surprised me so. She was not going to let me go get him, as if I'd asked to be allowed to, when what actually happened was that I offered to relieve her of a duty, or rather of an embarrassing explanation, that she was not by nature equipped to handle, whereas I can manage, generally, to talk to anybody and explain a difficult point of view with a certain understanding, and a certain tact. I'm able to assume that there is a hole in anybody's iron-clad armor, and that an entering wedge can be wedged in if it's done with patience, coolly, without undue excitement. I'm not sure why, but I can do those things, and I'd said I'd help, I'd assume responsibility for how things are and for explaining them.

"Do you think we should both go, then?" I said, after I'd recovered a little.

It was quite a while before she answered, but when she did it was quite firm.

"No," she said, "I'd rather go alone. I don't know why I ever said anything else. I can't think how it happened. Any of it."

I took it slowly, because obviously there was something askew here, and I might be required to use some of the tact I'd been hoarding for the airport.

"It happened," I said, "because it had to." I waited for a way to say it, and I had it: "Because an integer can't exist without integrity. That's what we are, together — a whole being, a fabric, a complex — we're completed. And our integrity — well, we need it, and we've got it. We have to fight for it, but we know that. Who knows it better?"

I felt good about linking up integer and integrity so precisely. There are ways of serving the people you care about, and I like to believe I'll never do Judith anything but honor in the words I use on her. I felt that way about last night — that I was finally communicating again with somebody I can get off the ground with. When she's the one who's listening I can feel what ought to be said and find ways to say it. If this sounds arrogant, I can't help how it sounds. It's my mite. I polish it up and give it gladly. And I don't expect it not to make a difference.

But she sat there and looked off somewhere in the same vague and intent way she'd looked at the cat during breakfast. And finally she said: "I've never really understood why you think we're so special. Are we?"

It was my instinct, when I heard her, to stop trying to hold myself together, just let go and fly apart. But I remembered just in time that I could not afford to — not if I didn't want to go around being half of what I should be the rest of my life. Nine months was enough for me.

"Take it on faith — we're special," I said. "Who else could have had our mother for a mother and our father for a father? Who else do you know that drives a Riley and owns a Boesendorfer, or even knows what they are. We didn't join Job's Daughters, or go steady with some clod, or live with the Alpha Kappa Thetas, because we never talked that language or thought in those terms. How could we? We can start living where other imaginations fail."

I let it hang there, and I heard Jude sigh. I didn't want it to get heavy, so I said: "And besides that we don't stick out in the wrong places."

"You don't stick out any place," Jude said, "it kind of scares me."

"Worry about me, will you please? It's things like that I need."

"Oh, I do," Jude said, "I worry a lot."

"Then just tell him, if you don't want me to, how it is — that we've got a big investment here, and it would be very irresponsible of us to sell it short. We've got to be true to ourselves and to a way of life that's right for us, however the hell it may look to anybody else anywhere. You know that, don't you?"

She didn't say. But she stayed where she was.

"Just try to remember our apartment," I said. "You don't go into a place like that every day. It's all the things we are. We put it together piece by piece. You want to know what my doctor said the first time she saw it? Yes you do. She said everything about it gives evidence of an informed taste. That's a quote."

"Who's your doctor?"

"Vera Mercer. She has informed taste."

"Where'd she get her training?"

"Yale to start with. Then she was at Langley-Porter for two years before she went into private practice."

"Langley-Porter? Why do you say doctor if you mean analyst?"

"Generic term."

"I'm for specific terms. How long have you been with an analyst?"

"Since about three weeks after you left."

"Why didn't you tell me?"

"I wanted it to be my secret."

"Does papa know about it?"

"I suppose. He gets my canceled checks."

"Vera Mercer," Jude said, as if she were trying to place the name, or else maybe fix it in her mind. "Is she good; I mean has she helped?"

She was being like granny again, with the attitude that if you go to any particular kind of doctor you should get some particular kind of results.

"I don't analyze her," I said. "She analyzes me. I don't ask whether she's good, but maybe she is. At least she's kept me from diving off the bridge, if that's good."

"You're kidding," Jude said in a way that meant she hoped I was. I decided not to talk about it any more, because I wasn't too sure, myself, how serious I was about the bridge, and to find out would require a good deal more analysis than I'd had.

"All right, maybe I am, and anyhow I don't want to talk about it. But about the apartment — it's what we've made it by being the way we are. Like the drawing in the bathroom — the Degas girl getting out of a tin tub. And the Nayarit figures. We'll always have apartments like that, and they'll get better and better."

"As our taste gets more and more informed?" Jude said

in a sort of flattish tone, more like me than her. I tried not to notice.

"You can't know how it was — being in our apartment by myself after you went to New York. Everywhere I'd look there'd be something we'd found together — not even counting the piano. Every single thing. Do you know, for example, that we've got a whole unopened tin of truffles in the refrigerator? I couldn't open it alone, but every time I'd look into the cold tray, there it was, just waiting. Like me, no good to anybody unopened, but unable to be opened up."

I felt the chill again, from thinking about the refrigerator, possibly, and remembering I hadn't defrosted it for two months. First thing I'd do when we got back.

"You're shaking," Jude said.

"I know," I said, "I do it every time I think how lonely I was in that apartment."

"I know what you mean," Jude said, again in that rather unemphatic throw-away voice. "I was pretty lonely there myself."

"When?" I said, quite emphatically. She kept surprising me.

She waited a minute, and then said, "All the time we lived there. You'd come home, take a bath, change your clothes, take the car and be away either all night or else most of it. That's how I got to be a pretty good musician; I had so much time to practice, waiting around for you to come home."

She didn't sound slightly angry, or vindictive, or any of the ways girls always sound in this kind of accounting. Just factual.

"But can't you remember?" I said. "Don't you remember what we were trying to do?"

"What were you?"

"Listen, when I say *we* I mean you and me, not me and anybody else."

"Sure," Jude said, "I know."

"Don't say it that way," I said. "We have to get straight on this or we're nowhere."

"All right, I know it wasn't anybody in particular. It was just more or less anybody."

I groaned. She can be so obtuse.

"You shouldn't remember any of that," I said, "because I don't think you understand what it was for me, or what I had to go through before I could tell myself I'd been through it."

"I know," she said.

"*What* do you know?"

"I know how you are. It's all right. It's one way to be."

I turned onto my stomach and thought a minute. There was no chill now. I was hot all over, like the day.

"I hope you do know how I am," I said, after a while, "because it's not the way I was then. That was my Rimbaud period. I was trying things for size. And the silly thing about it was that I knew all the time where I stood, what I wanted, how I wanted to be. I wanted to be what we are, at its best all the time — the way we were brought up, the way we were born — something very exclusive and very very rare. The way we can be now."

Silence up there above me. Nothing. Just heat. And I didn't want to say another thing until I'd had some sort of response. It was long in coming, but it came. I felt a slight pressure on the back of my hair and smelled the lime cologne very sharply, and I knew she'd leaned down and kissed me, the way you do babies.

"You'll be all right, Cassie," I heard her say, and when I heard it I turned over fast and looked up to see what sort of look went with it. Lovely look, very serious and sad.

"Of course I'll be all right," I said. "If I can just find my bag and take a bath, I'll get dressed and go with you. Maybe we can go early and have lunch at the Basque place in Bakersfield before the plane gets in."

"No," Judith said.

"No what?" I said, "no lunch?"

"I'm going alone," she said. "I thought I told you."

"You told me so many things," I said.

She waited a minute, looking back over her shoulder toward the pool; then she looked down at me, and said very quietly, "No, I don't think I really told you anything. It was all you, you did the talking, you made all the plans, and I, I don't know, but I think I got sort of drowned in it, or snowed under. When you hit your stride you're —"

"I'm what. Tell me. I absolutely have to know what I am when I hit my stride."

"You're overwhelming. It's some sort of crazy vitality and it goes out like rays. I'd forgotten what it's like to be with you — kind of a circus. Only —"

She stopped, and I wasn't quite sure I wanted to prod her. Maybe the best would be to keep her stopped, but before I thought how to do it it was too late.

"The trouble is that just when it's all fun, all high and wild, you do a switch and have to be rescued all of a sudden. I remember I was all to pieces laughing at something or other, and wham there you were telling me that if I married Walter Thorson, which is what you kept calling Jack Finch, you'd die in a booby hatch in a strait-jacket and I'd better believe it. And I couldn't make the transition all that fast, so I said, 'No, don't do that, don't die in a booby hatch in a strait-jacket, wear that dress you charged to gran at Magnin's, it's better on you somehow, looser.' And then — oh boy —"

She shook her head. "I guess I'm slow in my mind. I thought we were just batting things back and forth for fun the way we used to, but the minute I mentioned that dress I knew better. That's when I had to rescue you."

Her version was accurate enough in its way. It's true I was shattered about the dresses being alike. It was so degrading, somehow, for me to have fallen into such a shallow ditch, and when she brought it up later, even in the way she did it, I'd had quite a good deal of brandy by then and I opened up with everything I thought about everything — marriage, conventions, stodginess, short-sightedness, self-delusion, betrayal, and ended in a fit of sobbing. I couldn't help it. The day had been too much for me, seeing Jude again had been too much for me, and after I got the invective out of my system I wept, and Judith did what she always does when I'm hurt — she stayed with me, told me not to cry, brought me Kleenexes, told me she'd missed me, there wasn't anybody like me in the whole crazy world, and then cried too. It was the second time we'd both had to weep, and when it was over and we were lying there quiet I told her how it had to be and that I'd go to the airport and tell the boy, and I'd get rid of my stupid dress. That was when she said she'd get rid of hers too, and I was very grateful. I really did feel rescued, and I did make quite a few plans. It could be she didn't hear them all. She went to sleep quite a long time before I did. The last time I went to get ice I don't think she heard me come back at all.

"I know I never said I'd let you go get him," she said now. "You thought it up; and after all the trouble about the dress, I didn't think it was a very good time to get you all stirred up again. It was almost morning."

"*Stirred up*," I said, "girl, you do talk like granny."

"What do you want me to say — disturbed?" she said.

I felt a knife go in and twist around. For a moment everything stopped. Then I turned over again and lay flat and heard the pounding behind my ears, and felt the whirling in my head and the bitterness welling up out of my own personal well of bitterness, and I let it well. I think I may even have felt a certain relief, because nothing worse could happen now. I'd had the mortal blow, I'd received the Judas kiss with that word disturbed. I couldn't have believed that I could confide in someone so close to me, the only one — tell her I'd had to go to a psychiatrist for help three weeks after she'd abandoned me, and two minutes after I revealed it have her knife me with a word, the key word — disturbed. It was unthinkable, but I couldn't think anyhow. I lay there and listened to the roar, and once in a while some sounds would come down to me from up there where the assassins were hobnobbing with the traitors and hatching their plots, up there in the seersucker shirt. Who cares, it's over. But I kept on hearing my name in all its forms: "Cass, listen to me," and "Look, Cassie," and "Hey, Cassandra Edwards, don't make a big thing of this. Let's just not get into any more of these, shall we? Let's not. Can't we work up a little togetherness around here, and just accept the fact that I'm going to marry a man named Jack Finch, and his name isn't Walter Thorson, and I'm sure you'll like him very much, and that he'll adore you. That's how it ought to be, and that's why we came out here to get married — so that he'd know my family and they'd know him. Don't you see?"

But how can you see if you're dead, and I was good and

dead. I felt a little something when she shook me, but not too much at that.

"Come on, now," she said, very briskly. "Can't we stop dragging the heels and get with it? We've only got two days."

"Will you quit mauling me," I said, finally, because I was not up to so much jouncing around. "Just give me the *coup de grâce* and then have the grace to leave graciously."

"That's better," I heard the seersucker assassin say, and I heard a little nervous laugh that went with it. Relief, I suppose. I was somewhat relieved myself. It seemed to me for a while that I might never talk again. I turned my head and looked up.

"What happened?" Jude said. "We were talking and all of a sudden you just got terribly quiet. What did I say?"

I could tell she really didn't know, and that helped.

"I don't want to go into it," I said, "because it doesn't really matter. What matters is for you not to throw yourself away."

"I'm not. Maybe he is but I'm not."

"That's only one opinion," I said. "I had a long talk with granny at breakfast, and you know how she is — if you can't say something good about somebody don't say anything at all? Well, she didn't say anything at all for a while and then she volunteered that he has dreadful manners and disgusting personal habits and that he's rather repulsive looking, but that you probably won't be embarrassed by him until it's too late, and you're stuck."

Judith laughed in a wonderful way. It was such a big success that I decided to take it a step further. Or half step.

"And when I asked papa about him, he said he was quite endearingly self-important, — like a kid that's just got a

Little Country Doctor kit and can't wait to do an autopsy on every doll in the house."

She laughed again, but maybe not quite so spontaneously.

"You're cute," she said. "How can you think so fast, especially that repulsive part?"

"It's only what gran said. Remember I've never seen the boy — or man."

"Or kid with the kit," she said.

"Sometimes I think myself papa goes too far," I said, and the laugh was all free again, no strain, no constriction, and as long as we were re-established I felt entitled to a question.

"What did you mean about only having two days?"

"Maybe it should even be tomorrow," Judith said, "as long as you came home a day early. All we really have to do is get gran to get Reverend Branson to come out and read the service, and have a glass of champagne, and sign the certificate. It's not much of a production."

"You mean this?" I said. I was beginning to understand that ever since I'd arrived, I'd been climbing two steps and falling back five. Very uphill work with stubborn material.

"Cassie — do you honestly want to stop me?" she said after I'd been waiting quite a long time.

It was a tactless question, and I made her wait quite a while in her turn, before I dealt with it.

"You couldn't say it that way if you had the smallest understanding of what the problem really is," I said. "Nobody 'stops' anybody. It's a matter of realizing what things are worth. I wouldn't want to stop you because I shouldn't think I'd have to. You wouldn't deliberately set the house on fire and watch it burn down with everything in it."

She sighed, and after a while she said rather easily: "You mean you'll be burned up if I get married."

First tactlessness, then callousness. Nine months in New York had not increased my sister's sensitivity. There was no way to answer. I lay there in all the heat and wondered what it is that gets lovely simple things so knotted and gnarled up. What makes mistletoe move in on a tree and take over, what made the wild cells move in on Jane Edwards; why do weeds flourish and flowers give up? Why does papa have to prefer drinking alone on a ranch to the entrenched inanities of the university world? Where is there to go? Or barring that, where can you hide?

"Is it what you want?" I said, and I didn't load the question except that I may possibly have given a little accent of incredulity to the word *want*. Enough, at least, to get a much quicker answer than I might have hoped for or expected.

"I would never have let it get this far, if I hadn't been sure," Jude said. "We were going to do it Friday, but all morning I've kept thinking why not tomorrow? We don't even have to engage a church, because — did I tell you this last night? — because I've got this feeling, maybe it's crazy, but I've got it, that I'd like for us to be married in Jane's study."

That's what I thought I heard her say. In fact I knew I heard her say it. But I couldn't believe it. Not until she went so far as to enlarge on it.

"I haven't told granny, because you know how she gets about Jane. I thought I'd ask you first, if it seemed to you the way it does to me — that it would be a way of including all of us. Or do you think it would just seem icky like Memorial Day?"

I was in a state of shock. I didn't say a thing, and she went on alone.

"I asked Jack, naturally, and he said he thought as an

idea that it was about as sentimental as you can get but that where would we be without sentiment?"

I came to and said, "If the idea is to include all of us you'd better invite Current-cat and Rosie."

"Oh I intend to," she said. "I'd have the horses if they weren't so damned big. I mean it, strictly the family."

"Why don't you have it in the corral?" I said. "No, you couldn't, it would spoil the obscene mother-image background you're working on."

And this time I was the one who produced some silence. I felt the mattress move when Jude got up. I didn't hear her walk away but that was because she was barefooted. I lay flat and let her go, and heard the deck door close when she went into the house. She didn't even slam it.

Useless to imagine how I felt, because by this time I didn't feel. But I could wonder, in a dazed way, whether any of this was what she said it was — that she'd had no part in the plan to send me to explain at the airport, make the apologies, do the talking. Could I have been so hallucinated as to believe we'd talked it over together; or was she asleep, as she said, while I talked it over with myself between trips to the kitchen for supplies? No. Nobody who can go after supplies can be completely dreaming, no matter how well supplied. And I remembered with absolute clarity her saying the dress was wholly unimportant — she'd take it back — mail it back. That much I *did* know, she was with me on the dress question.

But she was in the house, and I was outside, where I now realized I'd been, figuratively, all along. I couldn't get up and go trotting in after her, or rather I could, of course, but I had a firm feeling it wouldn't do any good. I'd slipped up and got the door closed on me, closed and locked and double-bolted, and all I could do now was maintain a dignified silence and let her figure things out for herself, if she would. Or I could clear out if I wanted to, throw my things into the Riley and go back to Berkeley, but I was afraid it would only look petulant, from the outside, and not give a true indication of the depth of my trouble or the nature of the violation. If I left I'd be gone. But if I stayed at least she'd have to look at me sometimes, see me, and maybe make some connections.

"Stay," I said to myself. "Stay, Cassandra, it's all right. You used to live here, and nobody wants to exactly throw you out any more than anybody wants to exactly split an infinitive, or any integral unit. So stay. Be here. If you don't belong here, where do you?"

The truth is I was very tired, I've never been so tired. The mattress I was lying on seemed to be resisting me instead of letting me sink down and down with all the inertia there was in me. I wanted very much to sink, let gravity have its way with me, and stay sunk until I built up enough strength to go into the house and go to bed. I don't believe I slept after Judith left me but I did something that was rather like it — I resigned myself to letting the mattress hold me up and I drifted. In an odd way I became one with nature. I stopped thinking and turned into a heat wave, the kind you can see undulating above a field in the summertime in our valley.

I was still undulating when papa spoke to me. I turned over and looked up and I couldn't see him very well at first, the sun was high and there was such a glare over everything. But I got him located and smiled at him, and he leaned over and put his hand on my forehead and asked me how I was.

"Wonderful," I said, but I didn't try to sit up.

"We were worried about you out here in the sun so long."

"I was in the shade when I first came out," I said. "Who was worried?"

"That's the way it is with the sun," he said. "It moves. At least that's one theory."

"Who was worried?"

"Nobody," he said. "It's a good enough theory. It satisfies curiosity and takes most minds off the unimaginable complexities of the entire system. Besides that, it's neat and understandable and widely held."

No use to ask him again, just get him off the universe.

"Where is Judith," I said, and he said she'd gone, she wanted to do some shopping before she went to the airport, pick up some champagne and a cake before she picked up the other item — the bridegroom.

"She's gone?" I said and I must have sounded astonished, because I was. I knew of course she was going, but I didn't think she'd go, like this, without coming out or saying goodbye. Just go.

"What's wrong?" papa said. "Did you want to go with her?"

"No," I said, "but I thought she might like to take the Riley, and I was going to tell her."

"She's better off in my car," papa said, "it's air-cooled. No telling what champagne might do in the Riley on a day like this."

I closed my eyes. He was right about the day, a real firecracker.

"Did she leave any message, or messages?" I said.

"Not with me."

"Where's granny?"

"She's gone to Putnam to talk to the Reverend Mr. Branson. I told her to call him up, but she likes to look at people while she talks. And this is the kind of assignment that appeals to her a great deal."

"I know," I said, and I could see Mrs. Abbott with hat and gloves on telling Mr. Branson that Jack Finch stood first, at the very least, in his graduating class and had also passed his Wassermann brilliantly. And that Judith was all but slated for Town Hall.

"Papa," I said, with my eyes closed, "are you for this?"

It wouldn't make the smallest difference, papa said, whether he was or not, because when our grandmother decides to go in to Putnam rather than telephone, she goes, regardless of weather.

"Come on," he said, "let's go in. It's the first time I've been outdoors in a month, and I wouldn't be now if we hadn't got worried about you."

Full circle. Who got worried? Who did me such honor? I didn't ask again, however. I sat up and everything turned very black, but after a moment I got onto my feet and followed papa across the terrace, up the steps, across the lawn, up to the deck and into the dining room. The air-conditioner must have been going full tilt. It was like going into an ice compartment, and I couldn't make the change. I got as far as the counter in the kitchen, got onto a stool, and hung on there with my teeth chattering so noticeably that even papa noticed. And questioned me.

"It's probably some kind of a bug," I said, giving him the first cliché that came, and then expanding it. "Everybody in the University has it; classes half full and not an empty bed in Cowell."

I'd forgotten in the expansion period that classes were over, and examinations too, and that Berkeley was deserted, even by bugs, but if papa thought of it he gave no sign. He said instead that he'd been very much interested in what I'd been saying last night about the ancient skeptical drift in the thinking of current French writers (though of course he was the one who had said it, all I did was latch onto it and find some examples that pleased him) and that he wanted to talk about it at greater leisure than we had last night.

"So do I," I said, "very much."

"What are you doing?" he said, "having a chill?" and I said it was beginning to look like it and sound like it and maybe I was.

He looked across the counter at me, quite concerned, and then went down on his haunches and brought up a fresh bottle of brandy and poured me a pony and pushed it across the counter at me.

"It's what they give in the Alps," he said, and I took the little glass in my hand and shook an amount of it away, but got some as far as my mouth, drank it off and set the glass down again and made my excuses. What I really should do, I said, was go to bed for a while, take some aspirin if I could find some, drink a lot of water, take it easy for a while, and I'd probably be all right by evening.

"When will they be back, do you know?" I said, and papa said he thought by half past three or four, or maybe Judith said three.

"I'll be warm by then," I said, and I got off the stool and left the man; my dear father who wanted to talk about skepticism with me at some leisure; I simply left him standing there behind the counter, walked out and left him alone, where he was of course thoroughly inured to being.

There was a sound of thunder in our room when I opened the door, thunder and high waves. Conchita with her favorite appliance, the vacuum cleaner. She didn't of course hear me come in but I managed to get into a position to attract her attention and make the noise subside. And then I kissed her and said Qué tal, and Cómo se va, and Tengo frío, tengo resfriado, all the useful idiomatic expressions of both greeting and illness I could think of without strain, and of course I got it back a good deal more amply than I'd given it forth. She's nice, Conchita is, but she wanted to talk about Judith and Juanito, which I took to be Spanish for Walter Thorson, and granny and all the things there are. I told her, when my turn came, that I was so happy to be home, so happy, so happy, but that I had to go to bed now and if she would just forget our room I'd do it later. But she couldn't quite leave it as it was, she saw some paper sticking out from under my bed and she got down on her knees and looked under and pulled it out, yards of it, all ruffled and crumpled. And after she had it all out, she looked again, for more, possibly, and came up with a miracle — my clutch bag, my long narrow white clutch bag.

"Gracias a Dios," I said, and then more simply, "adiós." I took the bag, put it on Jude's bed, helped Conchita roll up the cord to the vacuum cleaner, pressed the tissue paper on her, opened the door for her, blessed her, closed it after her, and fell back against it for a moment after it was closed.

There's a push-in lock on the door to our bedroom; nothing very serious, you can open it from the other side with a nail file or a fairly stiff hair pin or a dime. But I locked it anyhow to keep granny from poking in when she came home, and to keep Conchita from any afterthoughts. It gave me a measure of privacy, however small, and I needed it.

I came back to Jude's bed, sat on the edge of it and looked across at my own, so beautifully turned down, so ready to take me in; I sat looking at it for a while; then I picked up the clutch bag, and possibly from association, clutched it — held it tight against me, as if it were a doll, and rocked it a little. I don't think I sang to it or anything quite so far out as that, but I do know I had a sense of having found a lost pet or teddy bear, one I couldn't really do without. I thought how nice it is to have an inanimate friend, one that can't get into a car and go roaring off to Bakersfield and places like that. This kind may hide under the bed and give you a bad time for a while, but it doesn't really run out on you. It stays where it is and waits until you find it, or Conchita finds it, and then it's back with you, just as it was. Just as it was, but I felt I should do a little checking anyhow, so I unsnapped it, then unzipped it, and then unzipped an inner pocket and dumped three bottles out onto the bedspread. The bottles were full; there was God's own plenty, all with numbers across the top, and dosage and usage overtly described: "One every six hours as needed for sleep," and "One capsule no oftener than every four hours as needed." I understood the reticence of the last one, I thought. It would be difficult for a great many pharmacists to write: "as needed for zest," or "as needed for zeal," or "as needed to encourage the minimum of tolerance for the brute stupidities of this world." It would also go against the grain to write simply "Pep pills." Apothecaries have their own sensitivities and some of them cannot go beyond a gentle "as needed."

The big question here was what's needed most: tranquillity, sleep, or zeal, and I didn't feel like deciding in any great hurry. Pull myself together a little bit first, because there would be some introductions later, and tranquil, zestful or asleep I'd like to be presentable within limits. I left the pills on the bedspread and went into the bathroom and started to take a shower and then changed it to a bath so that I could sit, and while I was sitting the thought came.

I don't believe I recognized it as a thought at first, simply as the dim stirring of an instinct, an instinct for peace — cessation of hopeless hope, or call it a war to end all wars. It can't be done on an international scale, too many embassies, go-betweens, attachés. But one single person — and I now felt very very single — can accomplish what he must face sooner or later anyhow — his own removal from the fray. It doesn't even take courage, because you don't give up anything if you have nothing left to expect. You bow out with dignity, looking presentable, newly bathed, scrubbed up, combed out. They can tell you planned it because the whole thing is so immaculately, so to speak, conceived. And there will be deep gratitude on all sides, and on the part of some — regrets laced with admiration.

I let the water out of the tub and later got out myself and dried off a little and caught a look at myself in the long mirror on the door. Thin, but I didn't think really too thin, somewhat boyish, but again not all the way. The dryad word came again. My dear papa, the great skeptic; and which skeptic was it that said the only thing better than dying young is never to be born at all? I didn't look bad, as a matter of fact. Just to look, you'd say young, and attractive, although an autopsy would probably reveal an incipient ulcer and all kinds of damage, here and there, if not the other place. In any case I decided not to hunt up something to sleep in, and I combed my hair and brushed it and just let it hang down my back, no pins, and pulled a couple of eyebrows, and brushed my teeth again, and let my face alone, because of the sunburn.

By the time I went back into the bedroom I had my mind made up. As I said, it wasn't really hard, because I couldn't stand what was going to happen, and I knew I couldn't, not now, keep it from happening. So go, girl. We should have been one person all along, not two, and this way the other one could live it out, possibly with some part of my spirit alive in her to the end of her days to make up for the part of her I might take with me today.

I brought a glass of water into the bedroom with me. I picked up the bottle as needed for it didn't say what and put it back into the inside pocket of my bag. Then I took the cap off the one that said "every four hours as needed for strain," shook two of them into my hand, swallowed them with water, and put the bottle back into the inside pocket with the other one.

The next was the last. It still said "as needed for sleep," but since it didn't make any adjustment for shorter or longer sleep, I had to stop and think what it would take to do it without overdoing it. I shook eleven pills out into my hand, because eleven is an appealing number, and then I put four back, because I'd already had two for strain, and because seven is another appealing number. Nothing's easy, not even this; calculation comes into it; you have to think, and I think I stayed with seven. Or eleven. Then I emptied the rest of them into the inside pocket of my bag along with the other two bottles, put the bag under Judith's bed and took the empty bottle to the night stand beside my bed. "Cassandra Edwards. One capsule every six hours as needed for sleep," I read, out loud this time, just to be hearing a voice I knew, and then I put the empty bottle on the stand with the cap off beside it, and got into bed and began swallowing capsules, one after the other. I took my time about it, and there was a period when it looked as if I might not have enough water. But I'd done enough getting up and down for one night and day, and I rationed it out and made it do. And when it had done I set the glass beside the empty bottle, slid down between the clean cool sheets, and arranged myself to wait.

I wondered, there's no reason not to admit it, what it would do to Judith to find me. She must have known I'd have to do something when she left without saying goodbye. But still — it wasn't my idea to hurt her. Oh not at all. And I'd forgotten to leave a note. Least I could do. It could say, "Please accept this token of my love with all good wishes for your future happiness." Like a card on a wedding gift.

I wanted very much, after I thought of it, to write the note, but by that time I was too tired to get up and look for a pen, and I lay there tracing letters on the sheet with my finger, trying to make myself believe she'd understand it without any note. I cried a little anyhow about not being able to make it — it would have been such a good note — but after a while that was over with and I floated easily without much caring what I left or where I went.

Last thing I can remember was opening my eyes a little and seeing the clown in the poster. I wanted to say something to him, and I think I did — something quite brilliant, like "Goodbye, you clown."

JUDITH SPEAKS

WE GOT BACK to the ranch later than we should have, because — oh for a lot of reasons, but mainly because I really didn't want to go back at all. The way I felt after a whole night and part of a day with my sister is difficult for me to describe and not easy to discuss. But I discussed it, anyhow, in the coffee shop at the airport, at some length and quite stubbornly. We sat in a booth for part of an hour and I tried to tell Jack everything I was afraid of, and more or less exactly what Cass's character is like, or what her problems are — problems and character being in her case so bound up together that you can't have one without the other; she's a problem character. He knew it all already, of course; I talk about her a lot too much, I'm afraid; but none of it ever seemed to worry him. He took the position I wished I could take — that once we were married, we'd be married; forsake father, forsake grandmother, forsake, please God, sister, and cleave unto each other someplace a long long way away from where the forsaking took place.

I had to be stubborn to get any of it told, really dogged, because when Jack got off the plane he was terribly full of new information himself, things about the hospital he'd been to, how there never was such a hospital, with every possible surgical extravagance, only the elevator he was in got stuck between the second and third floor. And how decent the director was after the elevator got fixed and they had the interview, and what a good place it would be to do a year's residence in with all that stuff to work with.

We were sitting across from each other in the booth, drinking iced coffee, and Jack was holding my free hand with his free hand. I felt as if he'd been gone for ten years, and that I'd personally put in the time at hard labor. The hand felt wonderful.

"There must be other places with surgical luxuries to work with," I said. "Places a lot farther away, where nobody can come to visit." And I could see he was still so taken up with the hospital that I added, "I don't mean visiting hours, I mean my family. Darling, listen to me, maybe we shouldn't ever even have children. I come from a long line of nuts."

"I've met them," he said, "all but your mother and your sister."

"They're the ones."

I felt I'd caught his attention, or at least got it away from me and onto what I was saying.

"You even want us to get married in your mother's study," he said, as if this were somehow an inconsistency, as if you can't have a tender memory of someone you just finished calling a nut.

"I was crazy about her," I said. "We both were; but — well, you won't find two mothers more different than ours was from Whistler's. She didn't seem like our mother at all — more like somebody's little brother."

"Nobody's managed to establish what normal is, even for mothers," Jack said, and all at once I could see what the effect of him would be across the desk from a patient, looking so kind and intelligent, making an inspired stab at a diagnosis. I set my coffee down and gave him my other hand, and he took it, thank God, and I stopped worrying for the moment and just looked at him. He had on a brown-and-black striped tie and a beautiful shirt with a gold safety pin holding the collar tabs together, and his jacket was on the bench beside him. His hair was so clean that each single hair had its own halo. Altogether a beautiful man whether or not I was in love with him. Which I was, unequivocally. I remembered the offhand way Cass said granny found him somewhat repulsive, and I bit my lip, and then laughed again, almost the same way I did when she said it.

"What's funny?" he said.

"My sister."

"I thought you were talking about your mother."

"Same thing. Jane was a good mother, though, in a way I don't think most mothers are. She kept us entertained. When she was home."

"What kind of a wife was she? Or don't you know?"

I looked at him, the doctor asking the questions, getting the history, and all I could think of when I looked at him was what kind of a wife I was going to be. Not like Jane. Not so entertaining, maybe, but devoted. Oh, endlessly devoted. It took me a moment to answer, to get away from me and back to Jane. And when I did I used the same word.

"She was devoted to papa," I said. "I think she practically worshiped him. It showed in kind of peculiar ways, though."

I got lost, thinking about Jane, and then about Cass, and then about papa; but not all lost because there were these scrubbed-up hands hanging on to mine.

"How?" the doctor said, and I came back to the question, but not until I'd looked at the backs of the hands that had mine. Very hairy backs of hands, and the hair was like the rest of him, so good-looking, so reassuring. It seemed silly to be sitting here in a coffee shop telling this man what his mother-in-law would have been like if he'd had to have one, but I decided to tell him anyway, because his own case history was so full of lacks. He'd never known his mother, and his father died when he was twelve. No home life at all, which is probably why he turned out so well.

"Well you've never seen a woman treat a man the way Jane treated papa, I bet," I said. "By the time he'd get a cigarette out of a package, she'd be there with a match. When she was home I don't think he ever lighted a single cigarette for himself. And she was always opening doors for him. I don't think I ever saw her pull his chair out for him at the table, but that was the sort of thing. When they'd play tennis or ping-pong Jane would shag all the balls, his side of the net, or hers, she'd chase them."

"Was there a big difference in their ages?"

"Three years."

"That's not much, for so much deference."

"I know. And something else — she was always bringing him presents or sending things when she was away — monogrammed pajamas, and gorgeous belts, and Hermès scarves, kind of thing papa never wears. But Jane did, sometimes. Last time I ever saw her she was wearing one of papa's monogrammed pajama tops, with the sleeves rolled to her elbows. She was in Mercy Hospital, looking very sporty. And being, too."

I didn't want to cry, not in the coffee shop or anywhere else. I turned my hands over, so that I could do a little holding. You might say clinging. And after a little of it I felt safe again. At least I knew I wouldn't cry, there'd been enough of that last night, and I didn't want to make a habit of it. There'd been enough of this booth, too, I began to feel, and enough of the big table-separation. I wanted to be in a room, on a bed, and not explaining anything.

"Do you have the license?" I said. It seemed to take a lot of breath to say it and more to add to it — "With you, I mean? I mean have you got it on you?"

He didn't answer. Just picked up his jacket, felt into an inside breast pocket and brought the paper out and laid it on the table.

"I read it last night in the hotel after I went to bed," he said, "about twenty times. I forgot to get a newspaper and all there was was a Gideon Bible and this, so I read this. It's short but you can read between the lines."

I picked it up and looked at it.

"Why didn't they give you a middle name, do you suppose?" Jack said, and I said I thought they were in such a state of shock from the day they found out there were going to be two of us that they couldn't find the energy to double up on names.

"Cass was born eleven minutes before I was," I said, "and when the nurse showed her to papa she was setting up such a howl that all he could think of was Cassandra wailing from the walls of Troy. So he named her that. They didn't name me for two weeks, and then they got mine out of the Apocrypha. But that's as far as they went. No middle names."

"I'm glad they took two weeks to yours. You got a good name."

"It looks good here," I said. My signature was very very legible. All clear and firm and brave. Jack's could have been anything. It was in physician's script, the kind pharmacists alone can read. But I could read it. John Thomas Finch, it said, and the M.D. was left off. I looked at it, and thought about it, and then looked up at Jack and asked him if what I wanted would be possible — get up from this table, pay for the coffee, pick up the license and take it to the City Hall and ask some magician there to turn me with all possible haste into Mrs. John Thomas Finch.

Jack took it calmly, but he did show a little surprise.

"Today?" he said, "right now?"

I nodded. It was all I could do after all the boldness.

"But you were all for having your sister be a witness, and your father give you away, and your mother's study be the place."

"I know I was," I said, "but I was wrong. That was a great big mistake I inadvertently happened to make."

"But your sister came all the way from —"

I cut in on him. "Oh I know, all the way from Berkeley a day early. I was terribly glad to see her, but I've seen her. Now all I want to do is get married, just very privately, before I have to see her again."

"We could have done it that way in New York," Jack said, and all at once I felt frightened, really scared, because I didn't want him to start thinking of me as erratic, or changeable, or impetuous. I didn't want him to start thinking about me at all from the outside, just love me and trust me to the end of time.

"Okay," I said. It was a little weak but I didn't want to do any pleading. I pushed the license back toward him, across the table, and he picked it up, and looked at it, and then at me and said, "Don't say okay, like that. I'm not trying to talk you out of anything."

"No," I said, "it wasn't a good idea. Forget I said it." I slid out of the booth and stood beside the table while Jack put the license back into his inside pocket, and picked up the check and dropped some change on the table, and while he was paying for the coffee I went on outside.

The heat after the air-cooled coffee shop dropped over me like a quilt, and I stood just outside the door trying to think what it was I was supposed to do in Bakersfield. Get champagne. Papa said get a case just in case, and be sure it was French. He wrote out a choice of brands and gave it to me, but I must have left it at home, or in the car, maybe, because it wasn't in my purse anywhere. I was hunting for it, though, and wondering whether Cass had ever found her clutch bag, when Jack came out and stood behind me for a minute and then put an arm around me and began walking toward the car. He didn't even mention the heat, not even when we got into the car and got hit by the accumulation that came from a half hour of sun through glass. He ran down the windows and sat there under the wheel and looked at me and asked me to tell him what was wrong.

"Start the car," I said, "so the cooler will work. Then let's drive around and find a champagne store. Papa wants a case for the wedding."

Jack started the car.

"A case should do nicely for four people," he said, "assuming your grandmother is still on the wagon. What's the matter?"

"The curse," I said, and changed it quickly — "I mean the old family curse."

"Your sister?"

"My sister. I don't know how she does it, but maybe you can tell me when you meet her."

"Maybe."

"She's so damned disarming. I decide everything's going to be one, two, three, no funny-business, and within an hour she's got me crying because she — oh it's too crazy to tell."

"Then tell it."

The air-conditioner was working by now. The car had cooled off and my spine was slightly stiffer and I thought why not, he might as well know, and I told him the whole dress sequence — how Cass had come up with a dress that was a replica of mine after all our years of trying so hard not to do anything alike, and how it humiliated her and made her break a glass all over the terrace, and go all to pieces herself.

"It was terrible," I said, "because when something ruins her, it ruins me too. I don't know why, but when anything makes Cass feel like a fool all I want to do is die."

"It's natural enough," Jack said. "You'll get over it."

"But she felt so awful, and granny thought it was so funny. Maybe it was, too, but all I wanted to do was die."

"Quit talking about wanting to die," Jack said. "Dying is a big thing."

"I know," I said. "Oh I know."

He turned and looked at me, and then pulled me over beside him and I came in close like all the high school girls we used to turn our noses up at. We were wrong. It's the only way to sit in a car. It gives you some confidence. You can confide.

"I told her finally that it didn't matter at all who wore what, and that I'd send my dress back, and then —"

"Then what?"

"Turn right, here. I think the champagne store is on this street, or else the next one."

He turned, and I sat close.

"Driving this car," he said, "gives me a feeling for a Park Avenue practice. Don't ever let me drive it again."

If I could have sat closer I would have.

"So did you send it back, for God's sake — your wedding dress? After I bought that suit?"

"No, of course not. I didn't really intend to — but I thought maybe I'd just wear something else — something uncontroversial — but that didn't do much good either, because — well, because Cass thought when I said I'd send it back that I meant —"

I couldn't say it, and I didn't for a while. But the way Jack kept still let me know I had to. So I did.

"She thought I meant I'd changed my mind about the whole thing — getting married. And she didn't give me any time to tell her what I did mean. She just said thank God I'd come to my senses and realized that people like us can't play fast and loose with their destiny, etc. etc. etc."

"Expand, please, on the etceteras," the doctor said, and again I knew I had to, even if it meant selling Cass out, and me with her, and papa and Jane and granny, and Tacky and the horses, and our whole life up to now.

"I think that's the store," I said, "the Metropole, on the corner down there," and after he'd parked and cut the motor, I stayed where I was against him, and he didn't move to get out either. With the motor off, the heat began piling up immediately, but we stayed together, and I told him, as fast as I could, which wasn't very fast, how it went, how Cass took over and planned on coming to the airport and telling him I'd changed my mind.

I think I told it all, without leaving anything out or smoothing anything up. But the hardest part to tell was that I'd let her think what she wanted to think for a while, because I could not bring myself to smash her up again — after all she'd been through with the dress business. I just didn't have it in me to pull the rug out from under her right while she was telling me how indispensable we are to each other, and how the marriage wouldn't last a year even if she let me go through with it.

"If she let you!" Jack said. "She said that, and you didn't put her straight?"

"Oh yes," I said, "I put her good and straight this morning. But last night she was the way she gets — pretty overpowering. I couldn't quite do it."

"She sounds to me like a bad bad girl," Jack said, and when I caught from his voice that he didn't include me I could not possibly have loved God more, nor nature, nor all bounty. And along with the relief I was flooded with forgiveness.

"She's not bad," I said, "she's just a little wild, a real Till Eulenspiegel by nature. You'll probably like her. It's very hard not to."

"Hand me my jacket, will you?" Jack said.

The jacket was on the other side of the seat, so that I was sitting between it and Jack. I picked it up and gave it to him and he took the license out of the pocket, and tossed the jacket into the back seat.

"I'm sorry I was so dense, back there," he said. "I think you're right, it was a mistake."

"Mistake?" I said, much too loud, because it was a word I wasn't expecting. It took a while for him to explain that he was only quoting me, that it had been a mistake for me to want to be married at home, at least in that particular home with that particular bridesmaid; but that we didn't have to stick to it, it was an error that hadn't yet been committed, very easily corrected, with the bridegroom getting what he'd opted for all along — a nice, private, civil ceremony in which the principals made their promises for no one's benefit but their own. He would have preferred

New York, maybe, but Bakersfield's a good town. Good and hot.

I ran down the window on my side but the air was the same outside as it was inside.

"Do you know where the City Hall is?" Jack said.

"There's a new one, I think," I said, "they were building it last time I came through."

"Can you remember where they were building it? Because that's probably where it is now, if they finished it."

"Probably so," I said, and started to laugh, and burst into tears instead. The tears came as a surprise to both of us, but more to me than to Jack, I guess, because he put his arm around me in all that heat and held me and let me cry and talked to me like a father. No, like a husband; like all good men, the very best of them, kind and good, and good and kind, telling me to cry, go right ahead, most natural thing in the world in heat like this, after a night like last night, and faced with a sudden important decisive change of plan. Who wouldn't cry? What woman, anyhow, and he didn't feel too strong himself.

"What about the ring, though? It's at home in the dresser drawer," I said, in a sort of wail, because it was a beautiful ring, broad and plain; I'd taken it out of the dresser drawer and looked at it twenty times while Jack was in Los Angeles and before Cass got home, just to see it and be glad we'd decided to fly in the face of convention and not label Jack as a husband with a big ring on, just one ring for me. And now neither of us had one, and I wanted mine very much.

"I'm not sure you need a ring," Jack said. "I think when the time comes the man says 'What token do you give, or have?' and then you give a token. It's usually a ring, but it probably doesn't legally have to be; it could be any old token. I could give you my Phi Beta Kappa key, if I had one."

"That's the only way I'd ever get one," I said. "But isn't there a part that says 'with this ring I thee wed'?"

"What about it? We could get the man to change it to 'with this Phi Beta Kappa key.' "

"But you don't have one."

"I know, but I belong to the club. I could buy one."

"I think the heat's hit you," I said. "What we have to have is a ring. And it's in the dresser drawer."

"I think maybe it has," Jack said. "The heat. There must be rings we could get. Just don't worry. We'll get one."

And we did too. We drove away from the Metropole without remembering why we'd stopped, and we found a ring in a variety store next door to the drugstore where Jack looked up the address of City Hall and made the call and got the appointment with the municipal judge for four o'clock.

I was very glad they'd built a new city hall, because when we went inside it felt like Ancient Rome — the halls cool and spacious, and the air calm and detached and formal. Above all cool. Above all quiet. We stopped a minute in front of a directory. Then I went to pull myself together while Jack found the clerk of the court. We said goodbye in front of a door marked LADIES.

"Five minutes," Jack said, and I said it back.

"In the judge's chambers."

"In the judge's chambers."

I watched him walk down the hall and turn a corner, and I pushed the door open and went inside and realized that I was within five minutes of becoming a different person, facing in a different direction, free to be myself for the one I loved. I washed my face three times with soap from a dispenser, dried off on paper towels, combed my hair, tucked in my blouse, decided against lipstick, and when there was nothing more to do and my watch said I still had a minute, I stood where I was and looked in the mirror, steadily and for as long as I had, and made my farewells to the one I saw there.

"Goodbye, Cassie; let me go now. And be happy, because I'm going to be, and you can too. I'm sure you can."

And then I turned my back, opened the door and walked down the hall to Room 120 humming "Sheep May Safely Graze," by J. S. Bach. I have no idea why I picked the music I did, but it was an altogether happy wedding march I made all the way from the dressing room to the judge's chambers, alone, on no-one's arm, all unattended. Jack was waiting for me in front of the door. He came forward a few steps to meet me and we went in together and came out, not much later, man and wife.

It was a solemn, happy, and beautiful wedding; and all the while it was taking place the maid of honor was in the throes of a solemn ceremony of her own — likewise unattended.

I knew papa would feel terrible about my forgetting the champagne, and that granny would feel worse about the cake. She'd wanted to make one herself, and I'd talked her out of it. It would have been different if we'd come home with something we could create a little diversion with; and by the time we got to the turn-off for the ranch, I was getting quite nervous and thinking maybe we could go on to Putnam and get some champagne, and a cake too, a little something to soften the blow.

"Your father can soften it with brandy," Jack said, be

cause he was against doing anything but going directly to the ranch and packing and getting someone to take us to an airplane that would get us back to New York and to the apartment that would be waiting for us. I wanted that, too, more than anything else in the world, but I was really worried now about how Cass would act, and how gran would feel about calling off the minister, and how sort of headlong the whole City Hall thing would look to papa, who never believes in moving fast, nor in moving.

"How'll we do it?" I said.

"Take it as it comes," Jack said; "go in, and get the introductions over, and when the subject comes up, deal with it. Then pack. Then blow."

"How would it be to phone ahead?" I said. "There's an emergency telephone booth along here somewhere."

"This isn't an emergency," Jack said. "We can tell them face to face." He waited a minute, and then said, "Can't we?" and I had to say of course we could, why not, we're of age, it's a free country, and it was my idea, anyhow, to go to the City Hall and get it over with.

We drove along between cotton fields, very green. The heat hung in wavy layers above the road and made it look like water.

"Get it *over* with?" Jack said. "That's no way to talk."

"I didn't mean it that way," I said, "I meant have it done, really accomplished, so that nothing that might happen could make the smallest difference, or stop it, or postpone it."

"Could anything ever have?" he said, and I told him the truth, that I didn't know, and that that was why I hadn't wanted to risk any sabotage.

"I can't believe it," he said.

"I can't either," I said, "I really can't. But I'm glad we're married. Aren't you?"

It took him a minute to answer and then he said, "Yes, oh sure," in such an absent-minded way that I might as well have been talking to papa.

"What are you thinking?" I said, and he told me. He was thinking about the blank wall you face when you open the door of our apartment, and how maybe the best thing would be to hang one of those long Chinese scrolls there, something to see when you open the door, nothing much, just something pleasant, because it's important to open a door and have a sense of who lives there. Maybe a little cabinet with a vase of flowers against that wall, something to let you know it's not just any door you happen to be opening.

"It won't be," I said. "We'll unlock it, and open it, and go inside, and it won't be just any door."

I looked up at him, and then on beyond him. We were passing a pumphouse with a long pipe sticking out of it and throwing a beautiful head of white water into a cement weir. I wished I could put my head into it, but I laid it on Jack's shoulder instead and thought about the door we'd open not so long from now.

"When do you suppose we can be there?" I said, and asking it I felt like a little girl asking for the fifteenth time how many more days until Christmas.

"I don't know," Jack said. "The schedule's at the ranch, but I think it's safe to say that by midnight tomorrow we'll be in our own house."

"In it?" I said.

"By midnight tomorrow," he said, "we might even have been in it for as long as two hours."

I sighed, deep and long, and at that moment I felt entirely equal to the ordeal of getting home and finding Cass and telling her we'd stolen a march, and equal to telling papa why there was no champagne and telling granny why there was no cake. I felt good. I felt up to it. And we drove the rest of the way without saying a word. Very thoughtful ride.

When we came into the driveway I saw granny standing in a flower bed outside our bedroom, shading her eyes and looking into our east bedroom window.

"I also come from a long line of peeping toms," I said. "Let's pretend we didn't see her."

"All right," Jack said. "I don't want to press charges. She'll grow out of it. Kiss me, will you, before we go in?"

"Of course," I said. "Of course," and before we knew where we were again, granny was tapping on the car window on my side, looking the way she looks when somebody's a half-hour late getting home. Worried, that is, but in a special way of looking worried that is very individual, very easily readable as high matriarchal worry. It's the look she always used to get when she diagnosed any of our stomach-aches as acute appendicitis.

I opened the door.

"You in some kind of trouble, Mrs. Abbott?" I said, and she said yes, she'd lost Cassie, that is she thought she was in the bedroom, because the bedroom door was locked, but she'd been there ever since I'd left for Bakersfield, and that's been a long time.

It's sad that alarmists always have the effect of calming any fears I might have. It seemed so much like old home week for gran to be worried about Cass that I could not take it seriously.

Jack got out of the car and came around to my side and I got out and said to gran: "May I introduce my husband, Dr. Finch," and gran apparently thought I was practicing up for when he would be, or else just didn't notice. In any case the alarmist look stayed on her face.

"I thought Jack might be able to see into the high window on the other side. The blind is pulled on this one."

"That's no way for Cass to meet her brother-in-law," I said, "it would give her a whole wrong impression. And I want them to like each other."

We went inside the house, and granny didn't even notice that we didn't have any packages — no cake box. I walked across the living room and took a quick look out the window at the pool, because it wouldn't have surprised me to see Cassie still there on the chaise longue where I'd left her. But she wasn't.

"She's probably taking a bath," I said. "She's a prolonged bath taker when she feels the way she felt this morning."

But I went into the hall, anyhow, and went to our door and tapped, and then tried the knob, and then tapped firmly, and after a while took a hairpin out of my hair and unlocked the door and went in.

It was so peaceful in that room, with no sound but the little stream of air from the air-conditioner, and the light cut by the blind, and the bed so beautifully smooth with the sheet turned back and Cass's hair coppery against the blue rosebud pillowcase. I remember thinking, God forgive me, that Cassandra Edwards asleep is Cassandra Edwards at her very best — beautiful, serene, trusting, and trustworthy. But mostly beautiful, in her own way, several steps this side of maturity, very young, incredibly young, younger, I felt, than I've ever looked. Much more like Jane.

Granny came in while I was looking at her, and I gave her a sign to be quiet, and then tiptoed over to her and led her to the door and then out into the hall and told her I'd like to be alone with Cassie for a while, wake her up gently and talk something over with her. But that I'd be sure to get her up, and meanwhile why didn't she give Jack a glass of lemonade or let him make himself a gin and tonic and cool off.

I went back into the bedroom, not being too quiet this time, then I rolled one of the wardrobe doors and let it bump at the end of the track. I did a lot of rather inspired things, meant not to startle but simply to unsettle; and as they got more and more inspired, and I began more and more to wonder, I felt the first stirring of fear and went and stood close and saw what there was to see — the beads of sweat on the forehead, the lack of all motion; and finally the empty bottle on the night stand, with the cap beside it and the empty glass, everything so neat, so empty.

I'm not sure what I did. Pulled back the sheet, though, saw she was naked, and also that she was not going to wake up, and then I ran to the hall and called Jack, and I don't know how long it took him to come, long enough to kill me, but it must not have been so long as I thought, because when he came he came fast, took one look, picked up the bottle, asked me if I knew what it was, and when I didn't told me to get on the phone to the drugstore, give them the prescription number and find out what it was. Then he slapped Cass and put his mouth to her ear and told her to wake up, wake up right now, no fooling around, come on, wake up, wake up, wake up. I left and went to the telephone in granny's room, and got a busy signal at the Berkeley drugstore, and when I came back to report, he had Cass half out of bed with her head low and her hair on the floor.

I don't quite know how I did it, but I managed not to howl or do anything but listen to what I was told; and I was told quite a few things — to put in a call to the doctor — Dr. Vera Mercer, person-to-person, and find out what was in the bottle — and to get gran to put two or three pieces of bread into the broiler and burn them black and make up a pot of strong tea and see if we had any milk of magnesia.

"Which first?" I said, and he told me to use the telephone next to the dining room and instruct gran from there while I got the call through, to make up a potion — two parts burned toast crumbs, crushed, one part strong tea, one part milk of magnesia, and get moving.

I got moving, but I had to call back "toast?" because I couldn't believe I'd got it right. But I had. Burned toast, and it works like charcoal, as a filter, but I don't know whether he told me then or later. I told gran so gently that she didn't get it, either; she's a woman who doesn't approve of burning toast.

"Please, Granny dear," I had to say, "if you love me burn some toast black, burn it to cinders, three pieces, and make some very very strong tea."

Gran rolled her eyes up, the way she does, "Who wants burned toast and strong tea?" she said, and I told her Cassie did.

"Oh, is she awake?" gran said, and I said no, not yet, but please please please burn some toast while I use the telephone. And I took the telephone into the dining room where gran wouldn't hear, and put in a call, person-to-person to Dr. Vera Mercer in Berkeley without knowing either the telephone number or the address. It took time, but there was a Dr. Mercer listed at two numbers — one office and one residence. I asked for the office and got it, finally, and did some fast talking to an interlocutor and then heard the doctor herself — cool, cagey, polite, and told her that a patient of hers, Cassandra Edwards, had taken a bottle of what I imagined to be sleeping pills, prescription number 736-719, issued by Dr. Mercer, and that the pharmacy gave me a busy line, and I wanted very much to know what the prescription was.

"Who is this, please?" the doctor said, and I said: "It's her sister, damn it, what was in the bottle?"

There was a moment when I couldn't, of course, know what the doctor was thinking, but when I heard her again, it was in a very different voice, and a very different manner.

"Judith," the voice said, "listen to me closely. It's most likely Nembutal — though she also has had prescriptions for Equanil and Dexedrine. Tell me this — is she conscious?"

"No," I said.

"Is there a pulse at all?"

"I don't know."

"Get a doctor as fast as you can," she said.

"We've got one," I said.

"What's he done?"

"Told me to call you and find out what was in the bottle."

"Tell him to try Universal Antidote first — two parts burned toast, one part strong tea, one part milk of —"

"We're making it," I said.

"Good," she said. "First try to get her conscious. Did the doctor bring a respirator?"

"No."

"What's wrong with him?"

"Nothing's wrong with him, he's doing what he can."

"I'd suggest a gastric lavage as soon as the patient can be brought to consciousness, or even before." And then she said, "Oh God," in a voice of real anguish, not cool at all, "why did she do it?"

"I don't know," I said, "but I think she had some reasons."

"May I speak to the doctor?"

"No, you may not," I said. "He's very busy; all he wants to know is what the prescription was for. She emptied the bottle."

"Tell the doctor to assume it was Nembutal — that's safe either way."

"Safe?" I said, a little loud.

"I mean to say it's safe to treat for. Tell me something —"

There was a long pause, and then she said: "Do you feel — how shall I put it — do you think she has a chance? Why didn't that fool bring a respirator? Don't let her die." There was an increase in pitch in everything she said, and I had problems of my own without having to deal with a hysterical woman. I had my information, and I hung up without saying goodbye, told granny to crush the toast fine as soon as it was burned and ran down to our bedroom to tell Jack what was probably in the bottle.

But I was so unprepared for what I saw in the bedroom that I could only stand in the doorway with my mouth open — and look. Jack was holding Cass, still naked of course, bent over backward in a deep dip, and he was leaning in over her like a vampire or a demon lover, possessed and possessing, his mouth to hers. Not oblivious, however. He knew when I came in, because he looked up with his eyes, in an imploring way, as if asking me to help him, to free him, get him out of the tangle. And I couldn't. I felt my hair stand on end and the scene became a nightmare I couldn't wake up from and couldn't do anything about — my husband gone mad, my sister unconscious — but very much together, the one and the other. I got the door closed, and I leaned back against it, still unable to look away, and it was then I noticed that Jack was not only imploring me with his eyes, he was signaling to me with short movements of his head to come closer; and when I came and stood beside him I saw that he was pinching Cass's nose on top of everything else he was doing. It was only then that my hair lay down and strength came back to my knees and I could see the words spelled out in our Primer of Life Saving: *As a last resort, try Mouth-to-Mouth Resuscitation.* It was the one part of the course we'd skipped any demonstrations of when we got our Senior certificates and here it was turning up in our bedroom ten years later. For real.

"Is it working?" I said, and Jack stopped blowing and unclamped the nose and listened for the return air but apparently couldn't hear it or feel it, because he went back to the blowing and clamping. And I left the nightmare and came back to reality, — which wasn't much better, but different.

"The doctor thinks it was Nembutal," I said. "And gran's burning some toast, but I haven't told her what happened. She's making the tea too. Shall I go and mix it?"

Jack stopped blowing and put his ear to Cass's nose again and shook his head, and told me to turn off the air-conditioner and get a blanket and see if we could get her warm. I tore the spread off my bed and got a blanket, too light, and then found a woolen one in a storage chest, and we got it around her and Jack kept up the blowing and listening and clamping and blowing, and told me, in one of the listening breaks, to call the Red Cross or a hospital and get them to bring a respirator and a tank of oxygen, and a pump and some tubes.

"Respirator, oxygen, pump, tubes," I said and went back to the telephone and got the hospital, told them how to get to the ranch and what to bring. The girl at the switchboard didn't know what I meant by pump and tubes, and neither did I, but she got me connected with someone who did, and I gave him a life-and-death speech and hung up the phone and faced granny, who had gathered finally, that all was not well in our house.

It's always difficult to tell about granny, how much she understands of what really goes on and how much protective gloss she can put between herself and what she knows. When I told her Cass had taken some pills from a wrong bottle I could see her wilt, but a moment later she had herself in hand and was taking the blame for leaving pills around where anybody might pick them up.

"I'd better go and explain to her which ones are mine," she said, and I had to stop her, tell her she couldn't see Cass, that Jack was taking care of her, and that all we could do was what he told us until the man came from the hospital.

"When the man comes, you can tell him how the accident happened, can't you? Judy?"

I started to say what accident, and then I said certainly I'd tell him, don't worry.

I opened the oven door, snatched a piece of burning toast from the broiler, blew it out, passed it from one hand to the other across the kitchen and dropped it into the blender and whirled it into crumbs.

"Cassie wants to give you and Jack a blender for a wedding present," gran said.

"She does?" I said. I went and got another piece of toast from the broiler, gave it the same business, and kept the conversation going, not to let her think too much. "Did she say so?"

Gran's voice was the voice of a woman crying. But her

face was composed. "Yes," she said, "at breakfast this morning. She said she thought you'd love one. And now we're putting burned toast in it. Judy, what's the matter with this family? Why did she?"

I wanted to stop and explain it to granny, tell her it was my fault for not knowing what I should have known — that people like us can't really be people and live happy lives. There's a cloud over us and we're caught in it together, then, now, and always. Unless, God forbid, death part us.

I shivered and then gasped. I'd forgotten what happened in Bakersfield. I turned my back, slipped off the variety store ring and put in into my pocket a moment before papa came up to the bar.

"Where did you put the champagne?" he said. "Is it still in the car?"

"Papa," I said, "Cassie's quite sick. Do you know whether we have any milk of magnesia anywhere?"

"I've got some Bromo-Seltzer," papa said. "It's better."

I thought for a minute I might go mad right there in the kitchen.

"Damn it, Papa," I said, "just listen to me and find some milk of magnesia."

I think I frightened him. He sat down on a bar stool and looked puzzled, and granny said she thought there might be a bottle in her medicine chest. There used to be.

"Hurry then," I said, and she went. I strained a half cup of tea into a measuring cup, dark red, very strong, and papa laid some filing cards on the bar and said he'd spent the afternoon pulling together some notes from Sextus Empiricus. He thought they might be surprisingly to the point in Cassandra's dissertation and he hoped she'd get over her stomach-ache and let him discuss it with her.

"Papa, you'll have to know. It's not a stomach-ache. Cassie took a bottle of sleeping pills. We're waiting for a man from the hospital, and I hope to God he isn't lost."

Papa looked at me, and after a moment he pushed the edges of the cards together and put them into his pocket. I went to him and took his hand and when I saw granny at the steps of the lower living room holding a blue bottle I ran and got it and brought it back to the kitchen.

"I'm afraid it's all dried up," gran said. And she was right. I ran some water into the bottle, held my thumb in the opening and shook it hard, and hard, and harder until I had a solution I could pour out and measure: one part milk of magnesia, one part strong tea, two parts charred toast crumbs. I was breathing fast, huffing, actually, and puffing, rhythmically and insistently; breathing, I realized, for two. I had just started to go down with my beaker of universal antidote when I heard the dog bark.

"It's the man," I called back to granny and papa, "it's the God-blessed man alive," and I ran to the door and brought him in — him and all his marvelous equipment.

I don't remember noticing when it got dark. It was a very busy afternoon. I spent it doing what Jack told me to do — things like adjust the mask, turn the valve, read the indicator, bring a pan, take away the pan, find some mustard, now the tube; then later, the strong coffee, no, not orally, from behind, now massage the extremities, the feet, my dearest, what's more extreme than feet? and let the family have a bulletin now and then, tell them the blood pressure is beginning to stabilize, because women the age and temperament of Mrs. Abbott have to be told something, they don't wait easily. Tell her to drink a pot of tea between bulletins or have herself a small glass of port wine, if there is any.

I stood still a minute and looked at him, on his knees by Cass's bed, sweat running down his face and drops hanging on his earlobes and the point of his chin. He looked like a holy man, and a true saviour. I got down on my knees beside him.

"You're a lovely boy," I said.

"Oh, so are you," he said, and there didn't seem to be anything wrong with it. He was holding Cass's wrist, feeling for the pulse and nodding sometimes. "We're very good together," he said, "I'm glad we're married."

I'd forgotten it again and it pierced me to know he'd kept it in mind through the ordeal of the afternoon.

"Oh, so am I," I said, and I was. More than that, I suddenly *felt* married. I picked a Kleenex up off the floor and wiped off the drops on Jack's earlobes and chin and dried off the back of his neck, and then stood up and looked down at Cass and knew I loved her, but that it was not the same thing as being married and feeling married, and that now it never could or would be. I felt very solemn about it, and some solemn words came into my mind. "Whom God hath split asunder, let nothing join together. Ever."

"What do I tell them?" I said to Jack. "The pressure is stabilized?"

"Stabilizing."

"Stabilizing," I said, "and tea and port, if there is any."

"Tea *or* port for Mrs. Abbott. I won't prescribe for your father, because I imagine he's taken care of it."

"Not so much as you might imagine," I said. "He's been reading to granny out of *Harper's Bazaar*, something or other about traveling, and she's been listening. Sort of."

I stopped at the door.

"Don't you think I might turn the air-conditioner back on now," I said, "and let you cool off a little?"

"Not yet," he said. "Heat's still the thing." He poked the blanket in behind Cass's neck with his free hand while he was saying it, and then looked up at me, so searchingly and curiously that it kept me from leaving. While I stood there he took his hand away from Cass's wrist, pushed her hand under the cover, looked down at her for a moment, then back at me and said: "You know, it's funny, but in a way it's true." He stopped there, looked back at Cass, and went on in a deeply perplexed voice: "It's a fact that I — uh — know my patient, here, quite a lot better than I know you. It's confusing. Maybe the heat."

I felt tears behind my eyes, a whole curtain of tears ready to roll, and I left the door and went back and knelt beside him again, and touched him gently.

"Poor guy," I said, "poor darling doctor. Don't think about it. Everything will fall into place and be all right. I'll be me, after this is all over; and you'll know it, because I know it."

He turned and looked at me, not quite so perplexed, and touched my face, and then went back to work, thumping Cass lightly on the cheek with his middle finger. I thought I saw her eyelids twitch when he did it, but he said no, when I asked him. No, they hadn't, not yet. He squeezed the bulb again, though, and read the pressure, and it had got up to 118 over 79 — safe, or close to it.

This time I got all the way out the door, and down the hall and into the living room with the report, and also with the doctor's recommendation of tea, or port wine, for Mrs. Abbott.

"I think we have some white port," granny said. "Cassie had some for breakfast, with her eggs."

"She *what?*" papa said. He closed *Harper's Bazaar,*

dropped it on the floor quite deliberately and said he thought the time had come for him to take a hand in the dietary habits of his daughters. And besides that we don't have any white port. Or red either, for that matter.

"Well don't worry about it, Jim," granny said. "I'd really prefer tea so don't go to town for anything, just for me."

"That's not the point," papa said, and I don't believe I've ever heard him bother to say anything so obvious to his mother-in-law. I went to the kitchen to start some hot water for tea, and papa followed me and sat down on a bar stool, where he could talk to me in the kitchen and granny in the living room, but mostly me.

"The point is," he said, "that you girls seem to have forgotten the *mens sana in corpore sano* ideal I tried to bring you up on. I don't think you live right."

I put three teaspoons of tea into a strainer, and considered saying that the big question had been whether one of us was going to live at all, right or not right, but I didn't, mostly because I didn't want granny to hear it. Or papa either, really. Or believe it for a moment, myself. We were over the hump and we'd stay there. The man had gone back to the hospital; we had a reserve tank of oxygen, in case we needed it, but we were over the hump, and you might almost say on the edge of being out of the woods.

"She'll be all right, Papa. She'll come out of this and be all right. Then we can talk about diet."

"She's much too thin," granny said, from the living room.

I was thinking about Jack and whether I could take him anything, some iced tea or a highball or a sandwich, and I decided against it. First things first, everything in its time; who wants to drink while doing great works? Not, in all likelihood, Dr. John Thomas Finch, not while saving the first life he ever saved. No, not he.

Papa was down on his haunches in front of the liquor cabinet now, taking inventory.

"I knew I didn't have any port," he said, "white or otherwise. What's this?"

He came up with a brandy bottle with no cork, held it up to the light and then took it across the kitchen, dropped it into a wastebasket, went back to the cabinet, brought up a new bottle, got out some soda and ice cubes and made himself a drink.

"Would you like something, Judith?" he said, and I thanked him kindly and said no, and that I was terribly sorry about the champagne, but that we'd simply forgotten to get it in the heat of — well, in the heat.

"Just as well," papa said, "in the circumstances. I daresay you'll want to postpone the wedding until your sister is feeling — well, more like it."

There were so many answers I could have made that I just got busy around the kitchen and didn't make any. But I did find a moment to slip my hand into my pocket and touch the evidence and feel secure, more or less out of danger myself; and very very grateful.

"Do you know why — why — ?"

Papa stopped there and I helped him. "Why Cassie did it, or tried to?" I said, and papa looked at me and said, "Was it because of you?"

I don't know why I always expect papa to be in some other age, unaware of present time, but I always do, and he mostly always is, so that when he says something that relates to living people doing the things they do it surprises me.

"My getting married, do you mean?" I said, and papa said yes, my going off to New York in the first place and now this.

I said I supposed that was the most natural thing to think of as the cause — not just that Cass and I had always been so close but that all of us had; as a family we'd been something of a closed corporation; nobody could buy in because we didn't need anybody. We would come home at night from a high school that never heard of Bartók and play the quartets on our own phonograph; when somebody wanted to run Cass for president of the girls' league, Jane read her Yeats's "Leaders of the Crowd" and she went back to school the next day and refused the nomination. Over and over it went that way — we had our own pinnacle to look down from. But when we went to college we couldn't quite keep it the way it was on the ranch. We tried, but it wasn't the same. We couldn't oppose the whole world, the way Cass thought we could and should, and finally I declared for getting out and into the stream, any stream would have done, but I knew music best and it seemed a good enough way of life until something came up I might like better.

I bumbled through it. I didn't know what to tell and what to leave out but papa was listening very thoughtfully, and not interrupting. There was more to say, the real thing was yet to say, and I wanted to stop, to go away now and see how it was going in the bedroom. I'd been away fifteen minutes, maybe more; and in that time Cass might have got her eyes open. But I stayed where I was and told papa why I thought she'd tried it — because she couldn't bring herself to try anything else. She couldn't believe she belonged anywhere but on a psychiatrist's couch, or with companions, call them that, girl-buddies, who were so inferior to her that they didn't count as human beings at all, just occupational therapy of no therapeutic value.

"She wastes herself, she drifts; all she wants to do with her life is lose it somewhere."

Granny's tea was ready, and I'd made a piece of unburned toast to go with it, but I didn't take the tray down to her yet. I sat down for a moment with papa and told him the saddest thing I know, because I had to say it. It had been heavy in my heart ever since we'd come back and found Cass and the empty pill bottle.

"There is only one thing that would help Cassie," I said, "really save her — and that would be for me to go to pieces in the same way she has."

Papa didn't say anything, and I wasn't sure he knew what I meant. But *I* did. If right now there were nothing for me but blankness and despair, meaningless loves, pleasureless drinking, no faith in anything except the decayed memory of us as a family, living in a fortress, being self-sufficient and superior — if it were that way for me, Cass would take over and get me out of it, bring me back, convince me, get me to the shore, turn me into a great musician, a whole-souled human being, a tee-total, anti-barbiturate, true believer. She would. She'd do it for me.

But I didn't need it, and I couldn't quite decide whether to rejoice for my sake, or regret it for hers. All I knew was I didn't need saving. Not any longer. I belonged somewhere, and Cass didn't. And probably never would.

"Do you remember, Papa?" I said, "when you read to us out of *The Anatomy of Melancholy* — 'Be not idle, be not solitary'?"

"It's the other way around, I believe," papa said. " 'Be not solitary, be not idle.' What about it?"

"Nothing, except I remembered it. It's why I left Berkeley and went to New York. I was stuck."

"I don't know why I should have chosen to read that to you," papa said, "I've always believed in solitude."

He looked down, saw his glass, recognized it, and took a drink.

"And in idleness too," he said. "I think the precept at the end of the book is more to the point. How does it go? Sperate Miseri, Cavete Felices. It's more for people like me."

"What's it mean?"

"You should know," he said, "it couldn't be simpler, it means: Hope, ye unhappy ones, Ye happy ones, fear."

"Touchée," I said, but only to myself, and I didn't feel it as any blow to my faith, but only as a hope for Cass, whom I now wanted very much to see.

"I want to take this tray down to granny," I said, "and then go and see Cassie and Jack."

I picked up the tray and took it down to the living room and found granny asleep upright in her chair, looking proper and composed but nevertheless asleep. I set the tray down, very quietly, and looked at my watch. A quarter to ten, and it was only then that I realized the lights were on and it was dark outside and that it had been a day for Mrs. Rowena Abbott, a day of blows and buffetings. I stood looking down at her wishing I could put her to bed without waking her up and while I looked she opened her eyes and said she was sorry, she must have dropped off for a minute.

"I think you'd do well to drop off for the night," I said. "Come on, I'll put the tray in your room."

"Oh Judy, you shouldn't have done that for me," she said, but she stood up and followed me, and called out to papa not to worry, to get a good rest, because our girl is going to be all right.

Papa didn't answer. It annoys him to have granny call us, either one of us, our girl, though it annoyed him worst of all when it was Jane she meant.

I felt some comment was due, so I called up to papa myself.

"Granny's going to go to bed now, Papa."

Papa's voice came back right away, "She is? Goodnight, Rowe, sleep well."

"I will," gran said, but in her room it was different. I had to talk her out of going to see Cassie; I had to assure her ten times that Jack knew she would regain consciousness, that he was no longer giving her oxygen, and that he wanted to keep her quiet and warm and stay with her.

"All night?" granny said and when I said yes, she bit her lip a little, thought a moment, and then said: "Judy, do you think that's the right thing?"

"Granny, he's a doctor, remember?"

"Oh I realize that," gran said, "but if Cassie's as well as you say I should think I might sleep in the other bed," and then added quickly, "and you sleep in mine. Wouldn't that be preferable all round?"

"No, Granny, it would not be preferable all around. We could get a nurse for tonight, but I'd rather have a doctor. Wouldn't you?"

Granny looked up at me quickly, very quickly, and said she certainly didn't want any nurses from Putnam coming out and poking around. It was bad enough having the man from the hospital knowing the whole thing and probably being quite talkative.

"What does it matter?" I said. "Anyhow I told him it was an accident, just the way you told me to."

"Thank you, dear. You've always been so kind to your granny."

I opened her wardrobe to get out her slippers and her nightgown and found all the floor space jammed with white boxes tied with white satin bows. I pretended not to see them, but granny gave a little gasp and said she guessed the cat was out of the bag — she'd planned a little bridal shower for tonight, just a few friends of hers, the girls she plays cards with — Sarah and Hannah and Kate — and that of course she'd had to call them and tell them not to come, with Cassie so sick, but that Kate's present had been here for two days, and the big square one was from Sarah, and Hannah was planning on bringing hers tonight, that is, before she told her not to come, and that it had seemed to her, even though she knew I was not much of a girl for parties and especially showers, that when other girls go into marriage with everything they'll ever need, there'd be no harm in just giving a very small party for a few very intimate friends.

"I don't have any," I said.

"I know," granny said, "but I do, and what's mine is yours."

I stood looking at the closet floor and shook my head. So many packages, and two of them from granny's friends, with one more to come.

"Are all the rest from you, Granny?" I said. I felt somewhat weepy, they looked so demure hiding in the closet.

"Well, yes," she said, and then added, "from me and Cassie; we more or less planned the shower together."

"You and Cassie?" I said. I couldn't believe it, and of course I shouldn't have.

"Well not in so many words," granny said. "You know how Cassie is; she won't come right out and say she thinks something is a good idea. But she thinks a lot, and I could tell she wanted to give you a shower."

Gran paused and looked off to the side, and said, "She'd also like you to have a church wedding, and invite friends."

"What friends?"

"Well, the teacher who took such an interest in you in high school — Miss, Miss —"

"You don't mean Mr. Rudholm?"

"Yes, that's the one."

"You can't ask Mr. Rudholm. He got killed in an auto accident."

"He did? When?"

"I don't know, two, three years ago."

"He wrote a letter to Jane about you; and he wrote to her about one of her books too."

"I know; he was nice. But he's not available."

Granny shook her head and took a sip of her tea. She was sitting in a little gray-and-gold brocade chair, a *bergère* I think, an elegant chair supporting an elegant old lady.

"Judy dear," she said, "I've been thinking all afternoon, ever since Cassie got so sick, how grateful I am that Jane died a natural death." She paused a moment and then said, "I mean nothing violent."

I started to say that lung cancer is not my idea of ultimate tranquillity, but I let her have it her way. I sat down, though, and listened, because I couldn't walk out on my grandmother while she was talking about my mother.

"I worried so about Jane," she said; "she was so headlong about everything. So dear and thoughtful and kind and funny; but so headlong. I didn't like her smoking so much, or driving an open car in the rain, and things like that, but I couldn't do a thing with her; and her friends were so — well so much like her. Remember that little actress that came to the ranch to see her?"

"Carol Leighton," I said. "I saw her in a movie last year."

Granny nodded.

"I think I worried as much about Jane," granny said, "after she was married as I did before. She never took care of herself, and when she had to be away from home, no one took care of her."

"But didn't we have fun when she was home," I said, and I stopped a moment to think about it, how there was a charge in the air when she was there and how slack it went when she left. I remembered the wonderful fights she and papa used to have once in a while, and how granny was always steering us off someplace, when all we wanted to do was listen to the bright blue exchanges that always ended with Jane roaring out of the driveway in cars and got roarier and roarier through the years. She was head-long all right, and we admired her. We admired papa too, but he never roared out of driveways.

"You know, Judy," granny said, "we could ask Carol Leighton to the wedding. She wrote to me when Jane passed away."

I almost said, "Don't say passed away," and I almost said there wasn't going to be a wedding because there'd already been one, but I couldn't do it, not to granny at this time of the night after such a day. Not with the shower all blown up, and all her plans slipped sidewise.

"Let's not bother with any movie stars," I said, "but I'll tell you what, Granny, before you go to bed, let's open a present. Just us. And just one."

It was a good idea. I could tell by granny's face. And voice. "Would you like to, sweetheart?"

"Love to."

"Then you shall," she said; "we'll just have a little shower all our own."

"Just one," I said; "just one present before you go to bed."

Granny got up and went to the closet and looked over her treasures.

"You pick it," I said, and she brought out the big square one.

"I'm terribly curious about this one from Sarah. It's heavy as lead and it comes from Bullock's Wilshire, so it must be nice."

It *was* nice too — a chafing dish, copper lined, with the *bain marie* and the spirit lamp, a full-blown, two-quart beauty among chafing dishes with a card wishing Judy and Jack all the happiness in the world in their new life.

I put it together on granny's dresser and looked at it and whistled, it was so beautiful. I'm not sure how I would have responded at an actual shower, but here alone with gran I said what I meant, all honestly:

"Oh, Granny; just what we've always wanted. I can't tell you how many times Cass and I have stopped in places like Fraser's and looked at chafing dishes. I don't know why we never happened to buy one, because Cassie has this big thing about crêpes suzettes."

"Cassie?" I heard granny say. "But sweetheart, this isn't for Cassie. It's for you. And Jack."

I walked backwards, away from the dresser, until I came to granny's bed. And then I sat down and spent a minute wondering what effect my speech would have had at an actual shower, the big kind, where fifty people listen to what you say. I felt like never opening my mouth again. But I did. I had to settle granny.

"It's very handsome," I said. "Jack will love it."

"Imagine Sarah," gran said, "I hope you can find time to write her a thank-you note; I mean not just tell her."

"Don't you worry," I said, "I'll write her ten pages. Single spaced."

Gran was taking off her stockings, but she looked up to say, "Wouldn't it be nicer if you wrote it by hand? I have some very nice notepaper."

"Even better," I said. I went back to the dresser, picked up the card, took the lid off the chafing dish, dropped the card inside and put the lid back on. The lid had a good weight to it, and it fell into place with the honest ring of a cymbal — such a good sound that I picked the lid up and did it again.

"Be careful with it, Judy," gran said, "Cassie's asleep."

And maybe not, I thought. Maybe awake. Just possibly, by now, awake.

I came away from the chafing dish, leaned down, kissed gran, told her to sleep well, and thanked her for the lovely party, picked up the papers and the ribbon and left.

I had put the papers into the fireplace and told papa I was going to look in on Cassie when we heard the dog bark. It wasn't aimless barking. Somebody was here. Probably some of gran's friends, I thought, mixed up about the shower, but before I got to the door I realized it was much too late for anyone to be coming to a shower. It was after ten, and the dog meant business.

I turned the entrance lights on and opened the door on an odd spectacle — a taxi, a conventional orange taxi, in our driveway. I went outside and stood between the lights, letting the moths bat me, as *bouche-bée* as a hick in front of a tent show; because though there are some taxis in Putnam, I've never seen one so far out in the country, certainly not in our driveway and I was unable to rise to the occasion.

It was the dog, our bristling Labrador, who finally brought me the power of speech.

"Knock it off, Rosie," I said, "until I see who it is."

The taxi driver didn't cut off the motor, nor did he get out. I suppose it was because of the dog, but he sat where he was, doing nothing, and let his passenger, a young woman, get out alone. I got a hand around Rosie's collar, and then both hands, and the woman stood by the taxi, looking at me, and said in a very clear voice: "Don't tell me." And then a second later, "Oh, you must be her sister."

"Take it easy, Rose," I said. "Yes, I am."

"I'm Vera Mercer, Cassandra's doctor."

I honestly couldn't think of anything at all to say to that, it was so improbable. And yet here she was, to all intents and purposes exactly who she said she was. And what. It was the same voice I'd heard over the telephone.

"How is she?" Vera Mercer said, and I said, a little stiffly, "Quite well, thank you."

It may have been because the taxi was still running that I thought it was a short call and that there was no reason to invite her inside, just fill her in on the medical aspects of the case, so far as I knew them, and send her off again. But she filled me in first — how she'd immediately canceled all appointments until Monday, got a private plane to fly her to the Putnam airport and called a taxi from there. Because she had to see Cass.

"Is is all right for me to let the taxi go?" she said, and I gave the only decent answer: of course, let him be on his way, some one of us could return her to the airport.

She smiled, just barely, and said the plane had gone

back, so it wouldn't be a question of getting her back to the airport, but that we could work something out, surely.

Surely, I said, with not much intonation; and she went immediately around to the other side of the cab and paid off the driver with one bill and thanked him, and then took a rather handsome piece of luggage — black canvas bound in tan leather, not particularly large but not exactly overnight either — out of the back seat, slammed the door, and nodded to the driver to be on his way.

I still didn't ask her to come in, and she set her bag down in the driveway and put out a hand and scratched Rosie on the head. She had gloves on but even so it was courageous of her, and I liked her better.

"Cassandra's all right?" she said. "Would you mind telling me everything you know about it? I don't mean why she did it — but what's been done since you called me."

"Everything, I think."

"Gastric lavage? Antidotes?"

"Other things too," I said. "Artificial respiration, emetics, and colonics, two tanks of oxygen and a respirator."

"Oh my God," she said, "it was that close?"

"It was," I said, "that close," and while I said it a big moth flew at me and I flew back at it all unnerved, and felt tears start and knew it was nip and tuck whether I'd get control or lose it beyond where I could ever get it again.

"I'm sorry," she said, "but I had to know. In a way I'm responsible. She's my patient and I should have known better than to let her come down here."

She put out a hand and batted a moth without looking at it, like an athlete with good reactions. The moths didn't bother her, the heat didn't bother her, she wasn't afraid of the dog.

"Did the doctor leave any further instructions?" she said. "Is she with a nurse?"

"No, the doctor's still with her. Don't worry, he won't leave. It's my husband."

She blinked at that, and I got it corrected, or uncorrected. "The man I'm going to marry," I said. "He's been with her ever since he got here, and there's also been a man from the hospital. And me."

I had the nip-and-tuck feeling again, and she knew it, and gave me a little bang on the shoulder.

"Let's go in," I said. "My grandmother's gone to bed, but my father's here."

"I'd like to see Cass, if you can persuade the doctor in charge that I'm a doctor, as well as a friend."

I picked up her bag, opened the door, and let her go into our house, but when she was in I wasn't quite sure what to do with her. Take her up and introduce her to papa, take her into our bedroom and spring her on Jack, put her to bed with granny, or tell her to go jump in the pool? I stopped in the middle of the living room, and she stopped behind me, and we stood a moment, quiet. Then I set her bag down, and made up my mind.

"Come and meet my father," I said, "and I'll go and ask Jack whether it's all right for you to see Cass."

Papa was sitting where I'd left him, with the brandy bottle, the soda siphon and the ice bucket in front of him. One glass.

"How is she?" he said, without taking any noticeable notice of the woman with me.

"I'm going to go and see," I said. "Papa, this is Dr. Mercer from Berkeley; she's Cassie's doctor. Dr. Mercer, our father, Dr. Edwards."

I don't know why I had to drag in papa's Ph.D. unless it was for purposes of confusion, of which we already had enough. But papa didn't seem to resent the title for once. He got off the stool, shook hands with Dr. Mercer, and was making her a drink when I left. I was free at long long last to go back to the bedroom, and I went fast. But I stopped in front of the door, took a deep breath, and tapped with my fingernail before I went in.

I couldn't see anything at first. There was a light in the bathroom and the bathroom door was open, but the bedroom itself wasn't lighted. It was a little like going into a movie in progress, the screen's bright but you have to wait before you can tell laps from seats. I heard Jack before I saw him.

"Where've you been?" he said.

"Some of the girls gave me a shower," I said. "How is she?"

"She talked," Jack said, "she asked for you."

"Oh God," I said. "Oh dear God, why couldn't I have been here?"

I could see him now. He wasn't on his knees any longer. He had a chair pulled up beside the bed. I could see Cass too, with her hair fanned out over the pillow and the blanket clear up to her chin. I crossed the room quickly and stood by Jack's chair.

"It didn't matter too much," he said in a low bedside voice, "whether you were here or not. I stood in for you, and she didn't know the difference."

"What?" I said in a voice a few tones up from bedside pitch. "What did she say?"

"Very groggy," Jack said, in the low voice. "Pretty incoherent. Contrite, mostly. She's nice. I liked her."

"Did she like you?"

"Oh God yes. Very determined. She's strong, especially considering what she's been through."

He looked down at her and then up at me. "I had to be a little strong myself," he said, and I nodded, because I knew what he meant. There's always been a little something of the tiger in Cassandra.

"What's her blood pressure?" I said, because tiger or not, I wanted it up.

"It's all right," he said. "One twenty over something like 85." And it was only then, speaking of pressure, that I remembered Vera Mercer.

"Her doctor's here," I said, close to Jack's ear. "I mean her analyst, the one who prescribed the pills, the one I called when I couldn't get the drugstore."

"What's he doing here?"

"She," I said. "Vera Mercer. I guess she cleared the couch and got hold of a private plane and took a taxi on out here."

Cass moaned, it was the first sound I'd heard her make, and I dropped down on my knees fast. "Don't worry, girl," I said. "It's me, and you're all right."

There was no answer from her except for a humming sound — mmmmmm — that went on continuously for quite a while and then broke.

"Where?" she said, after the break, and then stopped, closed her eyes, and kept them closed. I looked up at Jack and he told me to talk to her, try to make her talk back, work on it.

"Here," I said. "Where else? Right here at home in our house."

I was sorry I'd said it that way. I didn't want to give her anything I'd have to take away, and I knew we wouldn't be in this house forever. As soon as she was well, we'd leave. And she'd leave. I was supposed to be talking to her and making her talk back; I was supposed to work on it, but what was there to say? When you're well I'll leave you? Would she ever be well if I did?

"Go ahead," Jack said, softly. "Talk to her. Say things."

It wasn't easy. All I could say at first was her name, and tell her not to worry at all, just take things the way they come. But I kept it up. Cass, you'll be somebody; you're the brightest; there's nothing you can't do, so don't let *me* stop you. We're two separate people. Separate and different. I'm me; you're you; and there's no curse on us. We've got our lives to live . . .

I felt Jack's hand on the back of my head, and I stopped, because I didn't know why he'd touched me — to firm me up, or slow me down, or call me off — so I looked at him and then I knew it didn't have much to do with anything I was saying, but just with me and the back of my head. I turned away and looked at Cass again — so tired, like a little girl asleep after a long hard day picking wildflowers — and I got to my feet and stood close to Jack and asked him whether I should tell her, when she woke up again, about us and what we'd been pronounced this afternoon. We were very close together, not touching, just seeing and knowing and immersed in it I have no idea how long, and finally Jack said no, it probably would be safer not to for a while, wait until she's stronger; let the analyst tell her, as long as she's here; she'd know her patterns better, what to expect, how soon to risk it. Those people are trained in these things. They can chart reactions.

I thought of the other doctor. She probably had her gloves off now, and knew a lot about papa; and I didn't want her to see Cass, alive down here under the veils, safe now, breathing under her own power. Jack had breathed the breath of life into her, and I'd fanned the spark, and I couldn't help thinking it, or saying it — that after such miracles she belonged to us, not to some analyst just out of a taxi.

"You're mixed up," Jack said, "you're tired. Go turn on the cooler. Lowest volume."

I like commands you can carry out. I went around the foot of the bed, turned on the reading lamp over my bed and got the air-conditioner on and stood in front of it and pulled myself together and had some second thoughts. Very profound ones, and the most profound was that I was the one who needed the analyst if, after all I knew, I could fall so quickly back into the habit of thinking I had to protect Cassandra Edwards from strangers — strange analysts, strange linguists, and all aliens waiting to get her alienated.

"You're right," I said, "I'm good and mixed-up," and I left my station and went back to the bed and stood behind Jack and asked him to let me take the watch, leave us, I'll talk to her, you take a break, have a drink, go meet the analyst, she's up there with papa, walk around, stretch your legs, but come back some time.

I went to the bedroom door with him, saw him out, then closed it and came back to the bed and got down on my knees. This time I was going to do it, get the communications established, bring her all the way back. I reached inside the covers, found her hand, and was trying for a way to begin when she opened her eyes and looked at me pretty much the way she's always looked at me, straight in the eye, but from behind built-in baffles, the way cats look at you. And I suppose I looked back at her the same way, only wider-eyed.

She said my name. She knew who I was, and I couldn't

even tell her she was right. All I could do was stay in range and hang on to her hand.

"You find my note?" she said. It took her a while to say it, but the single words were clear.

"No," I said, "where is it?"

She closed her eyes and I thought she was going out again but after a while, with her eyes still closed, she said: "Maybe I didn't write it. Just my finger. No ink. But I — but I tried."

I swallowed, and said, "You don't have to write notes; you can talk."

"Don't patronize me," she said, in a good spurt, and then, much slower, "What happened?"

"You went to sleep, that's all; and then you woke up."

Her eyelids fluttered, and she got her eyes open, but her voice was almost nothing:

"I woke up — under — under something . . ."

"Under what, Cassie?"

"Wait a minute," she said. Her eyes closed again, and with them closed she said it: "Duress."

"No," I said. "No, Cassie, no, no, no. You've got a life to live. It's a duty. If you're born you've got to live. But the thing to know is — it can also be quite nice, quite good."

I meant it. I didn't think she'd answer, but after a while she did, very slowly.

"You memorized that; you've been coaxed," she said, and then fixed it: "— coached."

"No," I said. "I learned it myself."

"*I* didn't."

"You will. It takes time."

She didn't answer. I turned her hand over, took her wrist with my other hand and felt for her pulse, and found it. Slow, but strong.

"Listen," she said, and quit, and tried again: "Tell me
— where —"

"Here," I said. "Here at home."

"I know where I am," she said, "what I want to know
— is where'd you get so medical? It's nice. Thank you."

It was a big effort, costly, and the last one for a while.
She went slack and slept the deep sleep of the passed-out.
I dropped her hand, got up off my knees and pulled up a
chair and sat down and watched her sleep. The hand hung
limp over the edge of the bed and I took hold of it again
and sat there holding it and thinking, and then not thinking, hoping and then not sure, but finally knowing that all
my life, no matter where I was, I'd be wondering where
she was and what she was doing. And worrying about her.
Just like granny, in the old days, with Jane. And us with
Tacky.

But not like me with John Thomas Finch, nor him with
me.

It was better, now, in the bedroom. It was still cluttered
with supplies, but the light was soft, the air-conditioner
was making a little whishing noise, and outside, a million
crickets and frogs were presenting themselves in chorus.
What would our life be like, when we had one? I had a
moment, for the first time today, to think it over. We'd
live it, I knew, according to our vows — we'd love, honor,
and cherish; I'd keep me unto him, and he unto me, too,
within the limitations of his prior vow, the Hippocratic
oath, of course, which is to say I'd be alone a great deal.
But never quite alone, because I would understand the
reasons for separation, and I could make an art of waiting.
Even of waiting to start, I thought. I shifted Cass's hand to
my other hand, and lifted my free arm high, and stretched,
and yawned, and looked up at the clown in the circus

poster on our wall, and laughed, not at the clown, really, but because I remembered granny's shower, and remembered too that she'd forgotten to tell me whether she ever got the minister or not. Though I'd admitted to forgetting the cake. And the champagne too, even after papa had made me out a list of good years. I shifted hands again, and stretched the other one, and saw the clown and laughed again, and again it wasn't because of the clown (the clown's a real nothing) but because it came to me all in a rush that we were having quite a wanton wedding night — the bridegroom in conference with a heady psychiatrist at a bar up there somewhere, and the bride down here in the bedroom holding hands with her sister. Her own sister, that is to say, the one who almost died but, thank God, didn't.

"Wake up, Cassie," I said, but quietly, "wake up and talk to me. I'm lonesome."

"Me too," Cass said, and it scared me as much as if a doll had spoken.

"Have you been awake?" I said. "Did you hear me laugh?"

"What at?"

I thought a minute and said, the clown, the funny, funny clown, and Cass got her eyes open and said, "We're too — old for that clown. S'get rid of it."

"Huh-uh," I said, "Jane stole it for us, and it would hurt granny if we threw it out. We have to keep it."

"No we don't." She turned her head and looked away. "We ought to get rid — everything. Start over."

"We will," I said, and I knew I should not go on saying we, when sometimes I meant what she did, and sometimes I didn't. I ought to get it defined before she got too wide awake, float it in to her somehow, tell her myself, not farm it out to a professional. Keep it honest, cut the knot in a private ceremony, just as I'd tied the other one today.

"Cass, I'm going to tell you something . . ."

She moved her head, and opened her eyes as wide as she could and said, "Tell — little red goldihood," and slumped back into sleep, and I couldn't tell her anything, not that I was married, not that her doctor was here, not even that she had the title wrong — it was supposed to be Little Black Riding Locks, the story Jane used to make up out of The Three Bears and Little Black Sambo and Little Red Riding Hood, all mixed up.

"Cass," I said, "wake up. We'll get rid of the clown, and send the oxygen back to the hospital, and give them back their blood-pressure machine, and from this day on, we'll —"

She didn't hear me and it was just as well. I'd said it all. There was no conclusion to come to. I sat and looked at her and held on to her hand and the question came again, as it had before, the big question: why can't she love someone, the way I love someone? Why can't she love anybody but me?

I opened her hand and put it back under the covers. Then I got up, and walked to the window and stood looking out. The lights were on down at the pool, the moon was up. I opened the window, smelled the roses, and told myself that on such a night as this did someone swim the Hellespont and that I could wish it were as simple as that, just swim the Hellespont and find my love, my own true love.

And then I saw him coming across the lawn. The woman was with him. I could hear their voices, now one, now the other, very low and earnest. They walked across the lawn, up the steps to the side deck, and Jack held the door open and the woman went in and he went in after her, all very courtly looking, solemn, stately, and graceful, rather like a minuet in the antique manner. And then I couldn't see them, so I thought about minuets, and music, and how to make an art of waiting, but not for long. They must have come directly to the bedroom. There was a tap at the door and Jack came in, looked at me, looked at Cass, and then looked behind him and gave a nod and Vera Mercer came in.

She came directly across the room and stood beside the bed and looked down at Cass asleep, and I found I was watching her, not Cass, and seeing a face that surprised me — it was so open, so easily read, so full of concern — scarcely at all the face of a doctor looking at a patient. She seemed lost, troubled, deeply sad, and I looked away from her finally, and asked Jack, but without using any words, just eyebrows, whether he'd told her about us. He hadn't; at least he shook his head, and while we were communicating by signal, Vera Mercer sat down on the edge of Cass's bed, pulled away the covers, saw that she was naked, covered her again, and touched her face and said: "Wake up, Cassandra. Cass, darling, open your eyes."

A quick spasm went across Cass's face. We all saw it, and we all saw her eyelids twitch and tighten and stay closed. Vera Mercer didn't speak to her again, but she sat where she was on the edge of the bed and after a moment looked up at me and said, "Would it be possible for me to stay here with her tonight?"

I didn't answer. I couldn't. I couldn't think what to say.

"I'd like to be here when she wakes up," Vera Mercer said, in the manner, now, of a doctor, very sure, very direct, "and I should think you could stand some rest. You and the doctor both. Just let me take the night shift."

I looked at Jack, gave him the eyebrow signals again, but he said fine, if she felt up to it, and he didn't see any real reason for her to stay awake, just be here, sleep in my bed and be available if needed, but there wouldn't be any trouble; he'd feel safe enough in turning her over to a layman, but since we're long on doctors —

"Granny wanted to sleep here," I said, and neither of them even looked at me.

"I'll bring your bag," Jack said, and he left the two of us together. The three of us, counting Cass, who didn't count and couldn't vote.

"I didn't think about the domestic aspects of staying here," Vera Mercer said, after I'd looked at her for a moment. "I don't want to throw you out of your bed."

I suddenly realized I was free, in an unforeseeable way. I'd practically swum the Hellespont.

"No, that's all right," I said, "we've got plenty of places to sleep. Let me get you some sheets."

I stripped my bed and put on clean sheets, over Vera Mercer's protest. She didn't intend to sleep, she said. She only wanted to be here and give Cassandra some — well not advice, she said, she wasn't much for that — but maybe a few words of wisdom, if she could find some good ones, for her to take or leave alone.

Jack was back with the black canvas bag.

"I think I'll get the oxygen tank out of here," he said. "I'd just as soon not have her have to look at it when she wakes up all the way."

He wheeled it out into the hall and left it and came back, and started to roll up the armband of the blood-pressure thing and then decided to take the pressure once again. Dr. Mercer stood by and watched the needle rise and fall and flutter when Jack squeezed the bulb, and when it settled, they looked at each other and nodded in a way that made me remember what Cass made up this morning about Jack and his little doctor kit. They looked so earnest about their club, and I thought how difficult a matter true loyalty is when you're caught between the bright mockers and the altogether earnest. But when I saw Dr. Mercer roll up the armband and fit the bulb into the box and snap down the lid, I remembered another thing — Cass asking me how I got so medical, and saying thank you, it was nice. I thought I knew what she meant. It was nice to see somebody like Vera Mercer pick up something and put it away, very precisely, knowing how it fits, knowing what she's doing and doing it almost automatically. It was consoling, like watching good pianists work, and for the second time tonight I almost liked her.

The sheets I'd stripped off my bed were lying on the floor between the beds and when I leaned over to roll them up I saw the corner of Cass's bag, her white clutch bag, under my bed. I picked it up, and put it on the dresser, and told Vera Mercer to tell Cass I'd found her bag if she wanted it when she woke up tomorrow; she'd hunted everywhere for it this morning; she and granny and I spent most of the morning, off and on, looking for it everywhere, everywhere, that is but under my bed.

"I'll tell her," Vera Mercer said.

I took the sheets out to the laundry and dumped them into the hamper, and on the way back I went down the front hall to papa's rooms to tell him goodnight. There was no light under the door, and when I looked at my watch I knew why. I touched the door gently, asked God to bless papa and papa to bless me, and turned out the hall light and went back to our room.

The rest is confusion, up to a point. I held Cass up while Jack and Vera put a pajama coat on her; we folded the blanket and straightened the room, and I explained things to Dr. Mercer — that she should expect granny at about six, that she should introduce herself and explain that I'd — I'd what? I hadn't thought that far; and then it came to me — that I'd gone across the field to my mother's study to sleep.

I went into the bathroom and got my comb and toothbrush, and when I came back Jack was gone, and Cass had moved slightly. She was lying with one arm flung up behind her head, and the other outside the covers, relaxed on the spread, and there was no sign of strain, no sign of trouble on her face. I think I have never seen her look so tranquil, so exalted and above the battle; not all tranquil either, expectant, somehow, somehow waiting to come awake. I leaned down and kissed the top of her head. Then I thanked Vera Mercer, told her goodnight, and left.

I turned out the lights in the house, and found Jack waiting for me out by the pool. Then we turned the pool lights out too, and found our way across the field, through the crowd of crickets and frogs, to the door of the adobe house that was my mother's study. It was the place I'd thought of all along as the place where I'd like to be married. And after a certain point there was no confusion at all, not the slightest bit.

CASSANDRA SPEAKS

THE MAIN THING there is to say about pills is that they build up a world with flower-petal boundaries and then populate it quite thickly with everyone you know in real life, if you still think of it as real. After I did my thoughtful swallowing, all alone with nobody urging me on or calling me off, unless you count the clown, everything changed quite fast and I didn't have a moment to myself. I began hearing granny talking to one of her friends, saying with ringing pride that Jane passed on from natural causes but that we're all rather disappointed in Cassandra — other girls seem able to wait however long it takes for a natural cause to come along, but Cassie's always had this tendency to jump the gun. I had to work hard to stop laughing when I heard it, because in the first place I'd never heard gran use an expression like jump the gun in her life, and in the second place what a time to start saying it, when we all knew there was no gun involved here, and absolutely no jumping, just a tidy number of capsules, no bang, no drop. But granny is inaccurate, as papa used to say, to a fault, and when she gets hold of a phrase, she makes capital of it.

The clown, too. He kept getting in and out of the picture, telling me any grown-up woman who would steal a circus poster must be some kind of a nut, and anybody that has a nut for a mother must, in the nature of things, be slightly tinged, because it takes one to have one, if not two at a time.

And others, until I had a real overpopulation problem for a while — Sophie Myers there to tell me I'd just set back my spiritual evolution by something like three thousand years, and the tennis player with the name — Milvia Kralowek — saying I shouldn't even bother to get suited out if I'm going to be forever unwilling to charge the net. And Liz the lean, Liz the hungry, with the same old talon fastening from four years ago.

Oh they were there in force, the pick-ups and the retainers, and granny and the clown, trying to get a toehold and a headlock, trying to establish squatters' rights in what I wished to dignify as my last resting place, or next-to-last, and making an unholy commotion where none should have been. Who hasn't heard about the way it is when you're drowning, or the way it's said to be by those who have narrowly squeaked — that your whole life passes in review? But I always imagined it as a stately review, a pageant with pageantry, nothing like this keystone chase around my deathbed, and these lickety-split uncensored indignities.

So much for the passing in review. It was quick, I think — a great deal of it but soon finished, and then, though it's not simple, or even sensible, to try to reconstruct nothingness, I believe I almost achieved it for a while — a great stretch of purest black velvet, smooth, soundless, the very piece of black velvet I'd been looking for for so long. I can remember feeling it drop, weightless, over me, swathing and swaddling me and then becoming one with me so that there was no way to tell which was velvet and which was Cassandra. But I never made it all the way to nowhere; there was a dogged spark of consciousness, very small, very feeble, but dogged, and it could just as well be called conscience, damn it, as consciousness, because I knew in some beating depth that I was engaged in illicit communion with the one great howling beauty of them all, and that there would have to be what there always has to be in this kind of affair — repercussions. There would be jealousy, accusations, recriminations, the full deck of threats and noises. I couldn't stay all night, I'd have to leave by an inconspicuous exit and try not to kick anything over on the way out, and remember to pick up my things — my bag, my lipstick, all marks of identification, including the ostentatious monogrammed items my friends are forever giving me. Collect them and leave without lingering, because nobody will bless this union, not even granny, who will bless practically anything if you set it up right. No chance for me and the one of my choice, my calm sweet quiet black-velvet love — no receiving line, no friends to wish us all the happiness and success in the world in our new life, which of course is the wrong word, but how would they know enough to believe I could prefer the opposite number? How could they, when the best thing they can think of is life? And wish you all success and happiness in it, unless they happen to be tipped off that you want to marry a bolt of black velvet and you like it that way. Then they don't wish you anything; they shake their heads, they pity you, they say you jumped the gun. Cassandra Edwards took her own life, because the headlong fool could not quiet down and wait for a natural cause.

And even in the course, the very central core, of what seemed to be the terminal passion, there were murmurs that this can't be right, you can't do this, it's down in the book as illicit, not smiled-on, unsanctified, and unfixable by bribe. Just as always, only more serious. You've blundered into high-grade stuff here. You can't get away with it. Nobody's going to like it — not even God. It's not His plan, as everybody knows. His plan is for somebody from California to run into somebody from Connecticut, opposite sex and altogether fitting. And *then*, Lord, can the receiving line receive and the hosannas bounce off the back wall.

I knew where I was, approximately, once in a while. There was a female impersonator impersonating my sister at one point. I gave him as bad a time as I could, but there wasn't too much I could do, just tell him as grotesquely as possible that I loved him, play along and give him a small hint of how the other half lives. But nothing much, because I was somewhat nauseated, the way men always make me, even when they're impersonating women. He got quite rough. And sooner or later there was my sister herself, alone with me, getting inside and finding my hand, and finding my pulse, and kissing me at some neutral place on the head, as if that would change the world and set the stars back in place for me, as if by one neutral move she could break it up between me and black velvet. She told me something that sounded terribly well thought-out, but I didn't get it, or not entirely, about how if you're born you have an obligation to live, and I think the reason it eluded me was that within the terms of it I had no choice and no chance. I mean to say if I hadn't been born she wouldn't be laying injunctions on me. The only way I could cross her up would be not to be listening because I had ceased to live. But I'd tried that, and I hadn't, alas, ceased; I'd continued; I was doing a solid continuo for the other instruments to play across and over and against with the injunctions. The only good thing was that my attention span was never shorter. I could quit in the middle of anything and sink to the bottom of whatever it had become — my bed, I guess — and lie there long gone, short gone, rising occasionally but not to the occasion, most certainly not to the occasion when I saw behind the bars of my eyelashes my sister in the arms of this impostor-impersonator with the hairy hands. I wanted to do something about it, but what can you do if someone is bent on showing you a filthy picture when you've just finished failing to cease? Nothing except what I did, which was to stop looking through the eyelashes and bring down the lids. And wait. And sink again, and at once feel myself borne up by many arms and many hands, tossed from one to another, manipulated like an adagio dancer, pulled this way, pushed that way; you hold her, now this arm in this one, that one there, button it now, and there we are. That's it. But what was it all the time they were waiting for the shift to be found, and the buttons put through the buttonholes? Me, that's what it was; me in the showcase, on display in the dissecting-room, handed back and forth, looked over more than overlooked, aware of my nudity, conscious somewhere down there that a cold nude is a different matter from a warm one. But even so, sometime that night.

Sometime that night, very late, I think, maybe morning but not light yet, Vera Mercer asked me about it, why I chose to go out bare? We were in the classic position, she in the chair, I on the couch — my bed, in this case. She'd been doing the talking for a change, off and on all night in fact, and I'd been in and out of the world, but more and more in it, hearing most of what she said, which was nothing too imposing, just a human, low-voiced stream of what sounded like free association, possibly to show me how it should be done. But once in a while she'd throw me a question which I could either pretend not to hear or else go ahead and try to answer; and when she came to this one — why had I decided to die divested? — I made the choice to answer it honestly.

"Because," I said, "I thought I might as well go out with my best foot forward. I'm all I've got."

The bedroom began to throb with mirth — hers, and a little of mine too, but without sound, only the impulse of it, contained. And other impulses with it, beginning to come alive and be remembered.

I'd stormed her house, twice. Once she'd shown me the door; and once she'd let me stay — nicely under sedation in a room at the other end of the continent from hers. But she'd put me into a whirling bath the next morning, and given me tea, and orange juice with an egg whipped up in it. That's where I learned about froth. And we'd discussed the storm later that week in one of the regular sessions and written it off as a routine phase of analysis — to be expected.

Now she was in my house. Laughing, in a chair, in my room, with her sleeves pushed up. Talking to me all night, getting me interested, but sticking to the subject too, more or less, making me drink water and take deep breaths oftener than I cared to, and every little while mentioning that doctor, that marvelous boy who did every single thing that should have been done, and stayed with it and brought me back.

"I'll never be able to thank him enough."

"Then don't try," I said, "and don't expect me to. Did you meet my sister?"

"Yes."

"What did you think?"

She didn't answer it right off. Then she said it was

startling how much we look alike, astonishing at first glance.

"But after that I couldn't feel you have anything at all in common. It ends right there."

"No, I've told you. It's still the same. Take her away and I'm half of whatever we are."

There was another wait. I heard her draw a breath. And then she said no, I was wrong. "She's a nice girl. But you're Cassandra Edwards. And there's only one."

"One half."

"Don't believe it. I *know* you."

"From what I spill on the couch? I make most of that up to get your attention."

"I know that; but after I sort it out there's still enough left for three or four girls like your sister. You're really quite a girl."

There was a change in the air, but I didn't know how much.

There was something about the way she said it, and a certain charge in the air. At least I thought so, and the world began to look a little different if there could be the smallest possibility here.

"Why did you send me away?" I heard myself saying to her, all the way over there in the chair somewhere. "Why did you ditch me down the hall? How could you take such good care of me and then refuse to take care of me?"

I thought maybe she wouldn't answer. And she didn't for quite a while. Then it came.

"I'm overtrained. I know the rules."

"The thing to know," I said, "is when it's a duty to break them. Come here."

"What for?"

"Take my pulse. Anything."

I saw her stand up and go down to the foot of the bed. Quite slowly. I couldn't see her face, just the outline of her, very neat. She stood down there quite a while and then she said, "Take your own pulse. And don't talk to me about duty until you're grown up enough to have the barest notion what it is."

I caught my breath, somewhat stung, and in a minute she went on in a voice that was not a whisper, but very low and very cold.

"You could still die, you fool. Any exertion, any small slip-up, after all that lovely boy's good work. He saved your life. The least you can do is hang onto it."

I heard her take a breath, a long one, and go on with the lecture. About how little it meant to me that she might have been charged with an error. Because whether or not my life mattered to me, her profession mattered a great deal to her.

I pulled the sheet up over my face. But her voice got in, telling me, now, why she came here at all. Because she took her work so seriously that she didn't have the guts to wait and see if I'd pull through, that's why.

"Now I know," I said, under the sheet. "And many thanks. Goodbye, please."

"Oh I'm not leaving," she said. "I'll see you through the night. But if you thought you were going to maneuver me into forgetting why I'm here — If you thought I could let an impulse push me around —"

I pulled the sheet away from my face.

"Then that *was* an impulse?" I said.

I could feel her organizing an answer, and maybe re-organizing it. It took quite a while.

"Everybody has impulses," she said. "I have all kinds. Just about like yours. But I always hoped I could bring you to understand that there is such a thing as a whole life — a way of life — and a reason for being that is strong enough to protect you from every little whistling call of the wild."

"*What* reason for being?"

She waited so long that I thought I'd stumped her. Then she said, "Work, mostly. Work, and interest, and love."

"You've got all that?"

"Yes, I've got all that," she said, "because I found out how not to keep losing it. And I thought maybe you might find it too some day. I thought you might find out it's better to be going someplace than to keep running up and down side streets."

I don't know what else she might have said, but I was tired of listening.

"Don't stand down there pontificating," I said. "Come here. I've been sick."

"Then get well," she said in that same low cold voice. "Find out how, because the only impulse I have now is to quit trying to help you."

She went back to the chair and sat down and looked out the window. It was getting light and I could see her now, very small and dark. Quite different from us.

She kept on looking out the window, and after a while I said, "Oh, all right. Go ahead and talk."

"I did," she said. "I said it all and I'm through."

"Then where's my sister?"

"She's unavailable. Gone to bed."

"When?"

"Shortly after I came."

"Where's what's-his-name?"

"The doctor? He went before she did. I'm in charge. I want you to take some deep breaths and go to sleep."

"You take them," I said. "I've had them."

But I closed my eyes. Out in the tree the grown-up birds were beginning to be irritated by the nestsful of wide-open beaks. Get up, now. Give them something appeasing, because it's a new day, a big full twenty-four hours since the same birds got to me crumpled up here on this bed, getting an eye open to see Jude laid out over there in hers, asleep, unchanged in spite of everything, unassailable, though I didn't know it then; neatly covered, with her mind made up against me and the door already closed on me — willing, even in her sleep, to let me wander lost and alone after the kindnesses of the night. I moved one leg to a cooler place in the bed and let myself know that kindness can be a matter no more serious than tossing a dog a bone and letting yourself believe it will hold him. For good and all.

Same thing everywhere. The doctor sitting there in the chair. Why was she here? To protect her investment; to see that I didn't make a fool of her by dying. No other reason. Same thing everywhere I'd ever looked. Large amounts of safety; very few risks. Let nothing endanger the proper marriage, the fashionable career, the non-irritating thesis that says nothing new and nothing true. That's how they do it. They go along. All but papa, who prefers the skeptics and Five-star Hennessy. And me who what. Who nothing. Who less than nothing. Who tried, but didn't.

So let's have the frilling wedding. And dibs on being bridesmaid. I didn't mean bridesmaid. I meant maid of — what's the word? — honor. And go all the way, the sacrificial, sacramental hard way, worst way there is — stand there robed-up and watch myself in the form of my sister suffer myself to come under the yoke publicly in the presence of these witnesses, and marry the meddler who does everything right. Sleep a minute now. Take some deep breaths as instructed, get a little sleep, and then go through with it. Ring the cracked bells. Invite the cracked guests. If this is God's plan, let's for God's sake get with it. So mought it be. Mote it? So be it. But give the children a worm before the tree splits up.

It was a very nuptial production, the wedding.

I did most of the planning; with Jude, of course; that is, I told her how it had to be done. It had to be done right. First get Vera Mercer out of our house and back on a plane; she'd be a drag at a wedding. Then get the champagne, and the cake, and get on the phone and invite people. After all, granny's important around here — we should make an effort, for once, to do something the way she'd like it. Let's have Kate, and Sarah, and Hannah, and all the women from the other club too — the Current Topics Club — and your first music teacher, and our old swimming coach if he hasn't drowned yet, and Conchita and Tomás and their relatives and anybody else we can scare up, and have it at the church. And wear our sister dresses, because after all we've got them, and granny'd love to see us dressed alike finally after the twenty-four year campaign. Do the full-length red-carpet deal from the door to the altar, but not in Jane's study, because I cased it this morning and somebody's been sleeping in there, and besides gran likes churches and she's got Reverend Branson all set up and probably already paid off.

"Listen a minute," Judith said, "there's something I ought to tell you."

"Well, don't," I said. "Whatever it is, let's not kick it around. I'm not sure why, but the only thing I really want is — this wedding."

"Have you gone crazy?" Jude said.

We were out on the terrace. In the sun. I was wearing my old tank suit and I'd lost four pounds in the last two days. But I was wide awake.

"No," I said, "I'm about as sane as I'll ever get, and it's my fervent wish to see you married. Just forget yesterday. I can be pretty childish."

"Wow," Jude said, and I quote her verbatim.

"Will you?" I said. "Will you please do it the way I say — for granny, for tradition, for real?"

She looked at me a little cautiously, I thought.

"Let me talk it over with Jack," she said.

"Well naturally," I said, as naturally as ever I could, and off she went for a conference. I have no idea how she put it up to him. I don't think she knew how conscious and how unconscious I'd been through the long afternoon and the night. I wasn't too sure myself how much I'd heard and how much I'd dreamed and what was pure divination. And the result of the conference didn't clear it up either. The decision was to have the wedding — in the church, with the guests, with the dresses, the full fifty-two card deck. Fifty-three with the joker.

I took Vera Mercer to the plane myself, and before she got on I made a short speech about the sacredness of the doctor-patient relationship and how we must never let socialized medicine or anything like that threaten it, because think what it would do to the tenuous, delicate ligature of faith between the healer and the hurt.

"You'll never know how it touched me," I said, "your flying down to be with me. You'll just never know, so don't dare ever try."

She gave me a narrow look, started to say something and then raised her shoulders instead. Nothing really broad; you couldn't actually call it a shrug.

I watched the take-off, and when the plane was out of sight, I said, "Take care of yourself, Doctor." But I knew she would. It was something I could count on as firmly as a closing statement July first, and if I was looking for eternal verities I had one.

The wedding was at noon the next day. Granny thought of it as high noon, but I wasn't thinking much. I'd been pretty thoroughly put to sleep the night before by something through a needle — John Thomas Finch's idea of post-bungling care. Judith slept in her bed and we talked until I drifted off, but I don't know what we said except that jet travel has changed things to the point where New York and Berkeley are like Minneapolis and St. Paul. I didn't say it; she did. I was supposed to go to sleep feeling unseparated and unrejected, but I got partly awake two or three times in the night with the feeling that a chaplain would come along soon now and a guard would unlock the door and ask me how I'd like for him to pray with me before we go down the hall. And the next thing I knew the birds were at it, three days older and much much stronger. It was the wedding day, and there were things to do. For one thing find a place to have a reception, because you can't serve spirits in the social hall of the church, and where you can't serve spirits, papa won't go.

"Wouldn't it be nicer to have the reception here?" granny said. "In our own home?" This was at breakfast.

"No," we said, Judith and I, at exactly the same time, so exactly that gran thought it was only me, and suggested that I let my sister have some say. After all, it's her day. And papa said he didn't care who wanted it where, he thought he'd call up Berkshire's Bar-and-Grill and ask Jim Berkshire to let us reserve the bar and the main dining room from twelve-thirty to two-thirty, or three, or four, and that way we wouldn't have to listen to any vacuum cleaning or neaten up all the London Times *Literary Supplements* and wash the dog, the way gran feels constrained to do whenever she has anybody come and play cards or discuss Current Topics.

So we farmed out the reception but we kept busy anyhow, and by ten o'clock gran had given up on her feeling that the groom should not be allowed to see the bride before they met at the altar. Mostly because they'd already seen each other five times by nine o'clock, and there was no pretending they hadn't. She'd been packing her stuff with his, and he'd finished up her blueberry muffins and her bacon, and mine too, though of course there was no reason why he shouldn't see me and finish mine.

We kept calling people up all morning, too, as they occurred to us as good wedding guests to add to the list. Our doctor who double-diagnosed measles and whooping cough and chicken pox in their season. The pest-control expert who dusts our groves from an old old airplane. The lawyer who does the income tax and inheritance business, and H. L. Bickford of Bickford's Complete Market. And, naturally, their wives. Everybody accepted too, except the doctor and the dentist. But even there, we got the wives. It was, we all got to feeling, a social triumph — at least on paper.

Problems kept coming up, though — difficulties you wouldn't imagine, turning up where you wouldn't think it was possible. For the big instance, granny, it turned out, didn't think we should dress alike. She thought there should be a firm, strong, unmistakable differentiation between the bride and the maid of honor; she went so far as to say she thought it would look rather odd for us to be dressed alike.

"Now she tells us," I said, and did the eye roll, and Jude went along with it right up to saying that if we couldn't dress alike we'd just call the whole thing off and elope somewhere.

"That's right," I said, "that's just what we'll do. Go straight to Las Vegas."

"Or Bakersfield," Jude said, "that's even easier," and granny didn't try to make her point again. But she looked so crossed-up and helpless that I told her I'd wear my blue shantung even though my heart was set on the sister dresses.

"The blue shantung doesn't seem quite right, either," gran said. "Couldn't we just go to Fresno and start all over again? And get everything right?"

"And call off all the guests?" I said. "You know what they'd think? They'd think something or other."

She nodded, sadly. She's a woman who does not want people to get to thinking, at least not about any of us.

"What I'm worrying about more than that is the music," Jude said. "What will we do about that?"

"Do the usual," papa said. He'd been reading Thomas Hobbes straight through the blueberry muffins, but now he was listening. He was actually the one who suggested inviting the pest-control man. "Come in to Wagner. Go out to Mendelssohn."

"No," I said. "It isn't so simple as that. There has to be a musical prelude before the wedding march. Vocal. You have to get somebody to sing: Take thou this rose, this tender little rosebud."

"Cut it out," Judith said.

"Then what *do* you want?" I said. "Oh promise me that some day you and I will take our love together to some sky?"

"Look," Jude said, "all you had to do was say, Take Thou This Rose, and Oh Promise Me. You don't have to go through the whole damned lyrics when only the title is called for."

"Fine," I said. "Then it's 'Take Thou This Rose' and 'Oh Promise Me.' I'll write them down."

"No you won't."

"Oh?"

"Don't 'oh?' me," Jude said. "Get hold of the church organist — it used to be Hugh Campbell and maybe it still is — and tell him to play some Handel, and some Bach."

"K.P.E. or J.S.?"

"J.S. Anything he's got in his book ought to do while the people are coming in. And when everybody's there, go into the Wagner."

"And then you and papa come down the aisle?"

"No, you go down first. By yourself."

"That's me for you," I said.

"What was that about me?" papa said. "I didn't think I had to do anything but give her away."

"Wouldn't it make more sense," I said, "for me to give her away?"

There'd been quite a babble for a while, and now, for a moment, nobody said anything. Jude sat with her chin in her hand and her elbow on the table, looking at me, waiting until I'd got all the side-effects out of the way before we went back to the problem. And it gave granny an opening.

"What we need is a rehearsal, with Reverend Branson and the organist, and the vocalist."

"There isn't going to be any vocalist," Jude said.

"There isn't?" granny said, and Jude said please pay attention, there was going to be an organist if one turned up, or rather if we could find one, and that she'd do the tele-phoning herself and talk it over with him what to play, and find out who comes in when. It shouldn't be so hard. There's an order of procedure, very invariable.

"Oh I know there is," gran said, "but I can't remember just when the mother of the bride comes in."

I knew what she meant. Judith did too, and so did papa. She meant when did *she* come in — Mrs. Rowena Abbott — but it wasn't what she said, and it had a quieting effect on all of us.

"Ask the minister," Judith said. "No, I'll ask the or-ganist. I'm going to call him."

She left, and I told granny I thought she was supposed to be the last sitting-down guest to enter the church — before the lamb was led to the sacrifice, without even the brains to bleat.

"Cassie, what a way to talk."

"I know," I said, "and I'm sorry."

I left, and went out the side door. I was shaking. I was shaken. The mention of the mother of the bride had got me to remembering Jane's funeral, with everybody and his brother in attendance, and thinking that if I'd made good on my attempt this would probably be *my* day. Unless, of course, they'd been able to keep it quiet, which isn't too easy in a town like Putnam where they grow grapevines in the laboratory.

I walked across the lawn and down to the pool. One thing about being alive is that you can swim. Other things too — you can look at the clouds in the daytime and the stars at night and think of space as something you can't terribly care about conquering. Let it go on being spa-cious while it can. There's lots of time if you think in terms of light-years. So I was looking up at the clouds, the foamy ones we get in the summer, and I almost stepped on Jack Finch laid out face-down on a towel on the terrace. He didn't hear me. I was barefooted. I started to retreat and then decided not to. Another of the things about being alive is that you can step right over Jack Finch and dive into the pool.

I didn't do much swimming, just poked around down near the bottom, and came up and floated a minute and then climbed out by the ladder. He was standing there, and he handed me a towel, and asked me what my crazy relatives were doing in there, had they figured everything out?

It was up to me. I could let him go on thinking what he thought and find out a lot of things I really wanted to know — his opinion of me for the main one — but while I was deciding, he must have noticed something, the tank suit probably, that tipped him off and gave me back my identity, and as soon as I knew he knew who I was I didn't want it to get personal.

"What are you going to do for a best man?" I said.

"You know any?" he said, and I said no — no good, better, best. No men, and I'll keep it that way.

"That's a big waste."

"Listen, Jack," I said so that it sounded like Listen, Mac, "you saved my life, they tell me, and that's all right. I forgive you. I can let it go. But let's not get to talking about waste."

"Will you come and see us?"

It surprised me.

"Me?" I said. "Why?"

He picked his towel up off the terrace and began to fold it. He looked deeply preoccupied.

"Because Judith loves you," he said, "and I suppose I do too."

He didn't have to say it that way. He could have said because he loved Judith and he could hardly tell us apart. But it wasn't what he said.

"You'd better get dressed," I said. "We have to be there in —" I looked up at the sun. My watch was in the house. "Forty-five minutes."

We got there, too; people were going into the church, strung all the way from the sidewalk to the door, and no place to park. Judith and I were in the Riley. Gran and Jack and papa were in papa's car, because gran still felt the groom shouldn't see the bride before they met at the altar. Jude and I were both in white, because it turned out I hadn't brought the blue shantung after all, and gran didn't want me to wear anything old. But there wasn't much danger of our looking too much alike, no matter what we wore. Jude looked beautiful, and I looked the way I do — like a passport photo, quite tense and harried. But granny was the one — the real show-stopper with a little close blue forget-me-not hat and a blue forget-me-not dress and rhinestone buckles on her shoes and a corsage of white roses.

Jack went around to the side entrance of the church with an altar boy, and the rest of us stayed in the vestry with the Reverend Mr. Branson until we heard the town siren start low and rise to a sustained scream and fall to a dying wail to tell us our hour was upon us. It was noon. And ten minutes later, when all the stragglers were seated, another altar boy took us to the anteroom to wait for our turns.

We could hear the organ coming in nicely, playing "Jesu, Joy of Man's Desiring," and then fading without warning into "Sheep May Safely Graze." Our song — you might say — the one they played at Jane's mismanaged last rites. I looked at Jude and she looked at me, and she shook her head in answer to the question in my eyes. No, she didn't request it; it just happened. But granny didn't notice it; she had a job to do, and when the altar boy gave her the nod she lifted her head high, gave us a sweet sad smile, touched her hat with both hands and went in. I could hear a stir in the congregation, a tide of interest and admiration. I didn't even look through the crack in the door, but I knew what she was doing to them in there. She was giving them a Mother — brave, beautiful, transcendent, one they would not be likely to forget.

Then suddenly there was no more Bach, no joy, no sheep. Pure beating silence. I knew I was next, and I was right. The wedding march began. I thought a moment. Go nicely, now. Go gently. Don't break the spell your granny's cast. Play it out. But I didn't rush. I went back, kissed papa and told him not to wear the dark glasses. Then I looked at Jude. This should have been for us, this pomp. We've got stars named after us, and what's wrong with that? Nothing and everything, and the altar boy came and poked me on the elbow, and I stopped looking at her, and turned around and straight-armed the door and went in.

Jack was standing at the right of the altar — alone and looking quite sincere. When I'd got almost all the way down, he smiled at me and took a step forward. And then stepped back quickly and looked even more sincere. It was the first flub in what was being a nice-going wedding.

First and last, as it turned out. Dr. Branson waited at the top step in the robes of office, and when I reached my station, I turned and the music swelled and the door opened and the people turned their heads and then stood up, a few at a time, uncertainly, until everyone was standing in honor of Judith Edwards coming down the aisle on the arm of her father, James Murray Edwards, the ex-professor.

He looked beautiful, papa did, all black and silver, controlled and sustaining. I didn't look at Jude. I'd seen her, but I did look across at Jack, and this time he knew what to do. He advanced manfully to meet his bride and led her to the altar with no smiling, no backtracking, no double-shuffling. And as soon as papa and I closed in, the Reverend Mr. Branson looked out across the people, signaled for them to be seated, and said, in a voice of great resonance and sonority: "Dearly beloved, we are gathered together here in the sight of God, and in the face of this company, to join together this Man and this Woman in holy Matrimony; which is an honourable estate, instituted of God, signifying unto us the mystical union that is betwixt Christ and his Church: which holy estate Christ adorned and beautified with his presence and first miracle that he wrought in Cana of Galilee, and is commended of Saint Paul to be —"

And there he lost me. I turned and looked at papa and caught, in turning, a whiff of the sweet essence of Five-star Hennessy, though it may have only been whatever Jude was anointed with, and I reminded myself to ask papa some day, over a brandy and soda, what it meant to compare a man and a woman living in holy matrimony to the mystical union that is betwixt Christ and his church. If anyone could explain it, papa could; he's more or less spent his life drawing the line between clarity and obscurity, demonstrable precision and clouded sentiment, and he'd be quite sure to know which this was. I pretty well knew, myself, but I wanted to hear how papa'd put it. And I got back to the service just in time to hear the

minister say something I knew was in a wedding somewhere, but I wasn't sure where.

"Into this holy estate these two persons present come
now to be joined. If any man can show just cause, why
they may not lawfully be joined together, let him now
speak, or else hereafter forever hold his peace."

My cue, and I think Dr. Branson knew it, because he
swept the audience with a glance and ended up looking
directly at me. I looked back very thoughtfully, because it
had me thinking. But who's interested in just causes, shown
or unshown? What earthly good would it do, honest as I
am, to state my case again? I'd stated it often enough,
directly and privately, and with the single result that
this man and this woman were here getting joined. For
better for worse and for the good it would do them.

Nor would they acknowledge any impediment, of
course, why they should not be wed, though the minister
laid a warning very unequivocally before them — like
this, in these words: "I require and charge you both, as
ye will answer at the dreadful day of judgment when the
secrets of all hearts shall be disclosed, that if either of you
know any impediment, why ye may not be lawfully joined
together in Matrimony, ye do now confess it. For be ye
well assured, that if any persons are joined together otherwise than as God's Word doth allow, their marriage is not
lawful."

There was a weighty pause, and it brought no confession
of the smallest impediment, no avowal whatever. I pulled
a petal off my corsage, in my nervousness, and considered
that I'd really had the better part of this exchange, so far.
All *I* had to do, within the choice I'd made, was to hold
my peace forever. But Judith would have to answer at
the dreadful day of judgment when the secrets of all hearts
shall be disclosed.

Ah, religion, I thought, the great anonymous writer of threatening letters. But I knew Jude wasn't worrying much about the secrets of all hearts on judgment day. And I wasn't either. Papa and Jane had brought us up right. They didn't offer us freedom of religion, but they did give us freedom from it, and I could quit pulling my corsage apart now, because the worst was over, we were over the hump, the rest was clear sailing. John took Judith; Judith took John. Papa said "*I* do," in answer to the question who gives this woman to be married to this man, and then went and sat down with granny, and there were just the three of us there in front of the minister to finish it off. Finish it off for me, at least, whatever it did for them. There were ups and downs, prolonged genuflections when I could see the bottoms of both their soles, Jude's brand new, Jack's nicely weathered; there was the blessing of the ring, the taking of the bride's bouquet, the giving it back, the first marital kiss, and then, after more prayers — Mendelssohn! The triumphal procession from *A Midsummer Night's Dream*, and it got us back up the aisle, and out — two, and one.

We hadn't noticed the weather before the wedding, but we noticed it now. I dropped my corsage into the vestry wastebasket, and Jude tossed me her bouquet. I could have caught it, anybody could have, but I managed not to, and it landed in the wastebasket and I handed it back to her.

"You want to try again?" she said, and I said all I wanted was to get out of here and raise a toast. Or two, or three. And I'd see them at Berkshire's.

"Let's all go," Jude said, but Jack said he couldn't. He'd have to wait and settle with the minister, and the organist, but I could take Judith with me and he'd come along with granny and papa.

"Granny's already paid everybody," I said, but he said he'd have to be a man and make the gesture, and go ahead, take Judith.

She didn't want to leave him, that was quite clear, but she didn't want it to be too clear to me, so she came, and we parked the Riley in front of Berkshire's and went in.

It was cold in there, and dim. Dim in the bar, at least, and I didn't want to go into the dining room. Jude did, and came back and told me to come see it, beautiful flowers, lovely buffet; papa's idea could not have been nicer.

"Later," I said. "Sit down. I want to talk to you."

"What will it be, ladies?" the bartender said. "Champagne?"

"Double bourbon over ice," I said, and Jude said, "No, Cassie, don't get tight."

Catch the bouquet. Don't get tight. Come see the flowers. Come look at the buffet. Be nice.

"Sit down," I said, and she did, on a stool beside me. I could see the two of us in our wedding dresses in the mirror behind the bar. And I knew which was the bride. The one that didn't look like a passport photo. The one who was waiting for the groom to settle up and find her.

"I did some thinking during the wedding," I said. "You know, when I was just standing there without any lines?"

"Was it terrible?" Jude said.

"No," I said, "just thoughtful. How big's your apartment?"

"I don't know."

"Big as this bar?"

"Oh yes."

"Bigger?"

"Different shape," she said. "About as long, but broader."

"Anything like as big as ours — I mean mine — in Berkeley?"

"About the same," Jude said. "Smaller bedroom."

"Hell with the bedroom. I'm talking about the living room."

"Why?"

"I thought I'd like to give you my half of the Boesendorfer for a wedding present."

It was interesting what happened to her face. It began to look like a passport photo. Very tense.

"You can't do that," she said. "It's ours."

"Okay," I said, "keep your half, and I'll give my half to Jack. That way it's all in the family. Different family, but all in it."

"Champagne, ladies?" the bartender said. We were still the only customers.

"Yes, please," Jude said.

"Double bourbon over ice again," I said, and Jude said no, please have champagne.

"I'm not in a champagne mood," I said, "and anyhow what difference does it make which I have?"

"Champagne's nicer," Jude said, "it looks nicer."

"You're a beautiful bride," I said, "and a very conventional girl. I think you'll be very happy."

But I changed the order to champagne and she thanked me.

"You're quite welcome," I said, "a piano like that needs a pianist, it needs to be played. So please take it."

Judith blinked, took a sip of champagne, and then said no, not our piano, she couldn't do it. At least not right away. She stared straight ahead of her for a while and then turned to me.

"I think I'll tell you something I wasn't ever going to tell you," she said, and I knew by her face it was important. Also by how long it took her to follow it up. But she did, finally.

"It's about Jack," she said. "He doesn't care much at all about music. 'Clair de Lune,' and that's it."

There have been barroom confessions before, but not like this. I was stunned. My own brother-in-law.

"Gee," I said. It was all I could say for a while, but then I asked for details.

"How long have you known it?"

"Almost from the start. But I just couldn't do anything about it."

I moaned and said, "This is terrible."

"I know," Judith said, "but we love each other."

"How can you?"

"I don't know, but we do."

"Then this is no time to bring up impediments," I said. "You had your chance in the church."

"So did you. And thank you."

"You're welcome. Would you like a blender for the time being?" I said, and I'm not sure whether I'd have got an answer but I didn't get a chance to find out, because granny and papa and Jack came in then, and right behind them Sarah and Hannah and Kate, and then the doctor's wife, and the pest-control man, and we went into the dining room and stood five in a row — first granny, then papa, then me, then Jack, then Jude. The whole town came, more, I'm sure, than came to the wedding; and everybody that went down the line said it was a lovely wedding and they couldn't tell us apart, and asked Jack if he could, and if he had a brother, and there was quite an amount of kissing and handshaking and enough gaiety to strain a whole ceilingful of acoustical tiles. But for some reason I didn't have another drink. Because for some reason I didn't exactly want one. I didn't want anything much except to bow out, I mean to say not the way I had when Jude went to Bakersfield, but just out of Putnam, and the ranch, and the valley. I hadn't been able to give away my half of the Boesendorfer, and I rather wanted now to go back and see it, fold back the keyboard cover and work up my little Haydn piece and my easy Frescobaldi and my Bartók for Children, and take a quick look at my dumb thesis and see if it might lead into something less smooth and more revolting, or at least satisfying more than the requirements of the University. Papa was on my left and I had a question for him — who was it said life never offers us anything that can't be thought of as a fresh starting point just as easily as a termination, but I didn't have a chance in the din, and anyhow I remembered who it was — it was Gide, whom papa doesn't admire much except as an irritant. But it made me feel, for some reason, quite happy and quite easy, so easy that I broke ranks and went, after all, and got myself a glass of champagne. And one for papa and one for Jack. It wasn't that I was honing for a new start, because I never could be said to have started anything. It was just that I'd got a feeling for Berkeley again — all the fancy groceries and noon concerts and recorder groups and student demonstrations — all that progressive jazz. I was restless and ready. I'd had enough reception, and I knew we were getting to the place where the principals are supposed to duck out and make a getaway. It's supposed to be made difficult for them; but it wouldn't be much of a problem here. Nobody would try to abduct the bride. Nobody knew us that well. Nobody would let the air out of their tires or plant firecrackers under the hood. They didn't even have a car.

When the reception was over we'd go home unopposed. Granny'd go to bed at ten; papa'd get back to Thomas Hobbes. But Jude and Jack and I — what would we do — go bowling? They weren't leaving until the next day.

I thought about it through the rest of the reception, and the buffet, and the cake, and not all the champagne, but a respectable amount, and I began to feel that if the bride and groom could not make a traditional getaway in these circumstances, the least the maid of honor could do was honor them by making her own.

I milled around among the guests until I found granny and kissed her on one cheek and then the other.

"Cassie, how sweet. What for?"

"For having it the way you wanted it," I said. "It could not have been nicer."

"You couldn't have looked nicer, or acted nicer, either," she said, "either one of you."

"I tried," I said. "It comes natural to Judith." And I sidled off, the way it comes natural to me, and kept on sidling from one group to another until I'd sidled up to the side door. I was excited now. I'd made it, and I stood for a moment and looked at them — papa glowering over all the people, and Dr. John Thomas Finch in his serious suit, and Judith Edwards Finch surrounded by celebrants. And then I got out and drove back to the ranch.

It didn't take me long to do what I had to do. Just get the wedding dress off and into my bag, and separate the Italian shoes and put one in one side pocket and the other in the other, and put on a skirt and blouse, find my bag and my pillbox, and leave a quick note to tell papa I'd be back in two or three weeks to finish our conversation about my thesis, wish Jack and Judy all the success and happiness in the world and thank them for their contributions to my welfare, and run a string of x's for granny, and sign it your devoted sister, sister-in-law, daughter, and grandchild, C.E.

Next day was Saturday. I was down on Telegraph Avenue in the afternoon looking in the window of a music store and there was Liz Janko looking in the same window, staring at a guitar.

"How's your guitar, Elizabeth?" I said, and she told me she'd hocked it.

"That's no way," I said. "You were good. You've got true flamenco feeling."

"Maybe; I don't know. But the way I'm painting now, it's like a quarter of an inch thick, and that runs into a lot of paint."

She moved over to the other side of the window and looked at albums. She was wearing a tight blue skirt and a loose red sweater and her hair was very black. She looked a little like a painting herself. Girl looking in a window, call it, wearing sandals.

"See you around," she said, and moved off, and so did I, and ten minutes later we were both looking in the front window at Fraser's. There was a copper chafing dish on a table just inside the window.

"My sister got one almost exactly like that for a wedding present," I said.

"Jude?" she said. "Married?"

I nodded, and then said, "Yesterday."

"What are you going to do?" she said in a voice of quick sympathy, as if I'd announced something very different from a wedding. Doom, for instance.

"Oh, same thing I've been doing, I guess." I tried to

make it sound very matter of fact. "She's been in New York since September."

"I know," Liz said, "but I always thought she'd be back."

"Me too," I said, "but you've got to admit that's a very nice chafing dish."

"Yes," she said. "It's handsome. I'd like to paint it."

I looked at it a minute and thought maybe I'd just go in and buy it, but Liz had moved on and was looking at something else.

"How does it happen you're hanging around, not working?" I said.

She was looking at an espresso coffeepot, very complicated, and she told me she rented her studio to somebody on weekends, just in the daytime.

"Would you like to do something? Have some coffee? Go somewhere? I'm not doing anything much either."

"I wish you'd asked me this morning," she said. "I had something I wanted to do, but I did it. It took three buses and it would have been a lot easier in a car."

I waited a minute and she told me what it was — something she'd wanted to do for a long time and never had. She'd gone over to the San Francisco side of the Golden Gate Bridge and walked across it and looked out over the water.

She turned away from the window and leaned back against it and said, "The only thing I think about these days is light and what it does to things. Light on water is something to consider."

She stood there considering it, and then said she had to be going. And went.

I went too. Other direction, and after a while I went into a place and had a cup of coffee and sat looking at it and making different distributions of the salt shaker and pepper grinder and sugar shaker and napkin dispenser. I was inclined to build a tower, but I remembered how nervous towers always make my grandmother, and I laid off and drank my coffee and thought a little about economics and aesthetics, moving from the very simple to the slightly more complex, and wondering how it would feel to have to pawn a guitar, and how it would be to walk around until it gets dark and somebody gets out of your studio and you can go back in and go to work. The things that get in your way, the indignities you have to suffer before you're free to do one simple, personal, necessary thing — like work. If it has to be a quarter inch thick you hock a guitar, and when the supply runs out, hock something else, and no matter what you have to part with to do it you hang on to the hope of painting a good picture some day. And in time, others. That's painters. But for me it was pretty much the same thing. I could never write any of this until I could tear up the pawn ticket on the ghost of my mother. It's a different order of hocking but it comes to the same thing. Don't lean. Stand up. Find a way.

I kept on thinking about it, though, what she said about what light does to things. What light does to water, or possibly what water makes light do to it, who does what to whom, and I ended up walking across the bridge myself. That same afternoon. Just to see. I parked the Riley on the San Francisco side and walked almost to the Sausalito side. I took my time, stopped a lot and looked out over the water and down at the islands and the tankers on their way to China and the sailboats cutting around each other and kicking up little whitecaps, everything very bright and fresh and small-scale.

I was wearing loafers and socks and on the way back I was walking faster and one of my socks kept crawling down behind my heel. I stopped and pulled it up two or three times, and finally I slipped the shoe off and dropped the sock over the side and stood where I was and watched it go. Or tried to. It took immense concentration to stay with it. When I thought I'd lost it for good, the wind caught it far down and I saw it flash in the sunlight, once, and again, and maybe even a third time. But after that I don't know. It was out of sight a long time before it could have hit the water.

AFTERWORD

THE EDWARDS family is cultivated, charming, bohemian, and fun. They enjoy spending time together. And, as not many outsiders get invited to their ranch, it's a heady privilege for the reader to spend time with them too, during the weekend that twenty-four-year-old Cassandra drives out from San Francisco to attend, or possibly to prevent, the wedding of her identical—and very different—twin, Judith.

We meet, in addition to the twins, their grandmother, their father, and eventually Judith's fiancé, the ideal Jack Finch. Cassandra's remarkable psychoanalyst, Vera Mercer, also makes a late, brief appearance. The twins' mother, Jane, is a powerful memory, but she has died sometime before the story begins, as has the twins' most instructive pet, Tacky the cat. A few other figures are mentioned—fleetingly, though, and they seem entirely negligible, pallid and remote. *Cassandra at the Wedding* isn't long, but this is still a low ratio of characters, and their company, in the hermetic, rarefied atmosphere of the ranch, is intense.

The novel was first published in 1962, at a time when the prevailing culture of consumerism was stimulating critiques, implicit or explicit, in American art and social thought. And a lot of American fiction from that period which portrays characters from a privileged upper middle class (Cheever's, for example, or Yates's, or Salinger's) suggests the blight of an empty materialism. The Edwardses'

materialism, in contrast, isn't one bit empty—the family de-
rives substantial pleasure from their fresh orange juice, the
views from their house, their swimming pool, their closet
space and clothing, their pianos. It's a patrician American
idyll. These people aren't portrayed as grasping robots, but
as casual connoisseurs in Arcadia. The girls' grandmother,
Rowena Abbott, may be the object of her family's affection-
ate satire owing to her imperturbable propriety and un-
clouded bourgeois outlook, but on the other hand, the
welcome physical comfort of their world is largely of her
making. And in any case, the relative luxury of the Edwards
milieu is merely auxiliary; what they love best is the volup-
tuous pleasure of the probing intellect.

The daily life of the family is the life of the mind. The
twins' handsome, wonderful, Hennessy-saturated father is a
former professor of philosophy who has retired early because "it irked him to have to meet appointments" Cassandra tells us:

> It wasn't that way in Athens. A teacher in the golden
> age could stay in his bath however long he happened to
> wish to, and when he got out, some youth would be
> there with a towel... and by the time he was dry and
> robed, the word would have got around and the young
> men would have gathered to question and to be ques-
> tioned and end up convinced that the unexamined life
> is not worth living. We were raised that way ourselves;
> our father was Socrates, we were the youth and we sat
> at his feet.

Cassandra narrates the first and last of the book's three
sections, and she does so with great flair. She's aware of
her power to charm and dazzle, and aware, always, of

an audience. The book glitters with allusions to classical philosophy and mythology, as well as to poetry and music, some overt and some just winking out. But under an unforced and brightly associative surface, it's as tightly written as can be —uncluttered by arbitrary detail or random information. And by the time we get Cassandra's introduction to Professor Edwards, we already will have become sufficiently familiar with her anguished feelings about her sister and herself to think immediately of Plato's *Symposium* and his *Phaedrus*, in which Socrates discusses—with the youth at his feet—the nature of love.

In both dialogues Socrates employs the indelible conceit of love as the recognition of the long-lost other half of the soul and the unbearable yearning to reunite with it. Of course we hardly need to have read (much less understand) these fascinating and abstruse works in order to appreciate Baker's novel fully, but even the vaguest and most flawed notion of them will make us perhaps especially alert to the complex layerings of *Cassandra at the Wedding*. And a number of Baker's intricate jokes refract further in the light of the dialogues: "Whom God hath split asunder," Judith says to her fiancé, "let nothing join together."

The warmth of the family setting makes Cassandra's isolation starkly apparent, though it's obvious from the very opening of the book that something is terribly wrong. We are plunged immediately into an anticipatory, almost reckless haste as Cassandra prepares to drive out to the ranch, and it's right on the novel's second page that we read this:

> The bridge looked good again. The sun was on it, and it took on something of the appeal of a bright exit sign

in an auditorium that is crowded and airless and where
you are listening to a lecture, as I so often do, that is in
no way brilliant. But lectures can't all be brilliant, of
course; they can be sat through and listened to for
what there is in them, and if the exit sign is dazzling it
can still be ignored.

Hardly a page later, we learn that Cassandra is writing
her thesis on French female novelists who are more or less
her own age, although what she'd really like to be doing is
writing the novels herself. But she can't, she tells us; she just
can't, because her mother was a writer, and, we gather, an
accomplished one. And who, as Cassandra points out, wants
to struggle to measure up to a dead parent, whether you win
or you lose?

Cassandra is astonishingly adept at maneuvering argu-
ment to suit her needs and at disguising her crisp rationales
—to herself, at least—as disinterested, though decorative,
observation. So her submission to inhibition here is particularly striking and poignant. By casting writing as a competi-
tion with her mother, Cassandra has created a stalemate for
herself. She and her mother each have an unfair advantage
over the other—the one simply by virtue of being alive, the
other simply by virtue of being dead. As long as Cassandra
feels, as she seems to, that to become successful as a writer
would represent a betrayal or devastation of her mother and
that to fail to become successful would represent her
mother's mortification of her, she allows fear of writing itself to stay her hand. We understand that she's at a critical
moment. The wedding, or, as Cassandra sees it, the with-
drawal of her sister into marriage, her own retreat from
what is plausibly the work most appropriate and gratifying
to her, the scary consolation of suicidal thoughts—obvi-

ously it's all of a piece. How is she to proceed without being able either to write or to live with her sister?

In fact Judith has, in Cassandra's view, defected some time before, leaving their Berkeley apartment to live in New York. What has remained in the apartment is their splendid piano, a Boesendorfer, and although the instrument was bought jointly and its ownership is shared, the musical ability is Judith's alone. But the piano, intended for Judith to play, remains behind, like a mute stand-in. And it's characteristic of the paradoxes that Baker sends reverberating through the book that Judith narrates its central section.

Judith's voice is the clearer and also the fainter; its charm is reminiscent of her sister's, but Judith is far more direct and far less aggressive. Cassandra's theatrics keep us constantly and increasingly on edge: What sleight of hand might we be missing? Are we seeing, at this moment or that, the real person or are we seeing a performance? And what, in fact, is behind the curtain? Cassandra presents herself, even to herself, as a character, but the fact is that Judith, the twin who has, it seems, the more fully realized psyche and personality, can be heard only on the night before her wedding, while Cassandra is comatose from an attempted suicide.

Of course, nothing illustrates so vividly as family the essentially unsatisfactory nature of being a person. The first thing one learns in life is that the self is a partial thing; at the very moment of birth one is consigned to terminal separateness. The one attribute we can be sure that we all share is incompleteness. And perhaps that's our strongest suit, because without it where would we be? Off alone, each of us, in his or her own little tree house, complete, fulfilled, entirely happy in the perfection of solitude—no love, for example, and no family.

If we sought the company of others only for help, say, in building our individual tree houses, human associations would last no longer than it takes to pound some nails into a board. Surely, among the things that draw us together with such binding force is the painful longing to fit our own jagged, torn edges together with those of another, to become complete. And if we think of love as the oblique and approximate remedy for this painful longing which Plato describes so vividly, we could say that family is the arena in which we first encounter that remedy's comical and terrible disappointments.

A family, we could also say, is the place where there's not enough of anything for any one of the parts whose sum that family is. Shuttling along through the obstacles of childhood, one is made constantly aware, between the breakfast table and the bedtime story, that not only is the self not a unit, it doesn't fit nicely into a unit, either.

Whatever it is that one needs—talents, love, hope, happiness—there's rarely enough of it to go around, and what there is has to be apportioned among the members. If there are siblings, the problem is graphic: there's always the question of who is going to get what. Who gets to be "the musical one," "the intelligent one," "the sweet one," "the funny one," "the one with the flair for math"? Who is going to have to be "the difficult one," "the homely one," "the one who will never amount to anything"? A lot of us have spent a certain amount of our adult lives trying to sort out what is properly "oneself" from what it was convenient within the family that we be. And a lot of us have spent a certain amount of time learning to acknowledge in ourselves abilities that "belong" to some other member of the family.

Obviously the problems are ramified for identical twins. They're often the object of envy to the rest of us—a compulsory friend, someone who is bound to forgive our faults, to anticipate our needs, to understand our deepest, most inchoate feelings, a living laboratory of our own potentialities—we want one, too! But essentially, what we envy is their chimerical oneness, their beginnings as one, their separation by the mere detail of a second body. As expressions of our singular genetic material, we others feel that our isolation is irreversible, but that twins' degree of isolation is qualified, or negotiable.

Well, that's envy's view, anyhow. But the fact is that the contract regulating consciousness stipulates that it's one to a body, period. Whatever human mysteries and marvels identical twins may be, they're unavoidably, also, a metaphor for the riddle of self—or to look at the same thing from a hair's breadth away, the riddle of love.

Cassandra arrives at the ranch with a new white dress, perfect to wear at a wedding, she thinks (if she happens to be the bride, the reader might think). And the reader waits, flinching, to discover, along with everyone on the ranch, that the dress is identical to the one Judith has chosen. Cassandra then explains to Granny, who has never understood why their parents didn't allow her to put the children in adorable identical outfits,

> "They were concerned to have us become individuals, each of us in our own right, and not be confused in ourselves, nor confusing to other people."
>
> "That's right," Judith said, like an amen.

The twins' lifelong vigilance, however strenuous, is evidently something of a misplaced effort. And the dress—a ludicrous banality in itself—becomes more and more inescapably an emblem of the snares and conundrums of their relationship. At one point Judith begs Cassandra to wear it. Please, she says, "For Me."

"For you?" Cassandra answers, in a rather drunken rage, "Who's that?"

Cassandra may be the articulate, dashing, and reckless twin, but Judith actually *is* the musical one. She's also of course nicer, more prudent, more reasonable, more resilient. She's hardly short on virtues herself, obviously—though hers are blander. Sometimes, in fact, it seems that she is merely—for the author and in the "reality" that is the novel —sort of a casserole cooked up from the leftovers.

Judith doesn't complain, but the reader—so engaged by Baker in the mathematics of allotment—may feel it's a bit unfair. She's delightful, but she's just not as thrilling as Cassandra! But we understand, and both of the twins seem to as well, that the degree to which Cassandra domineers is the degree to which Cassandra, not Judith, is weak. It's a bit like someone who can afford a cook but can't boil an egg on her own and might starve to death if the cook were to take a week's vacation. Cassandra's powerful personality is not to be mistaken for real strength.

Judith is the more mature twin, clearly, and the one with the courage to separate. Or is it, instead, that she's running for her life? Perhaps she can't quite manage on her own, herself; certainly she has a better chance of an actual adulthood if she puts a little distance and a comfortable buffer, like Jack, between herself and her brilliant, devouring, hilarious, adored three-ring circus of a sister.

But the struggles, however ridiculous, extreme, or ineffectual, of a consciously terrified person like Cassandra inevitably seem more gallant than those of the person, like Judith, who seems somewhat better equipped for the challenge. Barely recuperating from her overdose, Cassandra perceives the romantic impulse her distraught analyst experiences and seizes on it, making an anarchic attempt at a seduction. "Come here," she says to Mercer, "I've been sick."

Does Cassandra really desire her analyst, or is she stalling, or competing with Judith, or persuading herself of her own irresistibility, or trying to prevent Mercer from articulating painful insights, or seeking the obliterating chaos of general catastrophe, or what? In any case, when Mercer refuses to respond to Cassandra's advance, Cassandra accuses the doctor, who has come to the ranch out of frantic concern for her patient, of ruthless self-interest. But even now, when we might be just about well and truly fed up with Cassandra's desperate antics, Mercer's stinging rebuke saves us the trouble. "Then get well," Mercer says. "Find out how, because the only impulse I have now is to quit trying to help you."

"To thine own self be true. And it must follow...," the twins' father has taught them long ago. But how is either twin to find out what exactly her "own self" is? Judith flees to the protections of conventionality. Cassandra flees to the protections of outrageousness, irony, and the fortress of the Edwardses' eccentric style of erudition.

Cassandra searches her reflections in the water, but what can she find, other than the self's dead end? If she gets any closer, she'll drown. Nor can she really ever truly subsume Judith through the surrogate affairs she apparently pursues halfheartedly with a variety of girls. It's hardly surprising that she fears men, as she puts it (or having sex with men, as we understand it) because love with a man would require relinquishing what is still an integral part of herself; she needs Judith, or feels she does, simply in order to exist. "Take her away," she says to Mercer, "and I'm half of whatever we are."

But it just isn't done, to marry one's identical twin. And even Cassandra doesn't expect to. The problem is *how* to make the unthinkable separation from Judith. "The bridge," she says at one point, "is the real project." It's a chillingly ambiguous comment, not only in regard to her intentions toward Judith but also in regard to the Golden Gate Bridge, which, blazing in the light, brackets the novel.

Suicide as a solution to her impasse seems pretty plausible at the point when we meet Cassandra, though given Cassandra's uncertainty about her identity, it's to be wondered who exactly she might feel is trying to kill whom, and who would be the witness to the act. Perhaps she has the sensation that she can dissolve her intransigent boundaries and be reborn whole. Still, it seems that there may not be enough room—on the spacious Edwards ranch, or in fact in the whole wide world—either for both Cassandra and her sister or for both Cassandra and the memory of her mother. And Cassandra is so strangled by her isolating egocentrism that she can barely breathe, let alone develop. What she actually needs is some way to sense that she herself is the locus of the bridge that can lead *from* herself out to something other than either stasis with her twin or death.

The sine qua non for a writer (other than pencil and paper) is a self—that protean, never truly complete entity. Cassandra is stunningly eloquent on the attitude her sister must maintain in order to properly pursue her music. She invokes their father's

pure faith of a skeptic. Maybe you don't believe in concerts but you believe in music; you care what happens
to it and you're willing to contribute what you can for
whatever it may be worth. Probably not much.

She is well aware that the grace of this sort of humility is
hard won, but she doesn't seem to be able to accept that it
could be available to her, too, if she could only achieve a
fairly reliable degree of autonomy.

Cassandra at the Wedding is a book that should never be
out of print. The Edwards family and their ranch is no less
welcome a retreat than they would have been when the
book was originally published, and Baker's writing is no less
masterful. The force, the fastidiousness, the brilliance are
sure to be a pure pleasure for readers and an exemplary one
for writers in the foreseeable future. It's one of the best
books I've read about the paralyzing terror of reaching maturity, and, as furious as Cassandra might have been about
it, Vera Mercer's barbed thoughts on the subject could save a
lot of people some pointless, painful time. "Everybody has
impulses," she says to Cassandra,

> I have all kinds. Just about like yours. But I always
> hoped I could bring you to understand that there is
> such a thing as a whole life—a way of life—and a reason
> for being that is strong enough to protect you from
> every little whistling call of the wild.

Also, it's a novel that should have a place with other
available works of fiction that examine doubling and nar-

cissim, such as James's *Turn of the Screw*, Hernández's *The Daisy Dolls*, virtually all of Kleist's work, Hoffmann's "The Sandman," Andersen's "The Snow Queen," and Mann's *Death in Venice*.

The end of *Cassandra at the Wedding* seems brightly, and perhaps somewhat improbably, optimistic, but in fact there are many tonalities to it. When Cassandra offers to give Judith the Boesendorfer, Judith seems slightly to panic and to grade over into Cassandra; are some of their qualities about to be redistributed? It seems a good thing that they're not losing a twin, they're gaining ambivalence, but it seems possible also that some of the terror that Cassandra has apparently cast off may come to reside with Judith, now.

We can't really be sure what will ultimately become of Cassandra, either. She has survived her panic, and her resurrection from quasi death seems to have enabled her to accept the wedding that she has become conscious just in time to attend. Also, we have her narration to indicate that she's lived into a future, and, at least in a sense, into a future as a writer—if, that is, we interpret the narration as "really" hers, and from a significant degree of future.

But we can't be sure what that sock dropped off the bridge is telling us—is the dropped sock a neatly placed seal to Cassandra's troubles? Or is it something stranger and more troubling—a charm, perhaps, or a bitter joke, or an experiment, or a threat? In any case, however satisfying that last moment is, it is colored by the sorrow of casting something, even a burdensome or tiny something, off.

What we do know is that Cassandra has to become a whole person in order to separate from her twin and in order to write. And she's needed to do it right now, on this summer solstice weekend of the wedding. The alternative is death, of either the body or the soul, and what we've witnessed in this very funny, very enjoyable, technically delicious book is nothing less than Cassandra's mortal struggle.

—DEBORAH EISENBERG

TITLES IN SERIES

For a complete list of titles, visit www.nyrb.com or write to:
Catalog Requests, NYRB, 435 Hudson Street, New York, NY 10014

J.R. ACKERLEY Hindoo Holiday*
J.R. ACKERLEY My Dog Tulip*
J.R. ACKERLEY My Father and Myself*
J.R. ACKERLEY We Think the World of You*
HENRY ADAMS The Jeffersonian Transformation
CÉLESTE ALBARET Monsieur Proust
DANTE ALIGHIERI The Inferno
DANTE ALIGHIERI The New Life
WILLIAM ATTAWAY Blood on the Forge
W.H. AUDEN (EDITOR) The Living Thoughts of Kierkegaard
W.H. AUDEN W.H. Auden's Book of Light Verse
ERICH AUERBACH Dante: Poet of the Secular World
DOROTHY BAKER Cassandra at the Wedding
J.A. BAKER The Peregrine
HONORÉ DE BALZAC The Unknown Masterpiece *and* Gambara*
MAX BEERBOHM Seven Men
STEPHEN BENATAR Wish Her Safe at Home*
FRANS G. BENGTSSON The Long Ships*
ALEXANDER BERKMAN Prison Memoirs of an Anarchist
GEORGES BERNANOS Mouchette
ADOLFO BIOY CASARES Asleep in the Sun
ADOLFO BIOY CASARES The Invention of Morel
CAROLINE BLACKWOOD Corrigan*
CAROLINE BLACKWOOD Great Granny Webster*
NICOLAS BOUVIER The Way of the World
MALCOLM BRALY On the Yard*
MILLEN BRAND The Outward Room*
SIR THOMAS BROWNE Religio Medici *and* Urne-Buriall*
JOHN HORNE BURNS The Gallery
ROBERT BURTON The Anatomy of Melancholy
CAMARA LAYE The Radiance of the King
GIROLAMO CARDANO The Book of My Life
DON CARPENTER Hard Rain Falling*
J.L. CARR A Month in the Country
BLAISE CENDRARS Moravagine
EILEEN CHANG Love in a Fallen City
UPAMANYU CHATTERJEE English, August: An Indian Story
NIRAD C. CHAUDHURI The Autobiography of an Unknown Indian
ANTON CHEKHOV Peasants and Other Stories
RICHARD COBB Paris and Elsewhere
COLETTE The Pure and the Impure
JOHN COLLIER Fancies and Goodnights
CARLO COLLODI The Adventures of Pinocchio*
IVY COMPTON-BURNETT A House and Its Head
IVY COMPTON-BURNETT Manservant and Maidservant
BARBARA COMYNS The Vet's Daughter
EVAN S. CONNELL The Diary of a Rapist
ALBERT COSSERY The Jokers*

* *Also available as an electronic book.*

ALBERT COSSERY Proud Beggars*
HAROLD CRUSE The Crisis of the Negro Intellectual
ASTOLPHE DE CUSTINE Letters from Russia
LORENZO DA PONTE Memoirs
ELIZABETH DAVID A Book of Mediterranean Food
ELIZABETH DAVID Summer Cooking
L.J. DAVIS A Meaningful Life*
VIVANT DENON No Tomorrow/Point de lendemain
MARIA DERMOÛT The Ten Thousand Things
DER NISTER The Family Mashber
TIBOR DÉRY Niki: The Story of a Dog
ARTHUR CONAN DOYLE The Exploits and Adventures of Brigadier Gerard
CHARLES DUFF A Handbook on Hanging
BRUCE DUFFY The World As I Found It*
DAPHNE DU MAURIER Don't Look Now: Stories
ELAINE DUNDY The Dud Avocado*
ELAINE DUNDY The Old Man and Me*
G.B. EDWARDS The Book of Ebenezer Le Page
MARCELLUS EMANTS A Posthumous Confession
EURIPIDES Grief Lessons: Four Plays; translated by Anne Carson
J.G. FARRELL Troubles*
J.G. FARRELL The Siege of Krishnapur*
J.G. FARRELL The Singapore Grip*
ELIZA FAY Original Letters from India
KENNETH FEARING The Big Clock
KENNETH FEARING Clark Gifford's Body
FÉLIX FÉNÉON Novels in Three Lines*
M.I. FINLEY The World of Odysseus
THEODOR FONTANE Irretrievable*
EDWIN FRANK (EDITOR) Unknown Masterpieces
MASANOBU FUKUOKA The One-Straw Revolution*
MARC FUMAROLI When the World Spoke French
CARLO EMILIO GADDA That Awful Mess on the Via Merulana
MAVIS GALLANT The Cost of Living: Early and Uncollected Stories*
MAVIS GALLANT Paris Stories*
MAVIS GALLANT Varieties of Exile*
GABRIEL GARCÍA MÁRQUEZ Clandestine in Chile: The Adventures of Miguel Littín
ALAN GARNER Red Shift*
THÉOPHILE GAUTIER My Fantoms
JEAN GENET Prisoner of Love
ÉLISABETH GILLE The Mirador: Dreamed Memories of Irène Némirovsky by Her Daughter*
JOHN GLASSCO Memoirs of Montparnasse*
P.V. GLOB The Bog People: Iron-Age Man Preserved
NIKOLAI GOGOL Dead Souls*
EDMOND AND JULES DE GONCOURT Pages from the Goncourt Journals
EDWARD GOREY (EDITOR) The Haunted Looking Glass
A.C. GRAHAM Poems of the Late T'ang
WILLIAM LINDSAY GRESHAM Nightmare Alley*
EMMETT GROGAN Ringolevio: A Life Played for Keeps
VASILY GROSSMAN Everything Flows*
VASILY GROSSMAN Life and Fate*
VASILY GROSSMAN The Road*
OAKLEY HALL Warlock

PATRICK HAMILTON The Slaves of Solitude
PATRICK HAMILTON Twenty Thousand Streets Under the Sky
PETER HANDKE Short Letter, Long Farewell
PETER HANDKE Slow Homecoming
ELIZABETH HARDWICK The New York Stories of Elizabeth Hardwick*
ELIZABETH HARDWICK Seduction and Betrayal*
ELIZABETH HARDWICK Sleepless Nights*
L.P. HARTLEY Eustace and Hilda: A Trilogy*
L.P. HARTLEY The Go-Between*
NATHANIEL HAWTHORNE Twenty Days with Julian & Little Bunny by Papa
GILBERT HIGHET Poets in a Landscape
JANET HOBHOUSE The Furies
HUGO VON HOFMANNSTHAL The Lord Chandos Letter
JAMES HOGG The Private Memoirs and Confessions of a Justified Sinner
RICHARD HOLMES Shelley: The Pursuit
ALISTAIR HORNE A Savage War of Peace: Algeria 1954–1962*
GEOFFREY HOUSEHOLD Rogue Male*
WILLIAM DEAN HOWELLS Indian Summer
BOHUMIL HRABAL Dancing Lessons for the Advanced in Age*
DOROTHY B. HUGHES The Expendable Man*
RICHARD HUGHES A High Wind in Jamaica*
RICHARD HUGHES In Hazard
RICHARD HUGHES The Fox in the Attic (The Human Predicament, Vol. 1)
RICHARD HUGHES The Wooden Shepherdess (The Human Predicament, Vol. 2)
MAUDE HUTCHINS Victorine
YASUSHI INOUE Tun-huang*
HENRY JAMES The Ivory Tower
HENRY JAMES The New York Stories of Henry James*
HENRY JAMES The Other House
HENRY JAMES The Outcry
TOVE JANSSON Fair Play
TOVE JANSSON The Summer Book
TOVE JANSSON The True Deceiver
RANDALL JARRELL (EDITOR) Randall Jarrell's Book of Stories
DAVID JONES In Parenthesis
KABIR Songs of Kabir; translated by Arvind Krishna Mehrotra*
FRIGYES KARINTHY A Journey Round My Skull
HELEN KELLER The World I Live In
YASHAR KEMAL Memed, My Hawk
YASHAR KEMAL They Burn the Thistles
MURRAY KEMPTON Part of Our Time: Some Ruins and Monuments of the Thirties
RAYMOND KENNEDY Ride a Cockhorse*
DAVID KIDD Peking Story*
ROBERT KIRK The Secret Commonwealth of Elves, Fauns, and Fairies
ARUN KOLATKAR Jejuri
DEZSŐ KOSZTOLÁNYI Skylark*
TÉTÉ-MICHEL KPOMASSIE An African in Greenland
GYULA KRÚDY The Adventures of Sindbad*
GYULA KRÚDY Sunflower*
SIGIZMUND KRZHIZHANOVSKY The Letter Killers Club*
SIGIZMUND KRZHIZHANOVSKY Memories of the Future
MARGARET LEECH Reveille in Washington: 1860–1865*
PATRICK LEIGH FERMOR Between the Woods and the Water*

PATRICK LEIGH FERMOR Mani: Travels in the Southern Peloponnese*
PATRICK LEIGH FERMOR Roumeli: Travels in Northern Greece*
PATRICK LEIGH FERMOR A Time of Gifts*
PATRICK LEIGH FERMOR A Time to Keep Silence*
PATRICK LEIGH FERMOR The Traveller's Tree*
D.B. WYNDHAM LEWIS AND CHARLES LEE (EDITORS) The Stuffed Owl
GEORG CHRISTOPH LICHTENBERG The Waste Books
JAKOV LIND Soul of Wood and Other Stories
H.P. LOVECRAFT AND OTHERS The Colour Out of Space
DWIGHT MACDONALD Masscult and Midcult: Essays Against the American Grain*
NORMAN MAILER Miami and the Siege of Chicago*
JANET MALCOLM In the Freud Archives
JEAN-PATRICK MANCHETTE Fatale*
OSIP MANDELSTAM The Selected Poems of Osip Mandelstam
OLIVIA MANNING Fortunes of War: The Balkan Trilogy
OLIVIA MANNING School for Love*
JAMES VANCE MARSHALL Walkabout*
GUY DE MAUPASSANT Afloat
GUY DE MAUPASSANT Alien Hearts*
JAMES MCCOURT Mawrdew Czgowchwz*
HENRI MICHAUX Miserable Miracle
JESSICA MITFORD Hons and Rebels
JESSICA MITFORD Poison Penmanship*
NANCY MITFORD Madame de Pompadour*
NANCY MITFORD The Sun King*
HENRY DE MONTHERLANT Chaos and Night
BRIAN MOORE The Lonely Passion of Judith Hearne*
BRIAN MOORE The Mangan Inheritance*
ALBERTO MORAVIA Boredom*
ALBERTO MORAVIA Contempt*
JAN MORRIS Conundrum
JAN MORRIS Hav*
PENELOPE MORTIMER The Pumpkin Eater*
ÁLVARO MUTIS The Adventures and Misadventures of Maqroll
L.H. MYERS The Root and the Flower*
NESCIO Amsterdam Stories*
DARCY O'BRIEN A Way of Life, Like Any Other
YURI OLESHA Envy*
IONA AND PETER OPIE The Lore and Language of Schoolchildren
IRIS OWENS After Claude*
RUSSELL PAGE The Education of a Gardener
ALEXANDROS PAPADIAMANTIS The Murderess
BORIS PASTERNAK, MARINA TSVETAYEVA, AND RAINER MARIA RILKE Letters, Summer 1926
CESARE PAVESE The Moon and the Bonfires
CESARE PAVESE The Selected Works of Cesare Pavese
LUIGI PIRANDELLO The Late Mattia Pascal
ANDREY PLATONOV The Foundation Pit
ANDREY PLATONOV Soul and Other Stories
J.F. POWERS Morte d'Urban
J.F. POWERS The Stories of J.F. Powers
J.F. POWERS Wheat That Springeth Green
CHRISTOPHER PRIEST Inverted World
BOLESŁAW PRUS The Doll*

RAYMOND QUENEAU We Always Treat Women Too Well
RAYMOND QUENEAU Witch Grass
RAYMOND RADIGUET Count d'Orgel's Ball
JULES RENARD Nature Stories*
JEAN RENOIR Renoir, My Father
GREGOR VON REZZORI An Ermine in Czernopol*
GREGOR VON REZZORI Memoirs of an Anti-Semite*
GREGOR VON REZZORI The Snows of Yesteryear: Portraits for an Autobiography*
TIM ROBINSON Stones of Aran: Labyrinth
TIM ROBINSON Stones of Aran: Pilgrimage
MILTON ROKEACH The Three Christs of Ypsilanti*
FR. ROLFE Hadrian the Seventh
GILLIAN ROSE Love's Work
WILLIAM ROUGHEAD Classic Crimes
CONSTANCE ROURKE American Humor: A Study of the National Character
TAYEB SALIH Season of Migration to the North
TAYEB SALIH The Wedding of Zein*
GERSHOM SCHOLEM Walter Benjamin: The Story of a Friendship
DANIEL PAUL SCHREBER Memoirs of My Nervous Illness
JAMES SCHUYLER Alfred and Guinevere
JAMES SCHUYLER What's for Dinner?*
LEONARDO SCIASCIA The Day of the Owl
LEONARDO SCIASCIA Equal Danger
LEONARDO SCIASCIA The Moro Affair
LEONARDO SCIASCIA To Each His Own
LEONARDO SCIASCIA The Wine-Dark Sea
VICTOR SEGALEN René Leys
PHILIPE-PAUL DE SÉGUR Defeat: Napoleon's Russian Campaign
VICTOR SERGE The Case of Comrade Tulayev*
VICTOR SERGE Conquered City*
VICTOR SERGE Memoirs of a Revolutionary
VICTOR SERGE Unforgiving Years
SHCHEDRIN The Golovlyov Family
ROBERT SHECKLEY The Store of the Worlds: The Stories of Robert Sheckley*
GEORGES SIMENON Act of Passion*
GEORGES SIMENON Dirty Snow*
GEORGES SIMENON The Engagement
GEORGES SIMENON The Man Who Watched Trains Go By
GEORGES SIMENON Monsieur Monde Vanishes*
GEORGES SIMENON Pedigree*
GEORGES SIMENON Red Lights
GEORGES SIMENON The Strangers in the House
GEORGES SIMENON Three Bedrooms in Manhattan*
GEORGES SIMENON Tropic Moon*
GEORGES SIMENON The Widow*
CHARLES SIMIC Dime-Store Alchemy: The Art of Joseph Cornell
MAY SINCLAIR Mary Olivier: A Life*
TESS SLESINGER The Unpossessed: A Novel of the Thirties
VLADIMIR SOROKIN Ice Trilogy*
VLADIMIR SOROKIN The Queue
DAVID STACTON The Judges of the Secret Court*
JEAN STAFFORD The Mountain Lion
CHRISTINA STEAD Letty Fox: Her Luck

GEORGE R. STEWART Names on the Land

STENDHAL The Life of Henry Brulard

ADALBERT STIFTER Rock Crystal

THEODOR STORM The Rider on the White Horse

JEAN STROUSE Alice James: A Biography*

HOWARD STURGIS Belchamber

ITALO SVEVO As a Man Grows Older

HARVEY SWADOS Nights in the Gardens of Brooklyn

A.J.A. SYMONS The Quest for Corvo

ELIZABETH TAYLOR Angel*

ELIZABETH TAYLOR A Game of Hide and Seek*

HENRY DAVID THOREAU The Journal: 1837–1861*

TATYANA TOLSTAYA The Slynx

TATYANA TOLSTAYA White Walls: Collected Stories

EDWARD JOHN TRELAWNY Records of Shelley, Byron, and the Author

LIONEL TRILLING The Liberal Imagination

LIONEL TRILLING The Middle of the Journey

IVAN TURGENEV Virgin Soil

JULES VALLÈS The Child

RAMÓN DEL VALLE-INCLÁN Tyrant Banderas*

MARK VAN DOREN Shakespeare

CARL VAN VECHTEN The Tiger in the House

ELIZABETH VON ARNIM The Enchanted April*

EDWARD LEWIS WALLANT The Tenants of Moonbloom

ROBERT WALSER Berlin Stories*

ROBERT WALSER Jakob von Gunten

REX WARNER Men and Gods

SYLVIA TOWNSEND WARNER Lolly Willowes*

SYLVIA TOWNSEND WARNER Mr. Fortune*

SYLVIA TOWNSEND WARNER Summer Will Show*

ALEKSANDER WAT My Century

C.V. WEDGWOOD The Thirty Years War

SIMONE WEIL AND RACHEL BESPALOFF War and the Iliad

GLENWAY WESCOTT Apartment in Athens*

GLENWAY WESCOTT The Pilgrim Hawk*

REBECCA WEST The Fountain Overflows

EDITH WHARTON The New York Stories of Edith Wharton*

PATRICK WHITE Riders in the Chariot

T.H. WHITE The Goshawk

JOHN WILLIAMS Butcher's Crossing*

JOHN WILLIAMS Stoner*

ANGUS WILSON Anglo-Saxon Attitudes

EDMUND WILSON Memoirs of Hecate County

RUDOLF AND MARGARET WITTKOWER Born Under Saturn

GEOFFREY WOLFF Black Sun*

FRANCIS WYNDHAM The Complete Fiction

JOHN WYNDHAM The Chrysalids

STEFAN ZWEIG Beware of Pity*

STEFAN ZWEIG Chess Story*

STEFAN ZWEIG Confusion

STEFAN ZWEIG Journey Into the Past

STEFAN ZWEIG The Post-Office Girl